THE OUTSKIRTS

■

THE OUTSKIRTS

■

A Novel by Stephen Stark

Algonquin Books of Chapel Hill

1988

Published by Algonquin Books of Chapel Hill
Post Office Box 2225
Chapel Hill, North Carolina 27515-2225

in association with
Taylor Publishing Company
1550 West Mockingbird Lane
Dallas, Texas 75235

Design by Molly Renda

LIBRARY OF CONGRESS CATALOGING-IN-PUBLICATION DATA

Stark, Stephen, 1958–
    The outskirts.
    "In association with Taylor Publishing Company"—
T.p. verso
    I. Title.
PS3569.T33576O98   1988   813'.54   88-3430
ISBN 0-912697-83-0

FIRST EDITION

■

APRIL

■

To my teachers, in particular
Peter Klappert and Marian Witcover

And to my wife, Rachael

THE OUTSKIRTS

Listen, listen.

The sensation is like fever. After the warmth has begun to rise and filter out through the bone and soft tissue, after everything has lightened and the street and the houses and the brittle green trees have dulled in the moisture and heat, it is hardly like running at all, but like a disease.

Listen, listen.

It is barely spring, but the heat is already immense. The bright, middle-Virginia winter has dissolved completely into this humid warmth, and the air feels like summer.

I close my eyes and feel the shudder of my body. Without looking, I know where I am—what block, which of the square, orderly wood-framed houses is sliding past. I know the exact texture of the street and how far I am from the woods. I know from the smell, from the way the heat hangs above the pavement, above the lawns.

When I open my eyes again, I turn from Augustine onto Parsons, and then I can see the woods, the tops of the trees over the roofs along the declining curve of the street.

It's here that the music begins. It's been following me all along. At the trees, it begins in earnest. It's something by Mahler that Kate played for me. I can't remember the title, but it's been running over and over in my head now for two weeks.

The music grows out of everything around me, as if it is a natural reaction of the sun against the air, against the trees, against the houses and the pavement. All of it—even the sound of the car that creeps up behind me on the road—begins as a source for the music, the melody building up and erasing everything piece by piece until at last there is nothing left but music, hard and clean and pure as ice.

I have no idea why it happens. I only know that all I have to do is hear a piece of music once, and then I can play it back measure for measure in my head just as it was performed. And it works best when I run.

I go along the edge of Parsons Street, heading for the footpath through the woods at Grant Park. Grant Park is three, maybe four miles long, and if you saw it on a map of Langston, which is west of the Roanoke Valley in a boat-shaped cusp of low, rolling stone mountains, it would be the jagged north edge of town. It's bordered on top by Division Highway, and on the bottom by the slow edge of Langston, the subdivision Grant Woods, where I live with my father. I run in Grant Park every day.

Once, when my father was still teaching, he took my mother and me on an airplane ride over the valley with a friend of his, a pilot, who owned a Piper Cub. From the window where I sat with my mother, I could see more sky than I ever dreamed possible. Everywhere was sky, hard and blue, even when I looked down. When the plane finished climbing and leveled off, I could see Langston as my father pointed it out. The houses and buildings were white and ordered and small in the nervous drone of the airplane. The whole town was bisected by the railyard and the gleaming wires of track that stripped out toward the horizon. Then I could see the woods at Grant Park, and the forest of the Outskirts. It was like a huge, unbroken ocean, spreading along the rippling Appalachians all the way to West Virginia. I stared down at it, as if the green could enter my skull and stay there, Langston gone, Roanoke gone, everything gone but the perfect green. I imagined that if the airplane fell, it would sink forever in the soft green. My father pointed out our house, my school, and Southwestern, the community college where he taught. I couldn't listen for staring down into the forest.

When we were back on the ground, I couldn't get the look of that forest out of my head. For months I dreamt that I was flying over it, the plane gone and just my body soaring over the flowing mountains.

In a moment, when I reach the trees, Langston, with its bright, neatly cut lawns, with its squared streets, will begin to dissolve behind me as if it has never existed, as if the only thing in the world is the deep green of the woods.

Even now, on the glassy pavement, I feel the woods closing up. Already the warm animal scent of the packed-earth path and the hush of the trees creep through me. I close my eyes again and let the music come up, as full and sweet and palpable as the sky.

The car tags along behind me, slow, persistent, the sound of its engine pulling at the edge of the music.

A moment away from the woods, from the end of the street, the car whips in front of me and stops in the cul-de-sac. Almost instantly, the music begins to break up. A balding man in a red sweat suit hops out, then jogs up next to me. It's Shaddock, cross-country coach at my high school. I know him from my freshman year when he was my gym teacher, when he first saw me run. I know him from seeing him through the classroom windows at the edge of the playing field, always in this red team sweat suit, always staring intently at his boys, shouting them down in the haze, jogging next to them and slapping them on the

backs, teasing them and coaxing them. I resent what he is, and
what he shares with them—the brassy sweat smell of his office,
the sound of their voices together in the locker room, the way he
stands with his hands on his hips, staying on them, staying with
them. And it makes me sad to listen to their voices barking back
at him, calling him *Sir,* calling him *Coach* like the words were
God or Father.

"Been watching you," he says, next to me now. In his voice is
that coaxing sound; it is here, but it is also on the field with his
boys.

I stop where the sidewalk falls off into the grass and the path
licks towards the woods. I wipe the salty moisture from my
mouth.

He stops too, and his fists find his hips. "You, uh, look pretty
good," he says. "Form's a little funny, but we can work on that."
His face is boyishly soft and free of wrinkles. Except for the bald
head, he could almost be my own age. He smiles emptily, and
stands close to me. He was only running for a second, but he's
already sweating. I look away from him. There is an ordinariness
to him that makes me forget what he looks like as soon as I turn
away. I face up into the bright green of the treetops, then to the
dark path beyond. In a moment, I look back.

"You know we could really use a man with your talents on
the team this year," he says. His voice has the same affection-
ate quality that it had last year and the year before when he
made this same come-on. "With the right kind of work, you
could even make it to state. How about it?" He bobs a little,
rubs his hands together. "Tryouts are next week—Tuesday afternoon, four sharp." He grins, pats me as if we are old teammates.
"You'll be a shoo-in, I guarantee it. All it takes is the right kind
of work." His mouth flickers between smile and uncertainty.

But I know that it takes more than just the right kind of work. I know it takes something I'm not ready to give him.

"Why?" I say. The word surprises me. I feel a twinge of regret that without meaning to, I'm being too harsh, too unbending.

He gives a startled, nasal laugh. A smile hangs on his mouth, out of place. "What?" he says, backing off a little, looking me up and down.

"Why?" I repeat, trying to soften it.

"What is it with you, Santamoravia? Huh?" He's expected this. He's known all along how I will react. It's a kind of game for him. He takes another step back and lets his eyes and jaw go hard.

I look away from him, from the shine of his bald pate. Even though my question is sarcastic, I really would like to have one good reason why. In my mind I can hear the other boys, running by him in the heat, shouting "yes sir!" to his commands, and all it does is make me sad. I think if he could give me just one solid thing that made sense, I'd probably go out and race for him.

He doesn't. He shakes his head and says, "You know it's been said that you're heading in the wrong direction, Albie. It's been said that you're heading for trouble." He stabs the air with his finger. "Let me tell you. Don't head in my direction because you'll be heading into a brick wall." His face is righteous, sealed up as tight and bitter as a persimmon.

A wire of adrenalin needles up in me and I want to hit him. I can see it. I can even feel it on the skin of my knuckles. But I don't. I like the way my silence affects him.

"You know," he says, feet planted, one hand pointing at me, "I've been trying with you, Santamor—" My name halts him. "*Albert*. I've been trying with you for a long time, *Albert*. You don't make it easy for me. You don't make it easy for anybody."

Sweat trickles into my eyes and the salt burns like acid. I let it come, let it burn, and Shaddock in his high school track uniform turns blurry like some big, stupid red fish. I stare at the blurring shape, listen to the sound of his voice, its rhythm and weight in the air. And then the music starts to come again. It surprises me at first. At first I think it's a radio somewhere, but it's too good, too pure. In a moment, it has grown. I look at him a moment more, but the sudden giddy surge of the music makes me give a little smile and start trotting in place, swinging my legs in and out. His voice stresses the air like claws, but I can't hear it any more, I can only see it, and I wave, turn and head off for the cool of the woods, the sweet canopy of trees. When I turn and wave again, he is gesturing, shouting, and his mouth moves like a red rubber band, *"What is it with you, Albert? What is it? What?"*

We are at the Outskirts, Emily, Kate, Carl and me. I am standing waist deep in the cold cold lake. The sky is blue and cloudless. Beneath the sun, the lakewater is green and has the vague smell of algae, of seaweed.

Kate lies next to Emily on the lake beach. Both girls are in bikinis, and both smoke Marlboros, from which smoke curls restlessly into the still air.

Carl and I have just raced back from the car, about three quarters of a mile through the woods. I can still feel the whip of leaves and branches against my skin. I can still feel the sprint of breath in my throat. In the heat and sunlight, in the drift of music from the transistor radio Carl monkeys with up the beach, I can smell lakewater on my skin, smell the tanning oil the girls use, and smell the cigarette smoke. Near me, a dragonfly skates over the water, its body the same color as the sky.

Kate's bikini is yellow; her hair is dry and smooth and long, a color like chestnut. Except for Carl, she has the best tan of all of us, and now and then, when I'm close to her and she swings her head and laughs, I can see exactly how dark her tan is—the bikini loosening for a moment, showing a strip of blue-white skin. Until now—until today or yesterday or the day before—I have seen nothing to compare with the curve of her body, nothing I've wanted so much to hold, to absorb. But there is something equally powerful that keeps me at a distance from her, some quality of looking and remembering that is in its own way more powerful, more believable, than the actual touch of her skin.

In a moment she gets up, picks up the air mattress, then floats it into the water. "God," she says, her feet in the water now. "It's freezing." I nod, distracted. She climbs onto the raft.

When she is near me I catch the scent of her. It's partly tobacco, partly perfume, partly perspiration. But it's something else as well. I look at the flat of her belly. My head is full of her.

She lies on her back and bends her head backward. "How can you stand it?" she says, squinting with the sun.

I don't say anything.

"The cold," she says.

"I don't," I say. "I don't even think about it. What's to stand?" I want to tell her that it's made my muscles stiff, that it's stood every hair on end, that it's so thoroughly iced every vein in my body that I can feel the cold creeping through me, even going through my brain. But I don't say it. It makes no difference. What matters is that she is on the raft. What matters is that her perfect skin, so smooth it makes my head reel, gleams in the sunshine.

"God, Albie," she says.

Carl gets up and throws stones into the trees; I hear them rip through the leaves. Some of them die in the air, others knock against the boughs of the trees.

"You know I got asked out," Kate says. She has weighed the sound and texture of her words before speaking, and they come out smoothly, neutrally, with a kind of musical precision. They are not immediately startling, but neither are they insignificant. "I got asked to the prom," she says, "if you can believe it this early."

"You must be popular," I say. I try to think of it, but it refuses me. Once, when I was little and still watched television, I used to think about things like proms—about the glamour of them. Now I can't make myself believe that such things exist.

She says nothing, but closes her eyes and puts her arm over her face. I touch the raft. The water moves me. I'm thinking about Shaddock, but when I look at her skin, when I look at the water and the trees and the sky, I don't believe in him either.

Carl throws a stone over us, and it says *Soon,* skips once, then twice. "Stop it," Emily says. He picks up a bigger stone, comes close to the edge of the water. The impact of it on the water is hollow, and the splash rises in the air, almost in slow motion, then rakes across Kate's legs. She looks up, winces, but says only, "God."

"Stop it," I say, watching Carl, my teeth held together.

Carl backs away. "Sorry, Kate. Sorry, Albie."

"Idiot," Emily says. Carl digs at his crotch a moment, then disappears into the woods.

I look at Kate. The sun on the water hurts my eyes. "What are you going to do?" I say. There is a long silence. I watch her face, then look away. In the length of silence I could live one life, two lives.

"What?" she says. She looks up at me and squints.

"What are you going to do?"

"Jesus goddamned Christ!" Carl shouts from the woods. His

voice carries on the water, flattens on the trees. There is a sudden riot of movement in the underbrush, and he shouts, *"Goddamn! Goddamn!"* Then there is a dead silence. I can hear his breathing, wild and heavy. We all turn to look, and when he comes out of the trees—his brown skin slowly materializing from the gray-green boughs and rustling leaves—he is holding something between both hands that looks at first like a stick, then, because it moves, like a long brown muscle. It wriggles against his hands, as if trying to climb the air. The underside of it is lighter, a pinkish brown. Its back is dull brown and colored with tan and black mottles.

Emily stands up and drops her cigarette. Her mouth opening, she backs toward the water.

"What is it?" Kate calls. I wheel around to look at her and she is sitting up on the air mattress, shielding her eyes from the sunlight. I turn back and Carl has one hand behind the snake's head, and the other on its tail. It is so thick in the middle that it sags with its own struggling weight.

"It's a goddamned *snake*," Emily shouts.

Carl laughs like crazy, an insane, shuddering laugh that sounds like nerves, like panic. "Goddamn," he says, again and again, whooping, whispering, the word becoming a part of his laughter.

And then, as soon as he's on the beach, at the edge of the trees, he moves his hand, and the head of the snake jerks away. "God," I say to myself, but there is no sound, only the brown muscle and tannish belly dropping a little and floating in the air for a fraction of a second, taking balance, then the great, wedge-shaped head, mouth opening, recoiling and flicking upward along its length, toward Carl's hand. I wait, staring, the soundlessness of the air going through me, into my chest and into my head. Then Carl's arm moves—suddenly, violently. His wrist snaps and the half-

coiled body of the snake whips out so suddenly that it is curled
out backwards. The head cracks with the momentum. Then there
is Carl's breathing again, hard, whooping, loud. His eyes are
fixed on the snake. He waits for it to rise again, but it wavers a
little, sluggish this time. He snaps it back again. Then he yowls
and jumps and begins to swing the snake around.

"Damn it, Carl," Emily says, not to him, not to anyone. She
backs away, searching the ground behind her. I look at Kate and
she is on her knees on the air mattress, the water flooding over
it, the ends raised.

Carl swings it once, twice, then brings it over his head. It
sounds like a rope hissing against the air. Leaning forward, he
smashes its head into a tree. The sound of the impact is obscene,
like a face being slapped. He winds up again and throws the
snake into the water. For a moment, he stands watching it, round-
eyed, mouth open.

And then Emily stands up, fists clenched, and stalks toward
him. Her narrow, freckled shoulders move with anger.

"Did you see that?" Carl says suddenly, looking at her, his
trance broken. "Did you see that?" His fists are balled, and he's
jumping, dancing. He looks at Emily, then at me. "I was—I
was in the woods. Jesus *Christ*. Goddamn." He hops a little.
"Goddamn it if he wasn't right there at my feet." He breathes
and his eyes go like crazy, dark and small as buckshot. "I can't
believe it. You saw it. I had to kill it."

"Goddamn it, Carl," Emily says, standing up close to him and
forcing her words through her teeth. I look to where the snake
hit the surface and watch it float in the wide circling of water.

Carl stands looking stupidly at Emily, amazed by her. Kate
comes out of the water, shakes out her towel and pulls it around
her.

"That was the stupidest goddamned thing I've ever seen. I never imagined you could be so stupid," Emily says, her voice crackling with anger.

Carl cuts her off. "What if one of us had stepped on it?" He stares at her, threatening her with his size and weight. "What? What? What then, huh?"

"And what would have happened if you'd hit someone with it?" She swings away from him and punches her hands to her hips. "Idiot," she says. "Idiot."

"Maybe you could have quietly cut its head off instead of making such a show. . . ." Kate says, watching Emily but keeping her own words soft and even. When she looks at Carl, she smiles vaguely, and it makes him laugh, low, embarrassed but proud. Kate's towel is tight on her shoulders and I see the white of her knuckles.

Emily kicks her own towel.

"I did what I thought was best," he says, moving toward Kate. He repeats himself, and he sounds as if he is mimicking someone else. It reminds me of other things about him. His face slackens.

Emily doesn't turn around except to glare. "You should have killed it in the woods. You should have done it where you weren't endangering other people. Use your goddamned head once in a while."

"Em," I say, then let it go.

"What, Albie? What?"

"Nothing," I say, shrugging it off.

Carl looks at Emily. "I should have saved it," he says, his eyes rolling at her. "We could have put it in Shaddock's mailbox."

Tired, sullen, we all make the long walk through the woods to the car close to one another, watching the leaves around us, expecting every stick to move in the gathering shadows. Once Carl jumps and says, "Look out," but no one pays attention to him.

In the back seat of the car, Kate sits close to me and I can smell her dusky hair, still scented with lakewater. Emily sits in the front with Carl, all the way to the right of the car, against the door, her hair going back and forth in the wind. She smokes furiously, pitching cigarette after cigarette out the window.

I hold Kate's hand. As always, it is cool. Her thights flatten out on the warm seat of the old Plymouth. She wears a T-shirt and cut-off jeans over her bikini.

"What have you been listening to? What have you been playing?" I say.

Over the rush of air, she says, "Mahler, more Mahler."

"No Bach?" I say. I watch her hair, watch, through the open window, the movement of trees overhead.

"No Bach," she says.

"Too bad."

"No," she says. "This Mahler is marvelous. Weight and joy."

The car hums along through the cool of the woods, beneath the overhanging trees. It lurches with the sway of the gravel road. Behind us a dust cloud comes up and lofts into the trees, into the weeds.

"Prokofiev," I say.

"Bless you," she says, but she doesn't laugh. I look at her, study the side of her face. I don't want her to be bored. What I want I can't say.

Then, testing her a little bit, I say, "Wagner."

"Elegant but vulgar," she says. "Maybe even profane. You know Mahler as a young man considered himself a Wagnerian. Wagner was wildly popular."

"Oh."

"I'm not sure how long the infatuation lasted, but you can see the scar."

"Yeah."

She leans forward and touches Carl on the shoulder. In the wind from the open windows, she holds her gathered hair in one hand. "I have to get home soon," she says. "Don't break any laws or anything, but I have a music lesson at six." I watch her shoulders, the way in the unseasonable humidity her T-shirt presses into fine wrinkles. I can see the outline of her bikini.

"What are you going to do, Albie?" Carl says.

I lean up, shoulder to shoulder with Kate, and look at Carl in the mirror. "I don't know. How about you?" I look at Kate's face; we are inches apart. Her skin has a texture completely unlike my own. In the rush of air, I can feel her breath, I can see the very pale, very fine down near her ears and on the sides of her neck. "I don't know," I say again, and stare at her. I let go of her hand because I know I can pick it up again.

I say, "Widow's walk, I guess. Emily?"

Tight-lipped, shrugging, Emily blows smoke out the window.

Carl pulls up at the stop sign and the trail of dust catches up and surrounds the car. Emily rolls up her window but no one else does. I taste the dust in my mouth and nostrils. Emily fans herself indignantly.

When Carl takes off again, gravel spits up under the floorboards. The car shudders and sways before grabbing onto the pavement. On the highway again, it feels as though we have materialized from another dimension into the one in which Langston exists.

Carl's mother sits in the warm stillness of their living room, in a green armchair that is as squat as she is. When the three of us come in, she looks at us for a long time, only her eyes moving.

And then, finally, her hands come out and tug at the hem of her dress. Her legs don't move. Emily, who is half a step in front of me, moves forward.

Opposite Mrs. Rieger, facing the street, is a huge picture window, across which she has put up brightly colored decals of fish—blue puffer fish, red sea horses, lavender octopuses, green angel fish. They catch the light from the setting sun and the colors blur, spreading and smearing on the opposite wall. Even on her there is a soft patch of blue. Next to her chair, there is a small wooden table, dark and polished, with a doily on top, and a leather-bound Bible folded open.

"It's nice to see you, Emily," she says, because Emily is in front.

"It's nice to see you, Mrs. Rieger," Emily says, her hand on the front strap of her purse, the thumbknuckle painfully sharp and white.

"Nice to see you, Albert," Mrs. Rieger says. I say nothing immediately. I am halted by her lack of motion.

"How are you?" I say finally.

"Very well, thanks," she says.

"We're going upstairs, Mom," Carl says. Carl's mother was almost fifty years old when he was born. Now, at sixty-six, she seems hardly like a mother at all, hardly like a human being.

"Why don't you fix your guests some lemonade?" she says. Her voice is thin, like watery broth.

"They're not thirsty," Carl says, curt.

Mrs. Rieger ignores him and smiles. Her face rides above her slack neck and smock dress like a buoy on calm water.

Carl's house is on a knoll, at the highest point of our subdivision. To the rear, beyond the Rieger's fence, is a series of fields. Beyond that, highway and woods. In front, beyond the driveway and the two small houses across the cul-de-sac, the land falls downward, and the town spreads out below. You can see the mountains on every side of town. You can see the smoky high-rise buildings in the downtown area, where my father works. Carl's house is three stories, and the widow's walk is on the top, reached through the attic. Mr. and Mrs. Rieger never go up there. Not any more. We have taken chairs up, and with our toes and fingernails and boredom have chipped away at the green mold that grows on the railings and on the bare tin and tar of the roof. When we were little, we used to chew the tar.

The first time I met Carl was when both of us were five years old. His family had just moved to town. His older brother—who is a doctor now, and so much older than Carl that they might as well not be brothers at all but distantly related—was washing a car in the driveway. He had no shirt on, and the soap suds in the sponge were white. Carl was on the porch—that was when there was a porch, before his father had the whole house taken apart and rebuilt, before the porch became the living room, before the roof was raised for the third story, before the widow's walk was installed. There was an old mattress there on the porch, maybe part of the detritus of moving, and Carl was jumping on it as though it were a trampoline. His hair circled around his head like a wig, and it seemed to bounce a little higher than he did. He was slender then, not thick and stocky the way he is now, and his pants were falling down. That's the way I remember first seeing him, going up and down, up and down, the porch screened in and sunny, his pants half-down and his white ass showing, his hair flopping. The sight stopped me, and I stood on the street, watching, a little envious of the comfortable disarray, the stacked boxes, the furniture on the lawn, the boy my own age tirelessly going up and down. His brother glanced up at me. I don't even remember what he looked like, except that he seemed huge and adult. And then he went back to the car he was working on, the wet surface of the paint gleaming in the afternoon. And I just stood there, staring, until Carl bounced around and faced me. His chest was wiry and his nipples were dark and tiny and eye-shaped, and he slowed when he saw me. Then he said, so loudly that the whole neighborhood could have heard, "Hey kid, come on," and whipped an arm around to motion me over. As I came up the walk, he started going again, but now faster, crazily, to show me how good he was, how good *it* was, going up and down, up and down, and I opened the door—I can still feel it in my fingers, the worn brass handle, the peeling paint smell on the jamb of the door—and I was jumping too as soon as I came onto the porch. The two of us went, grinning stupidly back and forth, giggling, up and down.

Now that afternoon seems like another life. None of it exists anymore. The porch was torn down and hauled away two years later, the same time my mother left.

Carl kneels and leans against the railing on the townside of the walk. His arms are up on the rail, and his thick shoulders knot like rope. "It's warm," he says.

Emily rolls her towel out on the roof and lies down. There's not much direct sunlight left. Her movements seem reflexive, a way of gathering space.

"Look," I say, pulling up one of the folding lawn chairs and looking out over the rail. "It's fat Mrs. Matlock." I point a big, broad-hipped woman walking along the drive. She wears stretch pants and a scarf to cover her curlers. She walks with the slow, sad deliberation of a cow prodded toward a livestock truck. As she heads out into the street, she reaches one hand behind her to scratch.

"What a pig," Carl says, loudly enough for her to hear. "Piggy piggy pig pig," he says.

"Hmm," I say. I can remember when the Matlocks moved into the neighborhood too. How we sat up here and watched them, their dusty things out in the yard, the sunlight making their bureaus and chairs look meager and spare. They had come from Michigan, and the sound of the word, *Michigan,* made me think, made me go home and look at a puzzle-map of the United States I used to play with.

"You guys sound like the Court of Neighborhood Injustice," Emily says, lying face down on the warm roof, not looking at us. "Mrs. Matlock," she says, mock seriously, imitating me, "we find you guilty of vulgarity. What's the sentence, guys? Going to go down and beat her up?"

"Shut up, Emily," Carl says.

"Maybe she *ought* to be punished," I say, knowing I don't believe it. "Maybe there ought to be a law against being fat and lazy and disgusting."

"Thank you, Mr. Albert Totalitarian."

Early in the morning, before school, in my running shoes and shorts, I meet Carl at the corner of my street. It is cool and damp; the grass is soaked with dew. We stretch, and in his yellow trunks Carl's legs look as heavy as logs.

"I knew I should have kept that snake," he says, running in place, waiting for me to finish stretching.

I say nothing but look at him.

"It might have been a good joke, you know? A really good joke."

"Maybe," I say, standing. "Maybe so."

We head down Main Street when we start off, away from our

neighborhood and toward the shopping mall. Carl starts out fast
and gets a block ahead of me, then waits on the corner for me,
running in place. I don't run very often with Carl. He wastes his
energy. I like to draw a run out; I like to bring up the music and
lose myself in the rhythm of breath and the sound of my feet.
Carl makes that difficult.

Shoulder to shoulder again, we turn off Main near the old rail-
road tracks and head through the Langston Garden apartments.
The morning air is good and cool and there is a breeze now, but
I have begun to warm already. The heat comes up in my hands,
dampening them. We pick up the pace a little. "Let's turn up
Highland," I say.

We pass the Baptist church where Carl's mother and father go
every Sunday—the two of them bundled and burrowing through
the daylight as strange as weevils—and head up the hill, to work
our way around into a wide circle. We go past a 7-Eleven, past a
clutch of cars hissing in the bright sunlight, go through the smell
of coffee and cigarettes and doughnuts and exhaust. And then
there is Emily, pedaling her bicycle up the hill. I nudge Carl and
he grins back at me, his thick, brown face going with the rhythm
of his body. We go faster, cross the street. Cars pass us, swing
wide for Emily. She shifts gears. She doesn't hear us yet. I run
out to her right, up onto the sidewalk, and then, soaking wet by
now, circle around and sidle up to her. "Hi, Em," I say.

Startled, wobbling, she says, "God, Albie, you about made
me pee in my pants."

When she turns toward me, Carl comes up from the other
side and pats her on the head. She swings around and her bike
wobbles again. "Goddamned funny," she shouts as we pass, her
face going red. She breathes heavily; she has just been to the
7-Eleven for cigarettes.

My shirt and shorts cling to me. I hear the jangle of Emily's bicycle behind us and the coarse whip of her breathing. I hear Carl next to me; the traffic. And then there are voices—a man's, then Emily's—and then a man's laughter. I see Carl turn and Emily raises a finger. Her bike goes *kunk kunk,* then falters and stops. A pickup truck pulls away from her. She jumps off, then stands on the curb swearing. The truck slides toward us, then past, toward the stoplight. Carl shoots away after it and I follow him, bounding weightless through the grass and over the curb. The pickup stops at the light ahead of us. "Bastard," Carl says.

With all the momentum of his run balled into his arms and hands, Carl dives through the open driver-side window and smashes the man. I can see it over the bed of the truck, through the back window. The pickup bucks and stalls. Carl's head is in the window. The door opens and Carl is pushed away. I jump up and lunge at the man in the opening door. He is about twenty-five, slender, thin-chinned, with full, bruised-looking lips. I hit him in the face once, twice, the sensation of the impact stinging through my hand and arm. Carl bashes him on the ear, pulls him the rest of the way out of the truck, kicks the door shut and throws him up against the closed door. Other cars pull up and stop; the lights change; drivers watch in fascination. And then Emily is screaming, but I can't tell what she is saying. I hit the man in the stomach, in the ribs, testing the way his body gives beneath my hands.

Emily lets her bicycle clang to the ground and rushes up behind us. "Stop it," she says. "Stop it."

Cars ooze around us, chrome gleaming like violence in the sun.

Carl holds the man against the truck, his fists pressing up on the man's chest. "Goddamned son of a bitch," he says. The man's nose bleeds, and the blood crosses his mouth. He has a fine moustache, and I can see the way the blood fans out in it. When he coughs, he sprays blood on Carl's shirt. His forearms are over his stomach in pain.

I look at Emily; she is shaking in anger. She stands behind us, watching, waiting to see what we'll do.

"What'd you say?" Carl says.

"Carl, let him go," Emily says.

"Shut up, Em," I say, turning to her.

"I want to know what you said." Carl brings his thumbs up and presses them to the man's throat. "Let me hear it."

The man's eyes blink and he coughs again. "Let go of me," he says quietly, almost apologetically. He stares at Carl like an infant.

"Carl," Emily says.

"Shut up, Emily," he says. *What did you say?* Carl presses him close and the man chokes a little, then Carl lets him go and kicks his legs out from under him. The man whoops, flails at the air for a moment, then lands on his hip and rolls. He pulls himself up against the wheel of the truck. Carl threatens to hit him again.

"I said," he stumbles, choking and halting, "I said, 'Nice tits.' "

"What?" Carl demands. "I didn't hear you." Carl crouches over him, his fists on his knees.

"I said, 'Nice tits.' "

Carl mocks him. " 'Nice tits.' Was it worth it? Was it worth it?" He slaps the side of the man's head. I almost expect the man to turn cataleptic there, the way he covers himself, the way he doesn't look at us but huddles against the truck.

"Stop it, Carl. Goddamn it, just stop it," Emily says, her voice sharp. She comes up and pushes his big brown shoulder. "That's just plenty. You touch him again and I'll kill you."

I turn around, back away, pick up Emily's bicycle and bring it to her. Carl follows, giving enough room so the man can slide up into his truck. As soon as he does, he starts the engine and speeds away. Traffic starts moving again. I bend down to wipe the blood from my hands onto the wet grass, then turn to watch the round, gaping faces in the cars as they go by.

Carl holds Emily's bicycle. She tears it away from him, saying, "Give me my goddamned bicycle."

"You could at least say thank you," he says.

"Thank you. Thank you for what? For beating that guy within an inch of his life? I should thank you for that?"

I look at her, my skin burning at the blank space the adrenalin has left. "Listen, Em," I say, pressing toward her with my eyes and whatever understanding I can bring up, "guys like that make me—"

"Make you what, Albie? Make you what? He was a coward. All right, so it's a drag that I can't go down the street without some asshole yelling at me, but it was only yelling." She fumbles with her purse, then takes out her new pack of cigarettes and tears it open. Cars glide past like big steaming fish.

"Well," I say, confused, angry. "I think he got what he deserved." I turn away from her. "I have no sympathy for him."

"You've got no sympathy for *any*body," she says.

"That guy was trash," Carl says. His breath is wild and he looks like he did the afternoon he killed the snake—like an inflated doll. "He'll think twice the next time he yells at someone."

"Yeah, well," she says, kneeling down to fix the chain on her bicycle. "I just hope it was worth it. I just hope it gave you a lot of pleasure." She spits the words. "And I'm just glad for your sake that he didn't have a gun or something."

Carl folds his arms over his chest. "Never would have got it out."

Scowling, wiping the chain oil from her hands on the grass, she says nothing, but gets on her bike and struggles the rest of the way up the hill.

The warm weather holds. The blue sky is as hard and constant as stone. Each day the leaves and grass get greener. Each day, Kate comes closer.

Again we are at the Outskirts. Carl and Emily are on the lake beach. From the clearing in the woods, Kate and I can hear them now and again, shouting or splashing.

We have been sitting in the clearing for more than an hour now. It seems like forever; it seems like nothing. She smokes and talks about music, about Mahler. I kiss her, and then I wait, and kiss her again. I can smell her perfume. On her mouth I taste the flavor of burnt tobacco.

"You're delicious," I say, and I'm surprised by the sound of my voice. My hand moves down her shoulder to her ribs. My voice is calmer than my heart.

When she breathes I can smell her breath and taste her saliva.

She points a finger and runs it across my cheek.

The air moves, and I let my hand fall away from her skin. She lies on her back and I lie next to her, looking up through the white-boughed trees at the sky. She lights a cigarette and blows smoke above us, blue as the sky.

"It's really gotten hot fast this year," she says, smoke rising, twisting, carried with the movement of the air. There is something in her voice I'm not sure I understand.

"Yeah," I say sleepily, a light edge of nerves making my thoughts slow. I look at her and she tugs at her bikini strap, and I think *Jesus,* but what I'm afraid *what I hope* will happen does not happen. In some small way it is a relief.

She is close to me on the ground, on the pungent, vaguely animal-smelling loam. Soon, when she stubs out her cigarette and flicks it into the trees, she rolls toward me, propping herself up with one arm. I watch her and watch the movement of the trees. Bits of twigs and leaves cling to her skin. For a moment, her body is still, the air is still.

"Once when I was little," she says.

"You going to tell me a story?" I close my eyes, tease her.

"Shush. Once we went to California, on vacation. We did all of the usual crap—Disneyland, you know—but we went north, to a place where you could see the condors. They're huge birds, absolutely fabulous. There are only about four or five of them left in the world. There were more then, I think. I remember more." She is silent for a moment and traces a finger across the line of my eyebrows. "I don't remember exactly. The ocean was near. I could be wrong. You could hear the wind in the wings of the birds. The sky—the sky was like it is today."

I roll on my side too and move up close to her. I kiss her on the mouth, and then, without thinking about it—or knowing that if I do think, there will be a million reasons why I should not— I sweep my hand up along her ribs and then like jumping from a high place, close it on her breast. I breathe and the forest breathes and there is nothing at all in the world but the sudden hollowness in my chest.

She brushes her lips against mine and seeks out my eyes. My breath is shallow and the blood is bright as neon in my head. And because of the way she looks, because of the hush of the woods and the joy of touching her, I reach up and pull the upper string of her bikini top. The fabric falls aside and she moves it.

I look but I can't look. Embarrassed, made stupid by the sight of her, I try to speak, but she covers my mouth. I roll toward her, press against her so she rolls onto her back.

She sits up suddenly, pushing me away, her forearms drawn into her body. "What's that?" she says.

I sit up and listen, my heartbeat making me rock. I watch as she slips up the fabric, watch as she ties the string behind her neck. "Sounds like a motorcycle," I say.

Carl calls, "Albie?" through the brush.

"I hear it," I call back.

In a minute, Carl comes crashing into the clearing, looking back and forth, banging his fists together. Emily follows behind. Kate is on her knees now, opening her purse, going for another cigarette.

"It sounds like it's heading this way."

I frown at Carl, swing around and listen again. It is still some way off. "Let's go," I say to him. Then to the girls, "Stay here."

Angry, my head still full of Kate, I race through the underbrush with Carl next to me like a thick, fleshy shadow. I try to think of Kate, but it's like an interrupted dream. I can see nothing but the fast jumble of the woods—honeysuckle, bramble, oak, laurel.

Near Carl's car we stop, crouch together and wait. The sound comes toward us, up and down, steadily rapping. I listen, and then I tap Carl on the shoulder and point toward the car. He looks up, then scuttles away around to the other side and disappears into the trees. I stay where I am.

The motorcycle comes along toward us slowly, stopping and starting. It cuts back and forth along the path, scoring the soft dirt with a long, zigzag scar. I smell the oily exhaust in the breeze.

The driver—I cannot see his face for his helmet—stops next to Carl's car and lets his bike idle; it raps like a chainsaw. He leans forward and looks into the car. Carl is nowhere in sight.

He shuts off the motorcycle. The silence is sudden, almost white with the scream of jays and the brattle of squirrels. My mouth is raw. I smell Kate on my skin.

The motorcycle guy pulls off his helmet and puts it on the handlebars of his bike, then kicks down the stand and gets off. He stands in the clearing, looking around. He is our age, maybe a little older. He has very dark, curly hair. His face is broad, sallow, and handsome.

Blood warms my face. My hands are stung up with adrenalin. I think of the man in the pickup truck, the way his face turned wet and soft, the way he fell away from me. And I think of Emily shouting like an old woman.

Carl circles around out of the woods, quiet and coiled as a cat. As soon as I see him, I stand up and walk into the clearing. My legs are unsteady a moment from squatting. The motorcycle guy looks at me, then wheels around when he hears Carl. "Well," he says, drawing the word out, looking back and forth. "Hi."

"What're you doing back here?" I say, folding my arms. The tone of my voice makes me uncomfortable. There is a coarseness to it that sounds unfamiliar to me.

"Well," he says again. As if politely, he takes a step backward. His voice is steady, deferential.

"What are you doing?" I say. My fingers move back and forth across the slick of my palms.

He shrugs. The smile stays. The smile is steady and measured.

"Just fooling around," he says. His words are buoyant and hang in the breeze. "You know, exploring."

Emily and Kate come out of the woods, all shyness and white skin. They stand away from us, close together. Their appearance angers me, and I try to control the flush of my face.

"What's your name?" Carl says, dropping his arms. I glare at him, but he is not paying attention to me. The motorcycle guy stands looking open-eyed at Carl.

"Martin," he says. As he says it, he looks at the girls and bows his head a little. His tongue crosses the last syllable of his name like a steel rod striking a cymbal.

"Exactly what were you exploring, Martin?" I say. The belligerence in my voice is not at all concealed. I don't look at Kate or Emily.

"You know," he says, sloughing off the question. "I was just fooling around. I just moved to Virginia."

I can't figure out why he makes me this angry. There's something about him, maybe something as simple as the dull way Carl stares at him—the way a child will stare at a television screen. My own impulse is violent, like a cool blue band of light.

"Listen," Martin says, his tone conciliatory, "if I'm intruding, just let me know and I'll turn around and take off."

Emily starts to speak, but I cut her off. "Do that," I say. "Take off." I can feel the burn of her glare.

Martin looks around, but when no one says anything, he nods. "Fine," he says. "Sorry to have bothered you." I watch his eyes, wide and dark and clear; I have seen them before. He looks at me as he puts on his helmet, and then, completely unperturbed, he smiles, gets onto the bike and starts it. When the thick, dark sound of it fills the clearing, I look at Kate. She is looking down, kicking the earth. I look at Emily. In a moment, the bike roars off down the path.

We all stand around motionless, as if we have just awakened. Emily says finally, as the sound of the motorcycle dies away, "Go to hell, Albie. Just go to hell." Then she turns and heads back for the lake.

Carl says, "He looked pretty cool to me." He stands a moment, his arms swinging a little, then he follows her.

"You could have been nicer," Kate says after a moment. She looks at me, not smiling, not frowning, only looking, as though she sees what no one else sees.

I come close to her and say, "I know." I want to be able to say something more, to explain, but I can't. I want to be where I was before the interruption.

Something has changed.

My father stands in the kitchen, still in gray wool trousers from work. He is a lawyer, though he has not always been. Before, he was an English teacher. He taught at Southwestern Community College, but that was a long time ago. He got his law degree when I was ten, three years after he divorced my mother.

I stand in the doorway, watching him do the dishes. I watch his shoulders and neck. People say I have my father's frame, and so I watch it to see how it moves.

"Hey," I say quietly, finally, to let him know I'm standing here. "What's going on?" It is late, and I can think of little more to say to him.

"Not much," he says, shaking his head. He does not turn to look at me but rinses a plate and puts it into the dishwasher.

For the last several years, I have felt peculiar around my father, unable to speak. Though I suppose we love one another, we are each other's greatest sadness. I don't like to be alone with him. I don't know what to say. I feel as if I'm open to intense scrutiny.

"So," I say, "how was work?" I come into the kitchen and lean against the counter. I put my head against the upper cabinets and look out the back window. In the dark, the lights from the Whalen's house smear against the dirty glass. I look for the fence, for the Whalen's little black dog.

"All right," he says. His tie is tucked inside the third and fourth buttons of his shirt, and I wonder why he hasn't taken it off and where he is going. He smells of aftershave, cigarettes, and peppermint gum. "Listen," he says, and the word plays a funny kind of harmony with the icy rush of water against the dishes. "One of your pals from school called me at the office today."

I look at him, but he looks straight ahead at his work.

"A guy named Shaddock. Know him?"

Sometimes I hate my father for his sarcasm. Maybe he's trying to be funny, I don't know. It comes out bitter. "Yeah," I say after making him wait a minute or two. I look at him because he will not look at me.

"He seems to think you're letting the track team down—and the school too—by not joining up."

I laugh, and try to make it sound derisive.

"Well?" he says, as if he has not heard me.

"That's just crap," I say. "I mean it's not like I was on the team once and quit or something. This guy just keeps following me around."

"He thinks you're good, evidently."

My father looks at me for the first time. He has fine, gentle, almost feminine features, practically the opposite of mine. I have my mother's face—strong, cold, arrogant.

"If I am, it's no business of his, or anybody else's either." I look out the window again. A light goes on. I try to remember the dog's name.

"Are you?"

"If you mean can I outrun everyone at school, I don't know. I doubt it. I've never tried."

"Would it hurt that much, Al, *to* try? Would it compromise you that much to join something, once in your life?" My father rubs his mouth when he looks at me, as if he is trying to keep something from jumping out. His eyes go back and forth.

It would be easy to get angry, to get excited. But around my house, the rule is soft voices, even tones. Everybody's rational, deliberate. "A *human being*," as my father likes to say.

"Look, Dad," I say, turning toward him again, the counter pressing into my side. "It has nothing to do with me at all. Nothing. If I were some retarded slob or something or an amputee—" I pick up a knife and slap it against my palm for a moment before dropping it into the basket of the dishwasher, "—Shaddock wouldn't have anything to do with me. He'd probably get all his track guys together and laugh at me." I sniffle a little bit and rub my nose. "He sees me on the street running and suddenly he's got ideas about me on his team. It's *crap*. I don't want anything to do with him, or anyone like him."

"Don't overestimate yourself, Champ," my father says. Sometimes I think I'd like him better if we did yell at each other.

"Don't—what? That's what *he* told me, the first time he followed me. I thought he was a goddamned pedophile or something." I stop, look at the floor. Perhaps my voice is too sharp, full of the same bitterness as his.

"Oh, Al," he says, scowling. After a moment, he says, "But you're not handicapped. You can run. Listen," he says, but stops and looks down into the sink. He shakes his head. "Even if you don't like him, it still seems to me that it might be an advantageous thing to do—particularly in consideration of the scholarship money that you could—"

"Oh Jesus," I say, and pace away from him. I stop at the kitchen door, then turn back to him, "I just can't see one good reason to do it. All right? If you want to run on the goddamned track team, go ahead. I don't want anything to do with it."

My father, with his neatly graying hair and his crisply laundered Oxford-style shirts, sighs. For a long time he is silent and I watch him, waiting. I listen to the on-off rush of aerated water, to the clatter of dishes. I wonder why every conversation with him has to be life and death.

It is late; my father has been working since seven this morning.

"I ordered out for pizza," he says finally. "Should be here any minute."

"What'd you get?"

"Canadian bacon, onions and mushrooms."

I stand nodding in silence, waiting for something to happen—for the world to explode, for the Russians to invade and shoot us all.

"Met a new guy today," I tell him.

"What's he like?"

"Rides a motorcycle. That's about all I know. Carl seems to like him."

My father hums, dries his hands on the towel that hangs next to the sink, then closes the dishwasher. "You like him?"

"Not much. I don't know."

He lights a cigarette and stands blowing smoke into the air. It drifts toward me. It is a smell that will always mean my father's presence. "How's Kate?"

"Good," I say. "Real good."

"Listen, Al," he says, looking at me—really looking at me—for the first time, "I just hope you're not letting yourself down."

When the doorbell rings, I answer it. We are both glad to be apart.

The sunlight is bright and intense but the air is still cool. For the moment the humidity is gone. There is no breeze, no sound but the double hiss of my breath and the *kiff kiff kiff* of my rubber-soled shoes. I warm quickly, the dampness beginning in my breath and moving out along my shoulders and suffusing the skin of my hands and face.

I run down Highland Street, where Carl and I beat up the man in the pickup truck. He was a small man, with fine, fair hair and a thin, boyish moustache. In my head I can see Carl's shoulder working, I can see his hand break one of the skirts of the man's nose. I can see the blood begin to form above his mouth and smear outward. I thought he might cry, but he didn't. He just stood there against the truck while we hit him again and again. Emily shouted; did Emily shout? He was smaller than either of us. He didn't defend himself, didn't struggle. Still, he deserved what he got. You can't go around yelling like that. I don't know what it is—a violent season—but it is in the air.

Everything is green, uneven, but unbroken. The yards are speckled with dandelions, bright as sulfur. In my mouth I can taste the scent of the green.

I pick up my pace when I see the woods. I look for the music, but it isn't there. Instead I think of this Martin, and his form mixes with the weight of the air as I go into the trees. He mixes with the colored sunlight that spikes and stabs through the canopy of leaves.

I cross the footbridge, listening to the sound of my feet, feeling in my legs the recoil of the wood as I strike it. Then I head up the path, the earth beneath me shiny and littered with smeared mulch and rotting, fallen leaves. There are birds all around, mad, suddenly, with spring, and their cries are like the leaves—close, constant. *Look at him, look at him,* they say. *Vulnerable, vulnerable.*

The path rises. I put my head down, curve my back. This Martin sits on his motorcycle and stares at me. His eyes are big and black, or such a dark brown that the difference is invisible. He does not blink, he does not speak. His mouth is crossed slightly, turning mockingly upward. He listens as I say, "What're you doing here, pal?" And I can feel the hollowness of my voice. I don't look at the others. Is it shame? There is no judgment in his voice when he says he'll leave. I search through it for bitterness, for pride, but there is nothing at all.

And then there is crashing in the underbrush—shredding leaves, popping branches. I slow up, startled, and run sideways, looking back in the direction of the sound, my arms still pumping. There is a sudden patch of red, moving up and down. Then a boy in white trunks and a red shirt comes bouncing through the trees behind me, running. He has red hair, and a wide, full mouth.

He is a jogger, come from another path.

He is lost.

I wipe the sweat from my forehead on my T-shirt. My feet scuff sideways on the path. The air changes temperature. Where the sun stabs through the trees, the air is warm, almost like summer. In the shade, it is cold.

Like a startled animal, he bursts over the brush and fallen trees and takes to the path several yards behind me. His red hair is curly and stands out on his head, trembling as he runs. He is fresh, dry; he has been waiting for me. But I do not know him.

I turn away again, but unconsciously, I've slowed enough to let him sidle up. "Hey, Santa Claus," he says.

I say nothing, only look at him up and down when he's next to me. He is breathless. His skin is white and puffy, like a little boy's. I search the woods for others, but I don't see anything. I have no doubt that I can outrun him. I smile, go faster, make him keep up.

"You're in trouble, Santa Claus," he says, panting, his words coming out the same fluffy texture as his hair.

I look at him, but still I say nothing. All I can think of is sarcasm, my father's voice.

"No kidding," he says.

Then another boy begins to break through the brush. The branches whip, the leaves flutter like birds. I see his legs first, white, the sun hitting them and making them gleam. He is also fresh. He picks gingerly toward the path, ahead of us. When we sweep along the curve of the path and go by him, I recognize him. He was in one of my classes last year. John, Jim, I can't remember. I didn't think he was a bad guy.

"You're a pussy, Santamoravia," the second one says too loudly, blurting the words. In a moment, he's on the path behind us, trying to catch up. "How does it feel to be a pussy?" he calls out. "Is it wet in there?"

The red-haired one laughs, but it makes him cough. "Yeah," he says, spitting, "is it wet in there?"

Vulnerable, vulnerable, the birds say. I search the woods again. If there are two, then there are more. I'm surprised by the feel of my legs, by the depth of my breath. I could run forever.

We are in some kind of sad dance, the two of them flanking

me. In our movement and in the still air, I can smell them, smell their bodies, the bitter commingling of sweat and soap; I can smell their stale and milky breath. Though they are certain they are going to beat me senseless, they have decided to do it in ritual time, waiting for the trees, the sky, the earth to tell them, *Now, Now,* waiting for the appearance of their friends when they could bring me down now.

I watch them and the woods around them. Their arms pump, their chests shudder with the impact of their feet. And then a third one scrabbles down through the trees, snapping and popping branches in the tight underbrush. I hope there are brambles. And then there's a fourth, thrashing in the trees farther up the path.

The red-haired one is to my right, and he looks at me, a crazy, bouncing smile on his face. The second one is on my left, even with me, the hair under his arms fanning out.

A fifth one shambles onto the path, and stupidly, they wait, all in a group, for us to get to them. I look around one more time; then I drop half a step behind the red-haired kid, plant my left foot, and smash my right foot down onto his calf as hard as I can. His heel has just begun to rise, and the muscle is flexed when I hit it. When he turns to me, I'm pulling away from him, heading in the opposite direction. His face is utterly blank, as though the skin has been pulled slack, and he falls forward as his leg collapses, hands and knees scudding into the dirt, head snapping forward with the impact. The others turn and crouch when he shouts in pain, but I'm gone.

The birds say, *Look at him, Look at him.*

In confusion, the others stop, and their voices circle in the air above them. "Goddamn it, go after him!"

In a moment, I hear them coming after me. I have no idea how many of them there are, but it doesn't make much difference. *Look at him, look at him.* Then, I hear them drop away. I kick the air. By the time I cross the footbridge and break out of the woods into the sudden heat and sunlight of the neighborhood, they apparently have given up.

I slow up when I hit Parsons, and halfway up the block, leaning against his car with his arms folded and his bald pate shining in the sun, is Shaddock. When he sees me, his arms unfold and he stands staring. I trot toward him, and when his expression changes, I speed up. He looks at me like I'm crazy. I tear towards him, thinking like Carl has said I ought to beat him up and keep beating him up until he leaves me alone, and it's not until I get right up to him and skid in the fine sandy gravel that I know I'm not going to fly into him. Wild with heat and sweat, I get up close and lean into his face. My heart is drumming in my chest and my breath is short and shallow. I'm as big as he is, and I like that. I don't say a word. I just look at him. I can see every pore, every acne scar. I can see his tear ducts and the blood vessels in his eyes. I want him to know that I could kill him, that I would kill him. Finally, I back up a little.

Taking the space I have given him, he scowls and leans back against the car. "What's the matter with you?" he says, not looking at me. "What is it with you?"

I turn from him, still silent.

"You a retard? You an animal? What's wrong with you, Albert?"

I take stride again, listening to the shrill of his voice.

"You'd better watch yourself," he shouts. "If you think this is the end—" but he is behind me now, and there is the sun and the gray-white gleam of the pavement and the sound of my feet.

Mrs. Rieger opens the door slowly, swinging it back as if it were of great size and weight, as if it were underwater. My breath echoes in the house. "Hello, Albert," she says. "Nice to see you. Carl is upstairs." Her words come slowly, widely, each a separate entity.

I nod and smile, overcome with politeness. I can see my face bobbing stupidly in the mirror above the hall highboy. I'm red with heat, my hair is stuck and slick with perspiration. "Thanks," I say. "Thank you."

Once, when Carl and I were six or seven years old, I walked into the downstairs bathroom while Mrs. Rieger was on the toilet. She was just sitting, her smock dress gathered in her hand, her thick, larva-colored legs straddling the porcelain. Except for the shine and echo of the room, she could have been sitting anywhere —in church, in the living room. She smiled politely at me and asked that I excuse her. In her broad-mouthed, broad-faced way, she stared at me as I backed away from her and closed the door.

Now, as I watch her recede into the living room—the sun having passed over the window and stung the fish to life—I hurry up the stairs before she is swallowed up by the room completely.

"We ought to have a chain—" Carl is saying when I come through the little door and onto the widow's walk. "Oh, hey Albie," he says, startled in a funny, defensive way. "Have a good run? We saw you coming up the hill." When he speaks, he compresses the words.

I stop. I can feel something going out of me. Like a corpse being drained of blood, I can feel my legs empty, weaken.

Dressed in jeans and a gray sweatshirt, Martin leans on the railing opposite Carl's chair. He looks at me without expression. Both of them look at me. I remember the way I looked in the mirror downstairs.

"You remember Martin," Carl says. His eyes are raised hesitantly, expectantly.

"Oh, hey," I say.

He puts his hand out for me to shake. I smile uneasily, wipe one hand on my trunks and take his. The skin is cool and tough and dry, like plastic. I drop it quickly and turn away, go to the railing. "What have you guys been doing?" I say.

"We were just talking about the cabin," Carl says. "I was just thinking we ought to do it, you know. With three of us, it'd be real—"

I look at him, run my tongue over the back of my teeth. "I just got attacked by Shaddock's personal army," I say. I glance at Martin to see if it has any effect. "They tried to ambush me in the woods over at Grant."

"I told you," Carl says. "I told you. We ought to get him one time."

I sit down on one of the lawn chairs and look out over the roofs that descend away from us. The trees are in sunlight; the green is very bright, very pale and pure, almost like painted metal. In my head I try to pick out the different colored roofs—rust, blue, tin, gray—and imagine them as they'd look if they were arranged according to color.

"Well? What happened?" Carl rocks in his chair and bangs the aluminum arm rest impatiently.

Martin is quiet. When he moves, he moves like a mink, his body all hinges and coils. Because of the coincidence of his face and his shoulders and his narrow hips, because of his hair and his eyes and his skin, it is easy to envy him.

"They were waiting along the path," I say. There is a falseness to my voice, and it occurs to me while I'm talking that I'm not really telling the truth. I'm telling what's happened, but the words are doing something else, almost independent of me. "I don't know how many of them there were exactly," I say, "but they came out one by one all along the path, chasing me."

"What'd you do?" Carl says. His voice seems perfunctory and not concerned; what should have been a good story has turned hollow because of Martin.

"I clocked one of them and went in the other direction." I lean forward into the breeze and let it take the moisture from my chest and arms.

"I don't suppose they thought you could outrun them," Martin offers softly. He leans out over the railing in front of me and rubs his chin as he speaks. I look at him and I don't know at all what to make of him.

"The goddamned thing is," I say, sloughing off the remark, "is that Shaddock was there with them. As if beating me up was some kind of team activity or something. When I came out of the woods alone, he was standing there, right in the middle of the street. I think he was surprised as hell to see me."

"You should have got him," Carl says.

I stretch my arms a little bit, look back and forth between the two of them. I shake my head. "I can't believe it, really," I say.

"Why?" Martin says. Again his voice is soft, even, without judgment. His question surprises me.

"Get him, nail him right to the floor," Carl says quietly, clenching his fists and punching the air.

"Why what?" We look at one another. I look at him longer than I think is safe. When I do, there is a funny mixture of things going on in my mind.

"Why does it seem so incredible?" he says. He folds his arms and looks at me, sanguine, assured, and yet, there is something there as wild and hot as madness.

I give a shuffling laugh. Then, after a moment of thought, I say, "Because of what he represents, because of who he is." My voice is defensive.

"But what does he represent? Really?"

"The goddamned school is what he represents." I look at him, lick the salt from my lips.

"But he represents the team, and isn't that just what you ought to expect?" His voice is reasonable, almost like my father's, except there's a place where it falls off that my father's never falls off.

I shrug, look away from him to Carl, then out over the rail. I feel a warm, stinging wash suffusing the skin of my face. My lips taste of salt. I want to do a million things, but I stay where I am, thinking. "Maybe," I say.

After a silence like dead leaves rattling in a breeze, I say, "What cabin, Carl?" My voice comes out like an accusation, which I don't mean, exactly. But I know what cabin.

For a long time—since we were little—we talked about building a cabin at the Outskirts. But it has always been the sort of thing I wanted to talk about and never to do. Talking about it, like talking about a dream, made it seem lovely and delicious and perfect, the way building it never would.

Carl looks up. His thick neck is slouched forward. "The one we've been talking about building for the last hundred years or so," he says loudly, in a blunt, musicless voice. His face is eager. "Martin wants to help. He knows about architecture and stuff."

My muscles have begun to cool, to stiffen. My chest seems tight, shallow. I laugh, squeeze my hands against the back of the chair. "Architecture," I say. "It's not like we're going to build an office complex or anything, just a cabin. You know. Abe Lincoln was born here. Home on the range, that sort of thing."

Insulted or annoyed, Martin turns away and looks off toward the fields. His movements are liquid, his arms are dark and ropey.

Secretly, I'm pleased with myself for making him turn away.

Carl doesn't pick it up. He keeps talking. I let the trees and lawns go blurred, I let the roofs smear out beneath me. I think of Kate, imagine her in the sweet, deep woods. The odd syncopation of Carl's voice thrums on the air.

"What about it, Alb? Huh? What about it?"

"What?" I say.

"I think we need the help. I think if we could all pitch in—"

"You sound like somebody's mother."

"I think we'll never do it unless we have help. We talk and talk. I want to do it. Martin's a good guy."

"You want, you want," I say, getting up and looking at him. For a moment I hate him. We have known each other all our lives, and I never realized how thick he is, how selfish. "What about what I want? The lake is my place. It's my place."

"It's not yours. It's no more yours than it is anybody else's."

"I found it. I took you there."

"So you found it," Martin says. "Hooray for you. I found it too."

I want to spit when I look at him. Instead, I get up. "Listen," I say, "you guys can do whatever you want." I turn away from them, then give a stiff little wave and head down the steps and out of the house. When I get out onto the street and start jogging toward home, Carl calls out, "Watch out, man."

The television is on in the living room, and though the sun is just setting outdoors—the back windows frame a late, orangish light—the glow from the television fills the room. I don't look at the screen, but the explosions of illumination are so sudden, so violent, that it seems as if the television is hurling the light.

My father paces back and forth across the living room, half of him shadow, half radiation. He pulls papers from the tops of the shelves and throws them into a brown grocery bag. He stacks the old newspapers that litter the coffee table and chairs and floor. He arranges and rearranges things while he stares at the television. Sometimes he laughs when the canned laughter jumbles out into the room.

I lean against the doorframe in the hallway, watching him. I'm behind the sweep of the television, in the darkness. The volume is up loud—a commercial now, a woman selling some kind of detergent for the bathroom. I ignore it except to notice that it makes my father's movements appear soundless.

For years, when my father and I walked together, we held hands. Partly it was out of affection for one another, and partly it was his concern for my safety. It never occurred to me, until only three or four years ago, to consider it embarrassing or compromising. I don't know what happened—or I do, but don't understand it.

When my father turns off the television, the silence in the room seems unnatural. He is a shadow now, moving slowly, wearily, without the metallic sheen the television gave him. When he turns on the light, both of us are surprised.

"I didn't know you were there," he says quietly.

I shrug. "Yeah," I say, "I'm here."

In the mornings when I was little I used to listen to my father as he got ready for work. I could predict where he would go next, what he would do—at exactly what moment he would shave, shower, just when he would start the coffee pot. I dreamt of my father, of the sound of his voice, of the smell of him and the touch of his clothes.

"I didn't mean to startle you," I say.

"Oh," he says, his voice vague, "you didn't. Really."

"How was work?"

"Work was work, Al," he says, his voice almost a whisper, as if it could scrape across the ceiling. "Work was work."

"You could tell me about it sometime," I say. I don't really mean it, but he looks tired, as if he needs something.

"There's nothing really to tell," he says. "I sit around an office all day with a bunch of other fun-loving people. We tell jokes, play cards, have a wonderful time." It is supposed to be funny, and he allows a weak laugh to escape him. I don't make a sound. He takes the sock he has been holding and throws it at the picture window at the front of the room. I wish it were a brick. I wish it would slam into the window and send the glass smashing and showering away from us. I'd love the gust of cool evening air, I'd love the sound of it. But the sock just slides down the glass and falls behind the couch.

"Hey," I say, "I'm going over to Kate's after supper."

"All right," he says, biting the corner of his mouth. "But listen." He stops and I look at him. His eyes fall away so that he doesn't have to look at me. "We have a meeting tomorrow, you and me," he says.

"You and me?"

"That's right. The two of us. Cozy, huh?"

"Who with?"

"Your—ah—Mrs. Schwartzmann."

Mrs. Schwartzmann is my English teacher. The only one of my teachers I like, and the only one who seems to be worth listening to at all.

"What about?"

My father pinches his lips together and squints. "About everything, I expect," he says. He sits down for a moment. "Since she's the only one who seems to be able to talk to you, your guidance counselor has turned your file over to her. So she says.

Something like that. It's all very complex. The inner workings of the high school bureaucracy."

"My file," I say.

"She thinks the three of us ought to get together and have a few drinks. You know. Get to know one another." He pats his breast pocket, digs out a cigarette. When he lights it, the color of the smoke is exactly that of the television light.

"Yeah," I say, weak inside.

My father gives his hands a little clap, then gets up and goes into the kitchen.

Kate sits at the edge of the carpet on a white stool. Behind her is a small black amplifier for her electric guitar. The guitar, one of several instruments in the room, is on her lap. I watch as her fingers go over the frets, sketching, scraping, halting and starting. She stops. A breathy laugh.

I sit on the carpet opposite her, legs crossed, leaning back in a state like nervous sleep. In my head I picture Martin, Mrs. Schwartzmann, Shaddock and my father.

The carpet is pale gray, like a dull sky. The walls are white, like bleached sand. There are photographs on the walls, and the metal frames look like windows. The piano I lean against is solid and black.

She wears khaki shorts, and the way she sits, her knees together and pulled up beneath her on the stool, the pockets of her shorts flare. She wears a sleeveless cotton T-shirt, and when she turns away from me to adjust the amplifier, I try not to look at the pale, pale skin that shows inside.

She flicks the strings. Her fingers are strong. On the left hand, they are coarse where they skate along the neck and frets.

After a while, she puts the guitar down on the carpet and turns

off the amplifier. In the silence I feel as if I could fall away
through the carpet and disappear.

"You want to hear something fabulous?" she says.

I nod, smile. Her skin and clothing stand out in the bright
room, against the white and gray.

She takes a tape off the shelf and puts it into the tape machine.
She flips two switches, then turns toward me. "I've been listening
to this almost constantly for the past couple of days. I made
it from a record at the library. It's by Mahler." She stands a
moment, looking at me, her hands held behind her back.

I am always looking at her body as though it is something I
have just discovered. I know but still I do not know the brown of
her legs, the fine spray of translucent hair.

"Close your eyes," she says, sitting down next to me, pushing
the piano bench away.

I close my eyes and lean against her, put one hand on her leg
as if for support.

"It's called *Kindertotenlieder,*" she says.

A woman's voice rises out over the music, sweet and sad and
lush.

"It means 'Songs on the death of children,' I think. One of
Mahler's poet friends wrote hundreds of poems after his children
died. I can't remember his name." She speaks softly, not inter-
rupting the music but coloring beneath it. "Mahler chose these
to put to music."

Maybe it's the music, or maybe it's just the day, but I begin to
feel light, weak. The darkness of the music is offset by a bright
resonance that moves through me with the shine of water. My
head fills with it. Like the beginning parts of sleep, like clouds
in a fast-moving sky, images cross and disappear.

Kate whispers, "Mahler had children of his own before he

finished the songs. His wife thought he was tempting fate by writing the last ones." She pauses and I listen for her voice in the music. "One of his daughters died. I think she was taken ill. After that, he shut up the house where the girls were raised and never went back. I think that's how it goes. God, his life was almost an opera itself."

I don't say anything. I think of Kate in the woods. I think of her half-dressed, and already that moment has begun to die in my mind. Because we are here. Because it's hard for me to believe in what's gone.

I feel the songs moving in me, making a place. Even though I don't understand the lyrics at all, I can feel the woman's voice echoing in my head, the words as full as if they had been sculpted.

We are silent for a long time, listening. "The last song," she says toward the end, "is supposed to have a brighter, more promising quality. Mahler's trademark is resurrection and redemption."

Later, when the music is finished, we go out onto her porch. I can hear the songs beginning to replay—the sad sweet soprano, the muted violins and reeds. I lean against the railing and look out into the dark. Kate sits in a wicker chair. The street is dark, and filled with lights, but I hardly feel awake. From the music, I feel as if I've come from another world, like I do sometimes when I've run too long and too far. I think of Martin too, standing against the rail at Carl's house, his shirtsleeves pulled up to his elbows.

After a while, Kate says, "How do you feel?"

Vaguely surprised, I turn to her. One leg is crossed over the other and she bends forward, holding her heel in her fingers. She doesn't look at me but out at the lighted street.

"I feel great," I say, uncertain. "I mean, I'm not sure I know what you want me to say."

She laughs through her teeth. "I don't *want* you to say anything." She looks at me but her smile drifts away. After a few moments, she pinches her lips together and looks at me straight on. "I mean how do you feel about the world? How do you feel about the president? about nuclear war? How do you feel about art? about music? about anything?" She digs into her pants pocket and gets out a crumpled package of cigarettes. When she lights one and blows smoke, she reminds me of Emily. "I mean," she says more softly, "sometimes you make yourself completely inaccessible, that's all. Sometimes I just wonder who you really are."

I look at her stupidly, startled, something going out of me, something dulling in the air. When I am unable to say anything, she continues.

"I'm—listen. I didn't mean that exactly. It's just that I—" She looks at me and then looks away, her eyes going quickly, nervously. "I mean, just forget it. Forget it. Most of the time, Al, you're just lovely, just perfect. Really you are. It's just the music and I don't know. Don't pay any attention to me. I'm a fool."

"I love art," I say emptily, meaning my words to be ironical. "I love music. I hate politics, I hate the president." I try to look at her, to search out her eyes. "What is it?" I say. "What?"

"It's nothing, Albie," she says. "I don't know. I don't even know what I meant." She waves her hand and the cigarette coal makes a trail in the air.

I look at my hands, at my legs. "I'm sorry," I say quietly. I want to touch her but I can't.

She stands up and kisses me, fast on the mouth. It's so quick I stand blinking, unsure that it has even happened. But there is the vague taste of burnt tobacco on my lips. She looks away. Again, I feel the river inside me, the inevitable movement of the current. She looks at me, then away out over the lawn and the glimmer of the houses beyond. She smokes, and the scent of it fills the air, still as the dead spot of a tornado.

After Kate's I sit on the front lawn at my father's house, by the sidewalk, listening to the night sounds. I try to figure out everything—school, track, Kate, Martin—and the music comes, slowly, quietly, the ringing of the oboe rising up in me, a perfect harmony for the woman's voice. I close my eyes and in the damp grass the music builds around me, a kind of salvation, a red warmth of sadness. It breaks things loose in my mind—images of Kate and Mrs. Schwartzmann and my father—and they come drifting up into my vision and away. When the music stops, I look up.

The motorcycle comes around the curve of my street, the headlight wobbling with the movement, with the rap of the engine.

It is only after the headlight washes over the lawn and catches me in its beam that I think of hiding in the bushes and waiting for him to go away. Instead, I stand up and watch it come close, listen to the roar of its motor. He stops where I am and cuts it off. The silence engulfs us, circles around and swallows us like a backwash from the current of the bike.

When he's taken off his helmet, he says, "How's it going?"

"All right," I say quietly, allowing nothing.

"This town's kind of dead," he says. If he said it differently, I'd almost take it as an insult, but he says it scientifically, as though it's only an objective observation. "I mean you walk down the street and hardly ever see other people. You see televisions on in living rooms, through the windows. But you never see people."

"Yeah, well," I say, trying to think, "it's an old town. A railroad town. Not much railroad anymore."

There is silence again, and it makes me feel like I am floating. I don't like silence.

"I've been thinking about your guy Shaddock," he says. "I mean after you left this afternoon, Carl told me a little." The motorcycle clicks in the space left between his words. He hangs the helmet over one of the handlebars. There's something apologetic in his words.

"I'm not sure he's worth it," I say.

He raises his eyebrows and cocks his head a little. In the dark, I can't tell if his expression is serious or only mocking. "I'm not sure you're right," he says, "but that's not what I meant."

I don't say anything, but watch as he knocks the kickstand down and leans forward on the bike, resting his elbows on the handlebars. I think of those old motorcycle movies and wonder who he's trying to emulate.

"When you were a kid," he says, biting the inside of his lip, "did you ever get into a fight on the playground?"

The question strikes me as funny, out of place, and I laugh at it. "I still do," I say. It is meant to sound defiant, but it sounds idiotic, hollow as a tin can banged with a spoon. "Sure," I say, "once or twice," and try to regain my balance.

"You know how as soon as the teachers heard what was going on, there was always someone to pull you apart and make you shake hands?"

I look at him and nod and wonder what he wants from me. At

the same time, I'm glad it's dark, glad the darkness hides both of our faces.

"What I was thinking about is that this guy Shaddock, while he's supposed to be in the position of pulling people like you and me apart—"

As he says this, I wonder what it would be like to fight him. I wonder if that's what he wants.

"—is instead getting his organization to ambush you, just to advance whatever goals he has."

I shrug my shoulders. There's a sour taste in my mouth. I'm not so sure I like the way that this is no longer a private problem. "So?" I say.

"I just think it's interesting, is all," he says, looking for the moment more adult than boy. "Think about war," he says. "Think about crime. Think about the difference between the way adults and children fight. Where's the line?" He looks at me and leaves his voice dangling in the air. "Somewhere along the line it becomes a matter of life and death rather than a matter of getting up out of the dirt and shaking hands. What I want to know is where the line is. The arguments can't be that much different, it's the scale that's different, the idiom. When do you start bringing in guns and knives and tanks and rockets and God knows what else?"

I shrug again. This is all very nice, but I'm not sure I see its relationship to me. I wonder why, after the way I acted toward him at the Outskirts, he should want to come around and solicit me like this.

Because of the silence, because of the high-pitched whine of the insects, I say, "I'm not sure I see what this has to do with Shaddock."

He smiles, and when he does, I wish I hadn't spoken. "It seems to me that it's guys like Shaddock who show us where the line is," he says. "And how to cross it." He looks at me and in the darkness it almost feels like we are the only two human beings in the universe. "Not that Shaddock is inherently evil— or that there is such a thing as inherent evil. Or even that he's particularly intelligent."

I shove my hands into my pockets and turn away from him. The evening is cool, the grass is damp. I think of Kate in the woods, and Martin's sudden, unwanted appearance. Suddenly he is becoming as much a part of the momentum I feel around me as my father or Shaddock or even Kate.

"Don't mistake stupidity for harmlessness," he says, and picks the helmet off his handlebars. "He'll try it again. Even the stupid learn from their mistakes."

"I can take care of myself," I say. I turn to him. He has a thin mouth. His lips are colorless and compressed. In the dark when he talks, his teeth and the whites of his eyes look blue, the color of the night sky.

He puts the helmet on and straps it beneath his chin. "Don't you think," he says quietly, drawing attention toward his voice with its low sibilance, "that he ought to be punished?"

It is an offer, an incantation. I shake my head and look down. I can't think of anything to say to him. If I say yes, I do think he ought to be punished, then we are intertwined.

After a minute of silence, he kicks down on the starter and jiggles the throttle. The motor catches and roars. Oily exhaust plumes out from the tailpipe and coils upward. It stinks, and makes my eyes water.

"See you later," he says, and I nod, knowing I will, but without the energy to shout over the sound of the bike.

* * *

My father flanks me closely as we follow Mrs. Schwartzmann from the cafeteria to the office. My father is as uncomfortable as I am, perhaps more so. The three of us, formal as funeral-goers, move through the mass of students as if in a cocoon.

As we go into the office, I see the red-haired kid I tripped in the woods, and he grins and elbows his friend, but his reaction doesn't seem to match my situation.

We go into the guidance office and Mrs. Schwartzmann holds the door for us, then lets it swing shut behind us. She says a few words to the secretary, and we follow her down another hallway and into a conference room. We take the chairs she offers us. The door closes with a sound like a refrigerator door.

Businesslike and smiling, Mrs. Schwartzmann puts my file on the table and folds her hands over it. She is a woman of real poise —every movement she makes seems elegant and considered. She has blue-black hair that is so perfect in color it must be dyed. She is the most intelligent person I know.

"What we're going to say today," she says, looking back and forth between us, "isn't going to go beyond these walls. It's off the record. Just between the three of us." If she is nervous, it does not register on her face. She looks at us, as if for agreement.

"To start with, why don't you tell me a little bit about yourself, Albert?" She looks at me and smiles. It is hard to doubt her sincerity. "I know a few things, but I want a fuller picture." She looks at me. "I know that for the most part your papers are quite good. And I know that you're doing well in my class." She smiles chidingly. "But I also know that it is perhaps the only arena that doesn't leave anything to be desired."

I look at her, but I look down at the table immediately. "I don't know what you want me to say," I tell her. "I mean, what do you want to know?" *The president, art, life*.

"Just give me some kind of idea what Albert Santamoravia is like outside of the classroom. You obviously have done some reading. What else do you like to do? Do you have a girlfriend? What are your hobbies?" She folds her hands over the table.

Violent, something inside my head says. *Albert Santamoravia is a violent person*. "I like to run," I say. "I run six, eight miles a day. Sometimes twice a day."

"My," she says.

"May I smoke?" my father says. His voice has a peculiar modulation to it. Each word is precise, careful.

"I'm sorry," Mrs. Schwartzmann says, turning to him, "but that's not allowed in here." Suddenly I feel sorry for my father, sorry that he has to be here in the house of children, sorry that he has to be treated like one of the children.

"I see," he says. "Fine." And the hand that hovered near his breast pocket drops to the table.

"Do you run for your health?" she says. "Are you concerned with fitness? With staying in shape? Or is it something else?"

I look at her and wonder who she's talked to, what she knows about me. "I do it because I like to. As far as I know there's no other reason."

"Do you enjoy other sports?"

"Running isn't a sport," I say. "There's no sport. No team, no competition. Like reading or listening to music, I do it alone."

Mrs. Schwartzmann stops, looks at my father, then gives the table a little tap. "Mr. Santamoravia," she says, "would you like a cup of coffee?" Her head is bent slightly toward him; a smile clings at her lips.

"Yes," my father says. "Yes. Black, please."

"Do you want a glass of water or something?" Mrs. Schwartzmann says to me. I shake my head.

When she's left the room, my father leans across the table to me. "I know you're uncomfortable, Al, but let's try not to be defiant, okay?" His eyes are red and the skin beneath them is loose, gray. "Can you please just try to be cooperative, all right?"

I look at him but say nothing. I want to tell him that I'm sick to death of hearing about my running, that it's no one's business but my own. In a moment, Mrs. Schwartzmann comes back into the room with two styrofoam cups of coffee.

"Well," she says congenially, "where were we?"

"We were talking about Al's running," my father says. I can see him trying the angle.

"That's right," she says. Her lips tremble as she sips from the cup. "Some of my friends who are joggers tell me that it can be very therapeutic. What do you think about when you run, Albert? Does it help you to solve problems?"

"I don't think about anything," I say. "Mostly I listen to music."

"You've got one of those little personal stereos that everyone seems to have these days?"

"No," I say shaking my head. "I just listen." Though I do not look at her, I can feel her looking at me curiously.

"Al," my father says, "has a knack for listening to music, then playing it back in his head, or so he tells us." I look at my father, then at Mrs. Schwartzmann. "He's been doing it since he was a child."

"That's very interesting," Mrs. Schwartzmann says.

"It's no big deal," I say. "It won't change the world."

"What do you listen to?" she says. "Who are your favorite groups?"

"Groups?" I say. I know what she means, but I am disappointed by her questions, and I want to make her explain.

"Bands?" she says loudly, as if I am deaf.

"If you mean rock and roll, then I don't like it very much," I say. "It's boring."

She gives a smile that rises up out of her like some kind of light. "I tend to agree with you," she says. "But if you don't listen to rock and roll, what then?"

I think of Kate sitting on the porch, her brown legs smooth as butter. I think of Martin standing in the darkness, his eyes cold and bright and blue as his teeth. "Mahler," I say. "I listen to Mahler most of all."

"Any piece in particular, or his whole oeuvre?" Her hands float like birds in the air when she gestures.

"The songs about dead children," I say.

"*Die Kindertotenlieder*?" she says. She seems surprised.

"I don't understand them—the words—but I like the singing, and the sadness."

"Well," she says, and brings a hand to her mouth a moment in thought. "Perhaps you'd like to take some German. Try to develop some more understanding of them?"

I look at my father. He wears his cooperative face. I look back at Mrs. Schwartzmann. "Why?" I say. What I want to tell her is that I know enough already, that I understand them perfectly well, that I don't need to know the words. What I want to say is that I'd rather *not* know the words. That would only ruin the sadness. But I can't explain it.

"There's a great body of wonderful German literature beyond

the songs of Mahler," Mrs. Schwartzmann says, folding the birds of her hands onto the table with something like impatience, "and though one can read a great deal of it in translation, reading translation is very limiting. You're not, after all, reading what the author wrote."

I try to right myself in the movement of the conversation. A moment ago we were talking about running, about music. Gears have changed, words are angling at me.

"There's Goethe, Thomas Mann, Rilke," she says.

"I like Rilke," I say.

"Good, then—"

"I don't want to take German," I say, shaking my head furiously. The anger that rises up in me and flushes my face is like a drug.

"The fact is, Albert," Mrs. Schwartzmann says, "that you have to do something." She opens the folder and takes out a piece of lime green computer paper. "This is the last semester of your last year. I realize that it's easy to get bored. So far, you've got a B in my class." She looks at me. There is no expression on her face, only dry searching. "Elsewhere the news is not so heartening. Now, something has to happen, or you're not going to be graduating. It's as simple as that." She shrugs, waves one hand in the air. "To be completely truthful with you," she says, "you're going to have to sit down and make a concerted effort to change things or all of this is going to pass you right by."

All of us sit in silence for a few moments. I can hear my father breathing, can hear the buzz of the bleach-white overhead lamps. Beyond the close walls, I can hear voices, hundreds of them, all melded together like some kind of powerful instrument.

"Exactly what are we talking about, then?" my father says. "Bottom line. What's it going to take?"

"It's hard to tell," Mrs. Schwartzmann says. She moves her eyebrows and her skin seems smooth and confident and eternal. "Albert is going to have to make a lot of friends." She laughs. My father smiles. "But the only classes he absolutely must pass are English and government. That's the bottom line. College is another question entirely."

"And what about college?" my father says.

"Again, it's hard to tell. Sometimes it's a lot easier for a student who's also an athlete, but since Albert says he's not interested in competition, then that's an alternative we can discard immediately." There is a hint of irony in her voice. Mrs. Schwartzmann draws her arms in close to her body and thinks a moment. Under the arms of her blue dress are dark crescents. "But there are plenty of colleges in the country," she says, "community colleges in particular, that will give all students a chance, no matter what their grades or circumstances." She gives a smile that seems vaguely medical. "Many of our less successful students use them as a stepping stone to the better universities. It gives them a chance to mature a little while they're improving their grades."

My father nods. His hands are folded in his lap, and he moves his head in a way that seems completely removed from his past. It's like he was never a teacher at all, like he doesn't already know these things. I hate him. I feel sorry for him. I don't know what to say to him, how to tell him what I think.

The weather dissolves and rain comes. The warmth of the air is gone and the sky is a steady, low march of gray clouds. The rain is full of the death songs, full of words—Martin's, Kate's, Mrs. Schwartzmann's and my father's.

I run but my legs are stiff and sore. The damp cool goes into me and rattles in my bones. The trees and grass are deep, wet green.

On my street, in the drizzle, I pass an old man with yellowish brown skin the texture of dried clay. He is working in his yard, pruning lilac, and wearing workgloves and glasses. He bends and stares as I go by. The sidewalk is littered with lilac petals, and the air is heavy with the scent. I smile but he only looks at me as if I were insane.

On Center Street, a woman stands with a girl in lavender stretch pants. Both are overweight, and watch a boy my age push a lawnmower through thick, wet grass. There are clots of cut grass in the yard. The boy doesn't seem to move. They all stand absolutely still in the rain, their eyes following me as I go by.

Soon I make the woods. My shirt is wet and clings to my skin. My shoes go *suck suck suck* in the wet earth. I think of the ambush, but I don't believe that those boys would crouch in the mud and rain-soaked leaves to wait for me. Still, it would make no difference. I'd be here anyway. I need the woods as much as I need the running itself.

When my father taught school—this was after the divorce, when it was just the two of us—we camped a lot. I suppose my father needed it. Sometimes, in spring and summer, we went almost every weekend. My father said if you stayed still in the woods, you could see anything you wanted. And so on our weekends, I learned how to hang in the trees, or hide in the brambles, or bury myself beneath the leaves. I remember spending hour upon hour patiently watching, waiting for whatever happened through. I remember crouching at the edge of the lake, watching the fish skate over the bottom in the shallows. They swam right up to where I sat motionless, and scattered when I moved.

In some small way, running in the woods is a part of the

same desire, just as is hanging around at the Outskirts. If I could become the trees, or become the electricity that moves between them—

I watch the leaves, watch the trees for movement. There is nothing, nothing at all but the chatter of squirrels, the empty woods, and the sound of my feet.

I circle around on the horseshoe path and come out across town, more tired than usual. The sidewalk is hard and startling after the soft of the woods.

At nearly half my usual pace, I turn onto Center Street and head toward Highland. Near the intersection, the red-haired kid, Roger, appears. He comes out from behind a white house on the hill, half a block away. He stands for a second in the yard, looking around, then pops down the little hill, over a concrete retaining wall and onto the sidewalk. I run between parked cars, start to cross the street to avoid him, but two more of them come out of the shrubs. I cross back up to the sidewalk and try to push myself faster. Behind me there is another, swinging onto the sidewalk from behind a row of lilac bushes. My breath is uneven, quick. I can't find my rhythm. All of them wear the same colors —red and white, the school colors. I look for my shadow but in the drizzle and overcast I haven't got one.

There's a coppery taste in my mouth. I slow up for a moment, let them close in. They come up quickly, the red-haired kid laughing, his hair bouncing on his head as if it were inflated. I look back and forth between them for an opening, but there isn't one. The grass is slippery. I can hear their feet. *Where is the line?* My heart hammers. I turn, listening to the sound of my own feet on the concrete, and head for the red-haired kid. He seems startled, and I watch as his face slackens a moment, then hardens. He hesitates, looks to his friends. Behind him is the long, cracked expanse of retaining wall.

When I hit him, he is turning, but there is nowhere to go. I hit him full on, with all my weight. He gives way beneath me and I can hear his breath push out, I can hear his knees go slamming into the pavement. I roll away from him, picking up sand and wet from the concrete. I slam him in the face with my fists. His cheek flattens and the skin turns white. He tries to get up again but I hit him in the mouth. I think I feel teeth giving way. Suddenly everything is sharp—the color of skin, of shirts and shorts. It is the violence. *Albert loves violence.* It seems like hours before the other boys get there. The red-haired kid's face is red and swollen with anger. I kick him in the legs, but lose my balance when a dark-haired kid with acne comes in between the cars and throws himself into the small of my back. I try to roll out of it, but there's a sharp kink of pain, and he pulls me down and my face is in the bright, spongy grass. I can taste the green, taste the animal-smelling dirt. The others scramble up. Somebody kicks me in the legs and I kick back, striking something, but I can't tell what. There are voices, muffled shouts. Their fists go like crazy. My mouth, the shallow of my ribs, the soft of my back. One kid takes hold of my hair and tries to hit me in the face. I hit him in the neck and he chokes, but someone pulls me up. Others grab my arms and I can't move. The red-haired kid moves in front to hit me, but I struggle them down, and they hold my legs, my face in the grass and wet and stink. His mouth bleeding, the red-haired kid winds up and hits me in the face. One of my eyes burns and I can feel blood. My stomach knots. I try to move but I can't. I kick up, try to punch. I'm wild suddenly with claustrophobia in the tight clutch of bodies. I'm wild with the stink of them and wild with a panic like drowning. I can feel the salt in my eyes and I know they are going to kill me. Their voices go like insanity, all around, whirling, becoming one voice, high, irregular, changing in pitch and modulation. I start to cough; there is blood in my mouth.

Then the high, changing voice is cut by another voice, this one rasping, dark and heavy. My body begins to lighten. I get closer to the grass, closer to the long, soft, moist blades. I want to sink down, lose myself in the sweet darkness of the earth. I think for a second of Kate, of the music. My lungs are high, gasping, bucking, but I don't feel it.

"Get up, goddamnit," someone says. I can't tell if I'm crying or breathing or bleeding to death.

"Al, get up."

"Come on, Albie."

They roll me over. It is Carl and Martin. The track boys are gone. I just lie on the grass, looking. My heart rolls back and forth in the hollow of my ribs.

"He looks like hell," Martin says.

"They beat the shit out of him."

"Nose is cut."

In a few minutes, I sit up on the grass, dizzy, and try to right myself. There's a rushing in my ears like wind in a conch shell. Martin's motorcycle is on the sidewalk and it seems to move. I shake my head and it feels like something is broken.

"Do you want to go to a doctor?" Carl says, touching my face gingerly, excited by the blood. "Do you want to go get those guys?"

"I want to go home," I say, and the childish sound of it makes me sick.

"I told you to be careful, man," Carl says. "I told you."

"Yeah," I say. My stomach surges.

"That nose is going to need stitches," Martin says, getting out a handkerchief and giving it to me. It burns against my nose.

Finally I get up. Martin gets onto the motorcycle and starts it. Like a giant wasp, the sound fills the air. Carl helps me on the back. The vibrato of the bike rattles through me. My face has begun to swell and the sound of the motorcycle is like the pain.

"Better hang onto me," Martin says, reaching behind him and taking my hands. "I'll go slowly. Wouldn't want to dump you on the curves." His voice is secure, like my father's. A point hard and dark. Haltingly, I take hold of his jacket. He lets out the clutch slowly and jiggles the throttle. The wind and drizzle pull blood from my nose all over my face. It spreads and thins. Everything seems like a dream. I watch Martin's neck and shoulders, but they seem at some remove from me, as if I were watching them on film.

My father sits in the bright examination room, his khaki poplin jacket draped over his lap, his elbows making round depressions in it. He says nothing, only watches wearily.

The doctor does not look at my eyes but looks downward as he stitches my nose. His hands are yellow, unreal, like a robot's hands in the rubber gloves he wears.

"There shouldn't be much in the way of scarring," he says. I watch the tiny inhuman blotches of blood on his gloves. "I had a similar cut when I was about your age." His eyes flash upwards a moment, then down again. His voice is like some kind of music, not really words at all but a series of tones set up in a fashion that's intended to soothe. "Right here," he says, touching a knuckle to the side of his nose, then pulling a stitch tight. "I fell off a bicycle." His smile is dry, antiseptic. I imagine if you cut his skin with a knife it would not bleed—there would only be more white, plasticky skin beneath.

The stitching, after the two painful shots of novocaine, is little more than a distant tugging at the skin. I want to tell the doctor I don't care about scars. I want to tell them both that I don't care about anything, but my mouth and my mind are as numb as my nose.

On the way home—it is late; our stay in the emergency room has lasted hours—my father stops for hamburgers. "You sure you can eat?" he asks. I nod slowly and watch as he gets out of the car and goes inside.

I watch him at the stainless steel counter while he orders. He looks out toward the parking lot, but I know he can't see me. Other people sit at the little, formica-covered tables, eating and drinking. Many of them are kids. They look happy, some of them in love.

I look at myself in the rearview mirror. My right eye is swollen and black. There's blood on my face and my mouth is swollen. My back and my arms and my chest and my legs—everything is sore and stiff.

When my father comes back, he turns on the car radio and we eat in the parking lot, him wolfing his hamburgers and me feeding french fries gingerly through my lips.

"Listen, Al," he says after a silence too much like a wall, "I can't possibly help if you don't tell me what's going on."

"You can't help anyway," I say, trying to hold my jaw rigid. "Just leave it alone."

"I just want to understand, son." He opens the cardboard box his cherry pie came in and slides out the pastry. "Damn it, this is cold."

"I know you want to help," I tell him before he has a chance to say anything more, "but I'd rather just work this out on my own."

"Then at least tell me who it was that beat you up."

I shake my head and wince. I want to tell him. I do, but I can't. I don't know how, my mouth won't work. I sit back against the hard seat of the BMW and a little bell in my head says, *Martin, Martin*. Finally, I say, "I can't tell you anything."

MAY

I could swear I smell rotting apples, but it is too early in the year for that.

I'm on the back of Martin's motorcycle, roaring down Division Highway. It's after school and we're following Carl across town. The air is cool and the sky is overcast; the trees off to the right of the highway, in Grant Park, blur together with speed and humidity. The wind rips into my face, into my mouth and nose and swollen eye, but I don't hear anything, I don't feel anything. I don't let myself. If I did, I'd think of the track boys, sniggering in the school halls at my bruises and stitches. In my head I'm listening to Mahler's First Symphony, and there is nothing but the music, the shell-white sky and the tearing wind. The road is close and gray and smooth. The moisture forming in my eyes makes everything seem unreal.

When we get across town, we pull off the highway and into a subdivision. Carl pulls the car onto a dead-end street, then turns it around and cuts the engine. Martin sidles the bike up to the car window and tells him to wait for us, to keep the trunk unlatched. I have my feet on the rear pegs of the motorcycle and my hands on the back of Martin's windbreaker. The music sounds like a waltz, or as I imagine a waltz to be—round and buoyant and deliberate. I pay no attention to what Martin and Carl say.

If it weren't for the wind and the shudder of the bike, I could

almost be in a dream when Martin lets out the clutch and swings
the bike away from the car. I watch Carl recede from us, watch
the earth speed up and feel the *chunk* of shifting gears.

We turn on a road called Nightshade Avenue, and Martin
buzzes along, looking right to left, watching the cars that pass
us, watching the cross streets and the houses. We turn again,
and I can feel the sway of gravity in my face and legs. We come
toward the Crossland shopping center and Martin speeds up. I
close my eyes and let the music well up like some narcotic gas.

We turn into the parking lot of the shopping center and speed
along the curb. At the far end is a supermarket. At the near
end is a drug store. People come in and out of the shops. In
front of a hardware store, where below the overhang there are
lawnmowers and seed spreaders set out on display, where there
are racks of garden tools arranged in neat gleaming rows, Martin
slows, passes by, then circles around and stops. A woman looks
at me when Martin, leaving the bike running, knocks down the
kickstand. We get off the bike and go to the tool racks. The
sidewalk is concrete and spotted with old chewing gum; there
is a smell like old leather and dirt and oil. The music swells,
horns standing up, racing with the strings. Point, counterpoint.
Then harmony. I find a chrome bow saw with a rubber handle
and put it over my shoulder. It is like I am looking through a
tube as we go, rattling the tool racks and searching through the
shine. I see nothing but what I look at directly. I hear nothing but
the music. A blue-shirted man stands by the glass doors of the
shop, watching me. Because of my bruises and stitches, I stand
out. I glance at him only in passing. I take the bow saw Martin
hands me and put it over my shoulder with the other. I pick up
a hammer, a hatchet and an ax. I see faces, bodies, but they
don't connect. Martin hands me more tools. *Three blind mice,*

the music says, slowing almost to a hush. I look at Martin and he nods his head. The blue-shirted man starts to move toward us when he sees us going for the bike, and suddenly we're running across the moving pavement, the tools rattling, and then we're on the bike, and Martin kicks the bike off the stand, yanks the throttle and rips away from the curb as quick as panic. The man starts to run after us, to shout. His words curl in the air in front of him, then hang like balloons. When I turn away from him, a hammer drops out of my arms and clatters across the pavement. Sparks. But then the music is building again, sweet and clean, blocking out even the high rattle of the motorcycle. In a moment there is nothing left but the music, the white inviolable calm in the center of my head. I clutch the ax and saws close to my stomach and lean into the speed of the bike and the flat of Martin's back. We hit Nightshade Avenue and race back to the car.

To make sure no one has followed us, Martin circles the bike around, and then, when he's sure, we dump the tools in the back of Carl's car and head for the Outskirts.

The three of us sit at the edge of the water, Carl throwing stones in the shallows. The ground beneath us is damp. My neck is stiff and so are my arms and legs. I listen to the sound of the stones falling into the water and get up stiffly. In the cool humidity, the thick woods seem all of one plane—thick and gray-brown and flat as a wall.

"Do you know where a street called Summerhays or something like that is?"

"Yeah," I say, nodding. "It's not far from Emily's. Real short. I think it's only about two blocks long." Martin stands against a corona of green. The features of his face seem indistinct.

After a moment or two, I say, "What about Summerhays?"

"That's where Red lives. Your friend Roger."

"Better dead than Red," Carl says, cackling. He sounds like a mockingbird—shrill, unreal.

"Shut up, Carl," I say.

"We ought to kill him. We ought to kill all of them," Carl says.

Martin says nothing. He stands with his arms folded and looks past me out over the glint of the lake and the haze and the white sky.

Martin's house is small and warm and cluttered. The kitchen blazes with light and smells of cooked vegetables, cooked meat. There are dishes in the sink and on the counters. The table is covered with neatly stacked papers and opened envelopes. A radio built into the wall near the sink plays classical music—Bach, I think.

From the other room, a woman's voice: "Marty? Mart?"

I touch the edge of the table with my fingers and think about my father. I've missed supper, and if my father cooked, he'll be angry. I imagine his face, but I'm here and there's nothing I can do.

"Hey, Mommalinda," Martin says leaning over the counter and opening and closing a breadbox.

I stand blinking, warmed and dizzied by the closeness of everything, by the unfamiliarity. Though the house is crowded, it is neat.

Martin leads the way into the other room, and we hover between the light of the kitchen, and the dimmer, yellowy light of the living room. "This is my mom," Martin says, pointing to the woman rising from the couch to greet us. There is a funny tinge to his voice, but I can't place it. "You can call her Mrs. Willman," he says, smiling, looking at her, "or you can call her Mom or Linda or even Delores." He laughs. She stares at him as she comes to us. Her curly hair is streaked with gray.

"This is Albie Santamoravia," Martin says. "You can call him Al."

She smiles broadly—almost too broadly. For a moment there is something about her that catches me off guard, but it happens so quickly that I can't figure it. I shake her soft hand.

"What kind of a name is Santamoravia?" she says.

"It's French or Spanish," I say. I've heard the question before, and I still don't know the answer. "It's American now, though."

"It's lovely," she says. "And it's a pleasure to meet you."

I thank her. She is pretty. Her face, unlike Martin's, is narrow, and her eyes are set in close to the blade of her nose. They're white and clear, and in a funny way, they almost seem transparent, as if you could look back into them and see her mind.

"We're going upstairs, Mom," he says.

Her mouth moves almost imperceptibly. Then she looks between us, as if someone's just come through the kitchen door. I fight the urge to turn and look. "Come on," Martin says, and takes hold of my arm. He seems different around her.

On the narrow landing at the top of the stairs, he stops me. When he leans close to whisper, I feel his breath. "You've got to ignore my mother," he says. "She's got a great sense of humor most of the time, but since my father died, she gets kind of sad sometimes." I watch the play of shadows on his face. As soon as he's said it, he sloughs it off, then turns and walks into his room. Below us, I can hear operatic singing. It's very light, very faint. It sounds like the radio.

Martin has the entire upstairs to himself. His bedroom faces the street, and on either side, the ceiling slants downward with the decline of the roof. His desk is against the window and there are books—some I recognize from school—lined up on top of it. Next to his desk is a packed bookcase. On the wall, there's a huge poster of Albert Einstein riding a bicycle. There are other posters and photographs all over the walls. Because of the look of the pictures, it is easy to tell that some of them are famous people, even though the only one I recognize is Einstein.

He pulls out the chair from behind the desk and sits down. Then he points to the neatly made bed and tells me to do the same.

"Who are all these people?" I say. The nervousness that runs through me keeps my arms in close to my body, keeps my legs close together.

"Most of them are philosophers," he says. "That over there is Nietzsche. The picture of the painting is Kant—ugly, wasn't he? That's Wittgenstein, and the one next to him is Richard Wagner, the composer, but I guess you know who he is."

Without meeting his eyes, I nod. I had not known from looking at the picture that it was Wagner. In the tiny space of silence, I shove my hands deep into my pockets and sit tightly, still scanning the walls. In looking, I'm hit by how much Martin knows that I don't.

Most of the faces on the walls seem stern and stony. In particular, the one he pointed out as being Nietzsche. "How can you wake up in a room with him staring at you?" I say, trying to be funny.

He ignores the remark. "I love that picture of Einstein," he says. "I read somewhere that what Einstein wanted most was to ride on a beam of light. Can you imagine?" He turns in the chair and faces me. I feel slow, out of place. "In a way, it kind of makes you want to envy the bicycle."

Puzzled, I nod.

"You ever read any philosophy?"

"Not really," I say, shaking my head.

"I have a little," he says. "My father was a philosophy teacher. Or a philosopher. He even wrote a couple of books." He raises his arm and sweeps it along the wall. "He used to talk about the great philosophers like they were his best friends. But I guess if you spend as much time reading as he did, that's the sort of thing that can happen. When I was little, I used to imagine that the people he worked with at the university were just like them—you know, whiskers and all." He laughs. "Kant was my father's favorite, I think. He used to talk about reason as if it were something as real as water or fire. He and my mother used to have these incredible arguments about reason. For the most part, she agreed with him, but she liked to wind him up, set him off." He stops and seems to study the wall for a moment, and then, before he speaks again, his eyes go slack, then jump to life again. "My father was a big talker, you see. Once he got started, you didn't interrupt him or try to change his mind. Once he got started, he was like a bulldozer."

"What happened to him?" Halfway through the question, I regret the decision to ask it.

"He was killed in a hunting accident." It surprises me how easily he says it, and I try to imagine the feeling of having a parent dead. "Got hit right here." He pats his chest where, if he were singing the national anthem, he would hold his hand. "A suitably irrational end. Never found out who did it, either. It went through him—it was an arrow—so fast that there was hardly a trace of blood."

"God," I say.

"Someone mistook him for a deer."

"I'm sorry."

"He never felt a thing, I'm sure." Martin gets up from his chair and stands in the middle of the room for a moment. "That's what turned my mother into a nihilist." The quality of his voice has changed. "From reason into nihilism. But it's a natural progression." He whirls around. "Hey, I've got something to show you."

He opens the closet and from within the neat cascade of hung clothing, he takes out a black thing that looks at first like a rifle. It is a crossbow. Black and sleek with a frame stock entirely of aluminum or some other lightweight metal, it looks, even without arrows, as deadly as a poisonous snake.

"Jesus," I say, "where did you get that thing?"

"My father got it for me. The four of us—my brothers Jack and Randy and my father and me—used to go bow hunting all of the time. Jack and Randy are both older. I was too little—too weak, really—to hold the string on a regular bow back long enough to get anything, so one of them would cock this thing for me." He swings the weapon up and shoulders it for a moment, then lets it drop back. "It's an extraordinarily accurate weapon. It's made in Israel. The Israeli soldiers use them in antiterrorist activities when they want to kill someone silently."

"God," I say again.

"Here," he says, handing me the weapon. "Take a look."

It is surprisingly light, almost like some kind of surgical instrument. I hold it up and look through the scope. I turn slowly and line up the crosshairs on Einstein's smiling, whiskered face.

"Pretty wild, huh?"

I think of his father, and of Shaddock, and suddenly uneasy, I give it back to him. The beguiling, almost erotic potential of the thing is dizzying.

"Ever shoot a bow?" He leans the weapon against the wall and hovers where he is for a moment.

"I used to have one when I was little. My father gave it to me for my seventh birthday. When we went camping, I used to try to spearfish with it. I loved it. Bows are great."

We stand in silence for a few moments. I feel uneasy, awkward. Downstairs, there's singing again.

After what seems like a long time, I say, "Do you go to school at West?" It is a question to which I feel I should already know the answer.

"Yeah, we just moved here. I had to transfer. I have two classes in the mornings, but I don't spend a lot of time hanging around or anything." He sits down on the bed and folds his hands together. "I'm just not into it, is all—the whole school thing, school spirit. You know. When my father died I missed a lot of school. I'd be in college now."

I nod blankly. I want to ask why he missed a lot of school.

"I mean I'll be nineteen in August." He looks at his hands as though there is something he isn't telling me. "In the fall I'm going to the community college. Study philosophy or something." He laughs. "Then I'll go somewhere else. I don't know." He says it without conviction.

In the backwash of silence, I go to the wall and look into the ancient faces there. It seems unbelievable that my own world could have any relation to these insane-looking, heavily whiskered faces. It seems impossible that they'd have any relationship to anything real.

"Let's go give it a try."

"What?" I turn around and he is standing now with the bow in his hand. "You go downstairs and stand under the window. I'll drop it to you. That way my mother won't worry her brains out."

"Are you serious?"

"Sure, why not?"

I can think of a million reasons, but I only shrug and look at the window, then back at Martin. "What do I say if she asks where I'm going?"

"Just tell her you're going home."

When I get downstairs, Mrs. Willman is sitting at the kitchen table. The radio plays softly some piece of music I don't know. She looks up, and her face is weary but lovely. "Leaving?" she says.

"Yeah," I say, nervous, watching her, "I've got to go."

"It was nice to meet you. Will you come again?"

I nod without speaking. In a way, I suddenly wish my father could meet her. He is roughly the same age, and has what seems like the same kind of intelligence. I am vaguely jealous of Martin. I wonder what his father was like.

"Well," I say.

"Come over for dinner sometime," she says.

I nod. Going outside is like coming up from underwater—the air is sweet and cool. Fighting the temptation to leave, I go to the wall of the house beneath the window. When Martin sees me, he drops the weapon into my arms.

We walk over by the high school. The movement does my legs good. It's been since I was beat up that I've run, and the bruises and the lack of movement have stiffened my legs.

We cut across the long, sloping lawn in front of the school, and I watch the ground in front of us as we go, the glistening of the heavy dew, the pull of our shadows in the purplish green coronas of the street lamps. I watch our shadows—mine stiff and angular, Martin's long and narrow, with the crossbow like an appendage.

I think of the first day at the Outskirts when Martin appeared, and I feel ashamed. I want to apologize for the way I acted, but

I don't. The words are right in my head, already formed, but I keep thinking of Mrs. Willman and the soft, lovely look of her face as I left.

We climb the fence to the stadium and it rings with the sound of our feet. In the middle of the field, we stop, and Martin cocks the weapon. I look up into the gray, ordered silence of the bleachers. I listen to the singing of the cicadas. He puts one of the little arrows into the bow, and I watch him.

"What are we shooting at?" I say, hands in pockets.

"The concession stand," he says. The head of the arrow is just a tiny flex of steel, blued and honed to a sharp edge.

He shoulders the bow, sights it for a moment. I watch the motion go out of his body. Then he pulls the trigger. There's a vague sound in the air like whispering, and then the faint *thunk* of impact. The quickness of it is astonishing.

He cocks the weapon again and hands it to me, then hands me one of the little arrows. "There's a safety on it right here," he says, touching the stock near the trigger, "but don't put the bolt in it until you're ready to fire, and never dry-fire it."

"The bolt," I say, nodding vaguely, feeling the weight and balance of it.

"Yeah," he says. "Just put it along the little groove, then notch it into the string."

I do as he says, then raise the weapon up and put it to my shoulder. I have to wait a moment for my eye to adjust. When I look down the sight and see the darkened field in the crosshairs, I get a momentary sense of panic. It strikes me clearly just how deadly it is. I lower it, then look at Martin.

"Pretty wild, huh?" he says, not really looking at me but waiting.

"Yeah," I say, then shoulder it again and bite my lip. I line up the crosshairs on the little wooden concession stand. When I touch the trigger, there's a click and a whisper, then a thin white trace in the air, and the *thunk*.

"Good shot," Martin says. He takes the bow when I hand it to him and we both walk toward the concession stand in silence.

"Beginner's luck," I say after a while.

After we get the bolts out of the concession stand—the tip of one of them breaks off in the soft plywood—we head back into the neighborhood, still in silence. I don't look at him, but I can feel him; I look at the moist long grass, at the dark hazy sky, at the way the light from the streetlamps sprays downward in the humidity.

We pass a woman walking a dog, but she doesn't look at us, and apparently, doesn't notice the crossbow. She only comes up out of the darkness, then recedes back into it like a giant bird floating by us on water.

I feel funny tagging along beside him like this—a little unnatural because of the silence—yet I keep going, because I know we're not going home yet.

We turn on Summerhays Avenue and walk on the unlit side of the street. I wonder what time it is; I wonder what my father is doing. I want to speak, but the silence has been so long that the whole idea of words seems crazy to me. I look for music and there is none. *Violence.*

Martin floats away from me, into a darkened yard. My hands damp with excitement, I follow him into the shadows and trees.

"You know," he says, crouching in a dry, grassless place between trees, "when Carl started talking about building a cabin at that place you all have—"

"The lake."

"Yeah." His voice is a whisper, yet even and considered. "I

knew that I had to be a part of it. I mean, still, if you don't want me to, then I won't, but it's been kind of a dream I've had. You know."

"Me too," I say, also whispering.

"It seems like the only way a civilization can go, if you know what I mean."

In silence, I nod. But I don't know what he means.

"Christ," he says, running his hand back up through his hair. "I mean if you look at everything in the world, everything that civilization stands for, it just makes you want to leave."

I breathe in the commingled scents of pine and honeysuckle, listen to the dark thrum of his words.

"My father, if he hadn't been a pragmatist, would have been a socialist. I mean he believed in the socialization of medicine and transportation and communication, but he knew human nature. He understood reason, and he understood people." He's silent for a moment, thinking. "I don't believe in any of that. I believe in self-sufficiency. That's why the idea of the cabin seems so great. It's the opportunity to test a philosophy. It's—" He stops, and his voice leaves a hush in the air. "Look," he says.

Across the street, on the porch of a white house with columns, with coach lamps gleaming against the shiny white paint, the red-haired kid Roger sits down with another boy on a pair of wooden lawn chairs. They both wear shorts, and Roger sits with his legs crossed. I can hear their voices—not what they're saying, only that they're talking. A dog barks somewhere.

"Here," he says quietly, cocking the bow. I don't know why, but it seems natural when he hands it to me, then hands me one of the bolts.

Without words, I take it and notch the bolt. I lie in the dirt, and lay the bow out in front of me. I know the feel of it now, just how sensitive the trigger is. And when I look down the tube of the scope, it feels like I've done it a million times. They're closer than the concession stand.

I sight the crosshairs just below the kid's head, but I don't even go near the trigger. It would be easy to do it, there is so much space between him and me. There is no relationship at all between the arrow and the boy on the porch, but the possibility that chance, that some sort of mechanical breakdown, could kill him, is intriguing. Of course nothing happens. With Martin lying here next to me in the dirt, I look down the sight and try to imagine what it would be like to die that way, what it would be like to have one of the razorheads rip through me. I wonder how Martin's father died. I wonder what it would be like for the boy on the porch. For a moment I can see it: the impact pushing him backward, against the wall, the razorhead crushing the bone, beneath it the muscle and lung giving way, and then the pain, coming in gusts at the same speed as the realization. And I can see him against the wall, pinned there by the bolt. Death rising like air in clear water.

Martin says, "My father," and laughs through his nose. "My father believed in global human responsibility. He thought we were all one great family, and each of us had a responsibility to the other. Do you know what he did? I hated him sometimes." He's close to me now, leaning to me as if telling me a secret, and as he speaks, I can feel the warmth of his breath. "Twice a month, he'd have us go—the whole goddamned family—down to the city shelter to work. We'd read to the drunks, wash bathrooms, do laundry. Can you believe it? This is when we lived in Richmond. I still can't believe it myself. Some of these people were so incapacitated by booze or disease or whatever that they couldn't even get up off the cots. There was one I used to see all the time, he wore a wig and makeup. Can you believe it? He was filthy, but he wore a wig and makeup. They were human garbage, and my father loved them. They had no right to live." He touches my arm and presses his words close to me. "I mean I never understood why they stayed in that horrible little shelter. Their lives were miserable. I wondered why they didn't leave, go into the woods—or even kill themselves. Anything would have been better than living like a parasite. I had no sympathy for them at all. None. People who can't take care of themselves ought to die, and they shouldn't be afraid of it. Sometimes it's the right thing. Sometimes it's the best thing."

He stops. I've been staring through the scope at the red-haired kid for so long that he has ceased to be anything real. His form is nothing more than a pattern of light wavering in the shadows. I blink and look away, but when I look back, it is still wavering, inhuman.

"The place stunk," he says. "You wouldn't believe how bad."

I take the bolt out of the crossbow.

"Their kidneys and livers and lungs were rotting right inside their bodies."

I hand the bolt to him and uncock the weapon.

On the telephone, Kate is distant. I missed her at school today and I want to see her. Her voice is difficult.

"Come to the lake," I say.

"I will," she says, "but not now. Tomorrow maybe." When she stops speaking, the phone line dangles soundlessly. I want to break into the silence, tell her that she doesn't understand.

"You have to see what we've started," I offer. "It's not much yet, but it's going to be something. We've already got a kind of foundation—"

"I will, Al, don't worry. Just not now." I can't tell if it's anger or weariness or annoyance in her voice.

"Can I come over?" I close my eyes. Involuntarily, the muscles in the wall of my stomach tighten.

"I'm tired, Al, please. And I have to practice."

"What's the matter?" I try not to let anxiety bleed into my voice.

"Nothing's the matter," she says. "Nothing." Then there is silence.

"All right," I say. "I'll talk to you tomorrow."

I wait a long time but she says nothing. In my head I imagine what she might say. I imagine her lifted by a flood and carried off. I imagine the receiver hanging in the rush of water. "Goodbye," I say finally, and when I hang up, I'm not even sure that she was ever there.

As soon as I hang up, the phone rings again.

"Where were you last night?" It is my father.

"I'm sorry, Dad. I was at Martin's." Unable to think, I feel like I'm drowning. The warmth of the receiver against my ear is maddening; angry suddenly, I have to keep myself from throwing the telephone and smashing it into a million pieces against the wall.

"Wait for me," he says.

I subdue my voice. "I was going to go for a run."

"Wait for me."

"Dad, I haven't run since—"

"Wait."

"God *damn* it," I say when I slam down the phone.

I stand in the street in the broad sunlight and wait for my father. It's late, but the sun is still high and hot. I wait, and moisture stands up on my face and chest. I remember when I was little and used to wait in the afternoons for my father to come home. That was when he still taught school. I try to remember my mother too, but nothing materializes except an image I've had for years of the fabric of a dress flattened between a pair of legs.

The air is still, and the neighborhood is silent but for the sound of children and the rush of cars in the distance. I look at our house, listen for the telephone, then look down the street. Still, he doesn't come.

I go inside and change into my running clothes. When I come out again, the driveway is empty, the street is wide.

I start to stretch. The grass is dry and stiff. Without willing it, I think of Kate—what she said about getting asked to the prom that day at the Outskirts. I don't know why it's never occurred to me to wonder before.

The prom. It almost makes me want to laugh. But all I can hear is the sound of her voice on the telephone–like a voice in another language, from another planet. I hear her saying *NO*, and it's like acid dripping down, eating up my insides.

Still my father doesn't come. I know what he's doing, and it makes me angry. For a moment, I'm so furious that I can hardly control myself. When cars crawl by on the street, I want to throw myself against them, smash the glass, make the sunshine stop gleaming. *Nihilism*, something says.

The sun moves. I stand up. I start to run, heading down our block in the direction from which my father, eventually, will come. When there is no sign of him, I turn off and head toward town, toward the woods at Grant Park. My body is stiff and sore, like something new and unused. Everything is painful.

I try to think of the woods, but I can't get Kate out of my head: *Kate at the piano, swaying through Beethoven; Kate at the Outskirts with her blouse raised; Kate in the music room at*

school, the sound going around us and through us like a river.
Without thinking, I turn off Parsons, then turn again and head
for her house. I have to look. I have to see.

I float above the heat and the pavement in the still air. The
warmth goes through me and softens the pain away from my legs
and arms. I get closer and I smell hamburgers cooking. I can
hear the death songs, but I don't know whether it is in my mind
or in the air.

Her mother's car is in the driveway. Her father's is at the curb.
The grass is long and needs mowing. The garage door is open.

I don't know what I expect, but there is nothing at all unusual.
I cross the street. I can hear the piano, and I can see her father
and mother moving in the kitchen window.

But suddenly I know by the sound of her playing that there's
someone with her, leaning into the sound of the instrument,
watching her move the way I have watched her. I start to go
faster. My legs are moving like they've always moved. Violence.
Speed. Who could it be? I wonder, but I know who—Martin.
Yet I know it's not true either. A little bell rings over and over in
my head.

Late in the afternoon—Saturday—after working all day cutting trees for our cabin, the three of us take off our clothes and
stand side by side on the beach. Carl is the first to go into the
water. His body strikes the green surface flatly, and the hollow
sound of it echoes out across the lake and back again. Beneath
the water, the yellowy shadow of his body skims out like some
enormous obscene fish. When the momentum of his dive ends,
he breaks the surface and shouts like murder. I look around,
across the lake in either direction. I wonder if someone will hear
us, but there is nothing at all, only empty lake and forest.

Martin shakes his head and smiles vaguely.

"Yeah, I know," I say. "I know."

"It's goddamned cold," Carl shouts.

"No kidding," Martin calls back. "What did you expect? It was cold yesterday and the day before." His voice is soft, not loud enough for Carl to hear. "Fool," he whispers.

"You ready?" I say.

"I guess," he says. "If you are."

"I don't know." I watch his eyes.

"Let's go," he says, eyes shiny. When he runs for the water, I tear along after him, then dive as soon as I get to the edge. It's like a gasp going through me, hitting me in the lungs and heart. In the shallows, it is warmer than it has been since Carl and I first went in back in March. But there are still patches of cold, icy water woven in among the warm currents.

Martin and I stand in the shallows, shivering lightly in the cool air. Carl swims out, way out to the middle; his head becomes a black dot against the glare of the late sunshine. I can smell myself and the water. I rub my arms, try to rub away the pine resin from our day's work. The resin does not want to come off. Martin says, "We'll have to send Carl in for some soap." Both of us laugh. I rub and rub until the skin blushes and begins to burn.

The cabin grows rapidly, awkwardly, both more and less perfectly than I had imagined it would.

We chose a spot deep in the woods—away from the road, away from the lake, a place so thick with trees you can't see ten yards ahead of you in any direction. Like a flower, the layers of the forest mount inward toward the clearing, heavy and sweet. Bramble, honeysuckle, grapes—you could circle the spot for hours, or sit in the woods and stare, but if there were no sound, and if you did not know it was there, you'd never know that there was anything but trees and vines and deep deep foliage.

While Martin and I cut the straight, narrow pines in the new forest, then carry them back to clearing (sometimes, we stand in the trees, suddenly stupefied by the thickness of the forest, wondering where we are), Carl drives back and forth into town to take things from his house or to shoplift, or to steal from construction sites. He is bored by the work, and when he is not driving, he does little but wander in the woods and piss like a dog on everything, or sit in his crazy beech tree talking nastily about Emily, or, when we come into the clearing, say how funny the cabin looks. "It looks like something one of the three pigs would build," he says, putting his finger into the crystal yellow ooze of pine resin. "I'll huff and I'll puff and I'll blow your—"

"Two pigs," Martin says softly. "Just two pigs."

"I've helped," he sneers. "Who got the plywood and the tar-paper? Who? Who got the food?"

It has been Martin and me who've cut and carried the sweet pines the half mile down from the new forest. It has been Martin and me who shaped and trimmed them, then notched them and put them into place.

Though it is small and hasty and incomplete, there is something about it that is deeply pleasing. Maybe it's only the work—or the feeling of the work in my arms and my hands and my head. Or maybe it is being away from Langston, from everything.

"You could do something like this for a million reasons, I guess," Martin says, slamming the axhead deep into the low part of the bough of a new tree. "But the best one, the only real one, is survival." He puts the ax down, spits into his hands, then looks at me.

I look at him, weighing the possibility. I don't say anything.

"I'm serious," he says, and his face goes dark a moment. He swings the ax again, then pulls it out with a squeak. "Just listen to this crap about peace and arms control. Just listen. It's all nonsense. Those people have never had any intention of doing anything. If they had, they would have done it a long time ago. It's all economics. They can't stop it, they won't." While he speaks, I think about the posters he had on his walls in his room. It seems like there are countless things he knows that I do not.

"They always have excuses. One week it's arms control, the next, it's balance of power. The fact is, they want to keep the stuff. They like the power." He shoulders the ax, then swings again. A big white chunk of pine flies loose and into the leaves. He swings deeper and deeper. I can smell the wood, and the commingling of our sweat with it.

"Yeah, I don't know," I say. "I guess so."

"The truth is," he says, not really paying attention to me, but breathing heavily with exertion, talking into the air, "that these people are contemptuous of the world. Utterly. And everything in it. Including you and me." He stops a moment, turns to me and lets the ax dangle in his hands. "Disgusting, isn't it? But that's the way the world is, and you have to be the same way, contemptuous of everything. My father thought differently, but look where he is."

My hands are blistered from my own ax. I rub them together gingerly, and listen to him. He is handsome, intelligent, angry, and there's something about the coincidence of those things that is enviable, yet when I listen, what I listen to isn't so much his words as the sound of his voice.

He swings one more time, then stands away from the tree and looks at it. "Come here and give a push," he says, not looking at me. We stand side by side and shove. Our shoulders touch.

It gives only slightly. Then again, and in rhythm. It begins to sway, a little at first, then the green plume of it begins to bounce. Suddenly there's a crack. I can feel it in the wood. The tree starts to fall slowly, then we jump out of the way and it picks up speed. Branches whip, crack, then snap off beneath it and tumble. It crashes down between the other trees and a great sound rails along its length.

Martin smiles, shoulders his ax again and rubs a spot of resin on his arm. "One more for today," he says, "one more."

After a few moments, when the silence of the forest has come back, I say, exaggerating, "I hate the world sometimes." I walk along the bough of the fallen tree, knocking off the low, dead branches with the back of my ax. "I just hate it."

"I don't hate it. I love it," Martin says. "I just hate the way some people treat it."

"Yeah, well, I guess that's what I mean."

"The question should be, do you want to survive?" he says when my back is turned to him. I don't turn around. "If you do, then you have to be ready to do what it takes."

Halfway up the bough of the tree, I turn and watch as he picks a new tree, then starts to swing. I watch his hair and the quality of his skin. I watch the ripple of his shoulders and back. I want to know what he means by contempt. I want to know what he means by necessity. I want to know if he includes friends.

"I've always liked this place," I say quietly, wanting to assert some kind of possession. "I used to come out here with my father when I was little. It's as close to paradise as any place I've ever seen. That's the only reason I wanted to do this. I wanted the place to come to. I don't know if that means survival or what."

"Isn't that what we all want," he says between swings of his ax, "in one way or another."

"I come out here to run sometimes. I get Carl to bring me. This week, in class, I kept thinking about the cabin. Here in the woods I could be anywhere, or anything. I could lose myself and never go back."

He lifts the ax to his face and looks at it, runs his finger along the blade. "You ought to have a better reason than that. Than wanting a little paradise. That's bourgeois. You ought to want to survive." He swings the ax again and sinks it into the tree.

I want to say I know, but I don't. I don't understand survival, not the way he has it. I want to tell him how sad the world makes me, nuclear weapons or no. I want to say how even seeing my father standing in a group with other suited and necktied lawyers makes me feel like I hate the world. When I see a group of people our own age walking down the street, the girls with small hands and tight pants and makeup and the air around them thick with perfume and chatter, the boys following eagerly, nodding, jabbering, poking out their hands to show something or touching their arms to feel their muscles or bragging on some foolish thing they've done—what I want to say is that I hate the way they dress, the way they talk, the music they listen to, the things they think are wonderful. What I want to say is that it's not hate, not really. It's something else I can't say. I don't know about survival. I come here to be away from the things I don't love and the things I do—I come here because I love the woods. But I can't say it. I don't know how.

"The thing is," he says, "that the world has survived on miracles for the last forty years. Fact." The word is like a rim shot. "They should have listened to Fermi and Einstein and Oppenheimer. The goddamned scientists should have listened to themselves." I'm surprised by the heat, the bitterness, that rides beneath his words. It's as if he feels personally cheated—as if he knew these dead men. "I'm sick of goddamned miracles. I don't want to live on miracles. They come too far and too few. I'm sorry. I've got to have something more real than that." He waits a moment. "See, it's a kind of selfishness you've got to have. But if everybody has it, then it's not selfishness at all."

Later, when we carry the logs back to the clearing, I tell him how I enjoy the work, how like in running I lose myself in it. "Work," he says, a log on each shoulder, me behind him and the branches and leaves sweeping over us, "will set you free."

High up in the trees above us, beyond the thick, wild run of bramble and blackberry and honeysuckle, beyond the still, humid air, beyond our own five static figures, the wind rides in the leaves like water over hot coals. It's Monday afternoon now, and the girls have just come out from town. They stand together, both of them wearing shorts and bikini tops. Emily smokes. Martin stands at the edge of the clearing, watching, his arms folded across his chest. Carl sits in his tree, his head dangling between his rounded shoulders like an ape's. I stand next to Kate, listening to the trees, to the breeze.

Kate says, "I don't understand why it has to be so far from the road."

"The farther out, the less likely someone is to stumble across it," Martin says, stepping closer to the girls, to me. "That's the point."

"But it's such a goddamned long walk," Emily says. "And I almost killed myself in that goddamned gully, by the way."

"Sorry," Martin says, his voice vaguely hostile.

"What about the roof?" she says, ignoring him.

"Plywood and tarpaper," he says, moving closer to her. His movements seem funny, detached, like those of a marionette. "We've got the materials. All we have to do is get them up."

"That means they stole them," Emily says to Kate, "in case you need the translation."

"And who asked you?" Martin says, standing close to her and looking down. Emily takes a step backward, but she doesn't stop staring at him. Her own eyes are cool and hard as glass. For a long time he looks down on her, and she stares back. Jays scream in the trees near us, riding the wire of tension that runs back and forth between all of us. It's like he's ready to jump into her skull, or suck out her heart, the way he looks at her. But then, abruptly, he turns away and goes back to the edge of the clearing. Emily glares after him.

I stand close to Kate, loving her presence against the woods.

Emily lights another cigarette and spits smoke.

For a long time there's silence, then Carl jumps out of his tree and stands next to Emily. "Who wants to go swimming?" he says. No one speaks, and he kicks dirt.

"There's no plumbing," he says to Emily.

"Thanks very much," she says, "but that's obvious."

"You have to pee in the woods," he says, coming close and staring at the side of her face. "With all the snakes and bears." He giggles.

"I wish you'd grow up."

"He's doing the best he can," Martin says.

Emily looks at Martin curiously. For a moment, there is a vague smile on her mouth, then it fades.

"I'm going for a run," I say, not looking at anyone, but into the trees.

"Can I come with you?" Kate says, her hand on my arm. "I brought some shoes and stuff. They're up at the car."

I look at her for a moment without understanding. When I first saw Kate, I wanted nothing more than just to look at her. I stared for hours, almost unable to believe the shape and substance of

her body. But after I had looked at her, I knew I had to touch her
—it was something beyond my own will. For so long, I dreamt
of the taste, the texture of her skin. And when I finally did touch
her, when she took off her blouse and led my hands to her skin,
I knew I had to have more, that I had to get inside of her and
own her. And I knew too that I couldn't allow anyone to look
at her the way I had. Now, watching her as I watch Martin and
Carl and Emily in the long green woods, I understand nothing at
all. But I stand close to her because I know—and this suddenly
—what will happen. I can feel it in the air, in the sketch of the
trees. She takes my hand. I hope she can't feel the tremble.

The air feels better, cleaner, when we get out of the clearing
and the others disappear. We can hear their voices, but soon, it's
only the two of us, cutting along through the trees, me leading
the way.

After a while, she says, "Martin's kind of a funny guy."

"How do you mean?" I know what she means, but I can't put
it into words myself.

"I don't know. Very protective is what I want to say, but I can't
think exactly what he's protecting."

"I know what you mean," I say, thinking more of the dampness
of her hand. "But he's all right."

"He's just so intense," she says. "It's like he's a couple of
degrees hotter than everybody else."

I nod. There is a silence. For miles there is nothing but us,
nothing but the birds and the snake-like sibilance of the breeze.

She says: "I'm sorry I've been so off lately, Al."

I don't know what to say, I want to tell her that it doesn't
matter, that I knew it was nothing. I don't say anything.

She clutches my hand tightly. "It has nothing to do with you,
really. I don't know. It doesn't really have anything to do with
anything." She laughs emptily. "Sometimes didn't you ever just

feel that the stars were against you? That everything was against you?"

It sounds odd, like something I've heard before. I don't know what she means, but I nod and hum anyway. "Yeah," I say.

"The thing is," she says, "sometimes I don't feel like I'm in control of my life, not really. You know? I feel like I do things just because I do them, and because I have to. I mean I feel like I'm being operated from without. That's why I wanted to run today." She's silent for a moment. We're nearing the car. "I mean, look at you. You're the healthiest person I've ever seen."

I want to tell her that it doesn't mean anything. I'm not healthy because of any conscious choice. I am just because I am. I do whatever I do just because it's the only place where things feel right and proper. She sounds a little like my father—always assuming that I am what I am because of some kind of choice.

"Besides," she says, "I really need the exercise."

The woods are quiet and the sunlight glimmers on the paint of Carl's and Emily's cars. We walk over a dip in the land, then up the little hill and through the underbrush. My whole body feels alive, aware. I can even feel the skin of my eyeballs. "I know I'll never be able to keep up with you," she says, "but just the same, you have to promise you won't go too fast."

"Don't worry," I say, distracted. My head feels light and my hands have begun to tremble.

When we get to the car, she opens the door and sits on the back seat with her feet out, on the ground. She takes off her sandals and exchanges them for cotton socks and running shoes. "Okay," she says, grinning, "I guess I'm ready."

I look at her and shrug.

"Do, um," she says shyly, "do you think this is okay?" She points to her bikini top, to her breasts.

"It's wonderful," I say. My throat is tight.

"What I meant was, you don't think it'll be too tight or anything?"

Almost laughing, I shrug. I feel vaguely nauseated. "It's okay," I say.

In a minute she closes the car door quietly and stands in front of me. I stare down at her. My arms burn from carrying logs down from the new forest. My nostrils burn with the scent of her. I stare, and I want to kiss her, but my mouth is dry as cotton. Finally I turn away.

"First thing you want to do is stretch," I tell her, and for a few minutes I go through the motions with her, showing her what to do. She giggles at me and makes fun. It's the first time I've ever felt like an authority on anything with her. Usually she teaches me. Before we start to run, she puts her hand on my arm, reaches up and kisses me. The sudden blush of her mouth rides through me.

The forest is like a drowning sea—long and deep, a constant bottle green. Starting off slowly through the creepers and honeysuckle at the edge of the overgrown road, she follows closely behind, and I can feel her running gingerly, trying to step where I have stepped.

"Why don't we run on the road?" she says as we get deeper into the woods. "Wouldn't it be easier?"

"No," I say. I start to say more, but I don't. The sensation of the run is beginning to rise in me and talking ruins it.

We go through skunk cabbage and laurel, through clouds of insects that hang in the irregular sunlight like gathered plankton. It may well be an ocean. It might as well be swimming.

Consciously, I make an effort to go slowly. I can hear her breath.

Everything is wet. The leaves and fronds still hold water from the morning's heavy dew. Everything is warm, tropical, as warm and wet as the thick air, the slapping leaves. She stays close to me, slightly back. In a little clearing, a rabbit stands walleyed, then dives into the weeds when we plod through. I look back at Kate; her breasts move with the riding motion of the run, and I see what she tried to tell me.

For me it's like floating in the softness of the rotting leaves —soundless, slow, steady, the sun glimmering on the surface of the forest and bleeding downward through the layers of air and moisture. Every sound we make dies in the air next to us. I start to warm up and settle into a rhythm. The leaves and boughs and branches drift past, and I no longer look but allow the green to blur until it swims past, cool and liquid and close as a tunnel. Things move around us, but I don't focus on them.

I look at Kate and sweat is showing on her face and arms. I slow up the pace a little, but still she begins to drop back.

It is no longer like movement at all but dreaming.

Kate on the porch at her house: Her feet are up on the railing, and her hair falls back over the chair. The look of her legs, the soft cream white of her arms and neck. I stand next to her in astonishment, hardly believing that either of us is real. I want to touch her but I can't.

The woods rise and fall like waves.

The air is too heavy, or the walls and the chairs and the windows stand up and say NO. I see her LAUGHING at the reach of my hands when she lifts her SHIRT over her head. She LAUGHS but I'm powerless as smoke, and my eyes are fading and my arms cross through her body and her skin melts into the air and the woods and the feel of the earth against my shoes. I look behind me, then speed up.

I'm creeping ahead of her—five yards, then ten, then twenty yards. Without looking back, I know where she is and how fast she's going. She calls out, "Albie!" between breaths, but I ignore it, and the forest swallows and swallows again. The underbrush thins, but the trees are still heavy. The upper branches snag at the slow-moving sky.

As my body loses itself in the rhythm, a tone rings through the trees. I had not expected music, but as soon as it comes, I begin to look for it, to heighten it. Kate shouts again, but I block it out. The tone is there, full and steady, so full that it seems surprising. It changes, moves up and down, then builds upward, layering in sketches of strings and reeds and brass. It is Mahler's First Symphony again, and suddenly I can see *Kate on the floor of the music room,* telling me about the composer, about rebirth and resurrection. The music begins to float and move, to carry me.

My stride lengthens. I cross over an old, dry creek bed that's edged with mountain laurel. The white and lavender blossoms are still damp. Then I go up a hill. We're near the new forest.

Then the music stops. *Albie!* I'm on the side of the hill, high enough to see the top sides of the leaves and the fall of the land behind me. There's no sign of Kate but her voice. That's not what's stopped me. Something is following us. Deep in the trees, exactly our pace, off in the west. *Vulnerable,* a jay screams. *Do you believe in God?*

Down the hill, in the thick of the trees, Kate is shouting. Her voice is lost, almost hysterical. Beyond us, surrounding us, the forest breathes. But there is something in it, watching, waiting. I can taste it, I can sense it, but I don't know what it is. I wheel around and scan the trees, but there is nothing. Except for my breathing and Kate's voice, there is nothing. Sweat stands up over my face and chest and arms. *Look at him, look at him.* My heart rattles in my chest like a stone in a steel drum. I think of the boys on the track team, and of the snake Carl found, but it is nothing like that. My skin gets cold.

I start back towards Kate, slowly at first, looking around in the trees, but then faster and faster until I'm only one step ahead of falling. Kate. The woods stand up and shout. Kate.

I go down the hill, across the gully, and the trees empty out into a clearing full of ferns and skunk cabbage. She stands there and sunlight falls like rain. She hugs her arms close to her and sobs. "Goddamn it," she says. "Goddamn it, Albie."

"What is it?" I swallow, look into the trees.

"You disappeared. I thought you were going to leave me here. I thought you were angry." She looks frightened, spooked. Her skin is pale and damp.

"I didn't mean to," I lie. "I'm sorry."

She puts her arms around me. Though we are in a clearing, the woods stand close. Beyond her shoulder, I see the place where I ran through the ferns, and only then does it occur to me that we are moving slowly, turning like a planet. Sunlight strikes her face in patches, and her tears taste of salt. I put my mouth against her skin, move it up to her shoulder, up the perfect arc of her neck.

"I'm sorry," I say, but she pulls my head toward her, closes her mouth on mine. The sound of blood in my ears is like thunder.

She does not speak, but I can feel her breath against me, and the dampness of her clothing and her hair.

We move toward the ferns, but I do not sense at all the movement of my legs. We are watched, but it doesn't matter now. There is nothing but the weight of my hands, and the fabric of her clothing. There is nothing but her skin and breath and the scream of blood in my head. *Why? Why?* a voice says. *Look at them, look at them.*

Each moment is like an awakening, but I have never slept. She is against me and her skin rises when the fabric falls. I can't breathe but I breathe Kate and the woods and the sky and the water that moves through the air. I move my mouth along her breastbone, uncovering the high, smooth skin, and the water moves beneath us. I move my feet. Smell my own saliva. But the blood takes the weight from me and I am like a shadow, pure sense, pure movement. My face against her ribs: her heartbeat is hollow, and the sound terrifies me. Yet my hands move downward, as if uncovering her is an art, an act of life and love that builds her in this place like she has never been built. Nipple. Belly. Mound. Slight sticking, then giving way, the skin rises under each follicle as white as milk or brown as bread crust. I move to taste her again. Bitter odor, then sweet. Closer and closer the forest is hushed around the spin of us, everything watching, even the beast, and the death songs singing. An image of Martin and Carl and Emily on the lake beach moving like a photographic transparency. I want to cry out with fear with love for the shuddering in my legs and chest and the soft diveaway of skin as I move forward against her, stupid and ineloquent as stone. My touch reverberates through the trees and against the sky. Blood. Then she is sinking toward the gully and the high ferns. She smiles, and her hands are on my skin, stumbling, hooking away my clothes. I know I'll die. The SOUND of her gasping. The wetness that covers the forest.

Rain comes, and we sit beneath the shelter we've made near the beach and watch the rain rattle the surface of the water. It drives in sheets, the wind taking it. Kate tries to speak, but she can't. I listen and there is nothing but the sound of the water. The gray skies jag like slow ice, spilling, subsuming everything, and soon the whole forest is full of water. I would drown.

I can't breathe. Kate is gone. I tear at my throat, at my chest. I go through the skin, all the way down to the bone. I tear open my ribs, and my lungs flutter out, then float mothlike the long way to the surface.

My throat is dry and sore when I wake up. Light from the

almost full moon bleeds down through the trees. There is a rustling in the trees beyond the clearing, but I can see nothing. Birds, probably, or a raccoon.

I sit up in my sleeping bag for a long time, listening, staring into the woods, and for the first time ever, I'm scared of being so deep in the woods and so alone.

Carl and Martin are in the open cabin. When I finally get up, I look at the two of them. They don't move; but for the sound of their breath, they could be dead. The crossbow is against the wall, uncocked and unloaded. I look at it, and look at Martin's face.

I go into the woods to take a leak, and when I come back, I get the crossbow and razorheads from the cabin. I slip back out again and cock the crossbow. There is rustling in the leaves again, and the feel of the weapon in my hands makes me a little steadier. I put a bolt in and swing it around. Silence.

I stand and listen. I could swear there is a cigarette burning somewhere nearby, but the scent is elusive—like the sense I have that I'm being watched, that I have been watched. I wait and my stomach feels empty and dead.

Then there is a noise again in the woods beyond the clearing. A branch pops. I float away from the cabin, toward the far edge of the clearing. The place where the fire was is still warm. I raise the bow and it feels like sleep in my hands, or a million years. I move it toward the darkness. My skin is cold and blood shrills in my head. I wait for the next sound.

I imagine laughter. *You won't shoot me. You couldn't.* I will. *You're nothing but a child.* The leaves slither. I will. Laughter.

The razorhead slips through the trees with a sound like water.

"So what did you do with her?" Martin says, leaning against the cabin wall.

I don't look at him, but the question takes me by surprise and flushes my face. For a while I don't say anything, thinking maybe he'll let it pass. He doesn't. I run my hand over the top of the roll of tarpaper that Carl stole from a construction site, and when my hand is sticky, I say, "What's that supposed to mean?"

"What did you do with her?"

It's hard to discern the tone of his voice.

"Nothing."

"Nothing. Nothing? Don't tell me that. I can see it. I can smell it."

I look at him. "See what?" For a moment, I have the impression that he is clairvoyant, that because the images in my mind are so vivid, he can read them on the air.

He puts his teeth together and lowers his head. "Why don't you say it? Why don't you say what's obvious?"

"If there was something to tell, it wouldn't be any of your business," I say. It sounds childish, defensive.

"But it is," he says, then does a funny sort of pirouette, comes forward and stops inches from my face. "Why?"

"Stop it," I say, backing away from him.

He grabs my arm. "*Why?*"

I shake off his hand and push him backward, but he bounces on his heel and comes forward swinging. His closed hand catches me on the side of the face. The trees flutter, a tiny hole opens in the sky and a red light burns through.

When I catch my balance, I back away. My whole body trembles. In my eyes everything is sharp and focussed.

"Why?" he says again vacantly, quietly, rubbing his hand as if it is stained.

"I have nothing to say to you," I tell him, unable to keep the trembling from my voice. I want to kill him. *Hatred. Disgust.* I want to say more. Without willing it, an image of splitting his head open with a stone swims through my head.

"I'm sorry," he says, turning, looking at me. His eyes are soft. "I didn't mean to do that. I don't know why I—" He stops, looks at his fist.

There is silence for a long time. Even the birds and insects are quiet—as if they've dissolved into the wetness of the woods and the air, as if they're waiting to see if I will kill him.

He smiles finally. "You want to take a shot at me?" He runs his hand through his hair. "I owe you one."

I shake my head and turn away from him. "No," I say. I feel weak in the backwash of adrenalin.

"Listen," he says, "I have something for you." His voice is contrite, at a polar opposite from where it was five minutes ago. "Wait just a minute."

I breathe through my nose and watch as he steps out of the clearing and goes in the direction of Carl's car. I'm alone in the clearing when he has disappeared completely.

When he reappears—silently, as if he's just solidified out of the trees—he's carrying a compound bow with a rack of aluminum razorheads clipped to it. The handle is metal, with a shape like a twisted root. On the top and the bottom, fitted into slots in the metal, are two laminated pieces of fiberglass—the flexible parts of the bow, the parts that give it its power. There are black metal pulleys at either end, and, transversing them, is a cable that crosses back and forth and attaches to the bowstring.

"This is for you," he says. "I think it's about time we started getting our own food. Time we started being self-sufficient."

I take the bow from him when he offers it to me and test the feel of it in my arms. The handle twists into my hand and lays like a glove. I pull the string and feel the power of it in my arms.

Then, halfway through the pull, the pulleys kick and the string breaks and becomes suddenly light. "Wow," I say.

"That's the wonder of a compound bow," he says.

I can feel it in my chest. I ease the string back.

"It was my father's," he says. "But he doesn't have much use for it now." I look at him and his face is without expression.

"I can't take your father's bow," I say. "It's—"

"If you think you can't take it because it has sentimental value, you're wrong. I don't believe in that crap. It doesn't. Take it. You need it and I don't."

"What about Carl?"

"Carl has his own now. He got the money from his mother."

I'm surprised by this news, mainly because I know nothing about it. I try to remember what Carl was like a year ago, or ten years ago, and I can't. Yet it makes a certain amount of sense; Carl could always get money from his mother. I could never have gotten money from my father.

I feel the current of the air move around me, I listen to the rustle of the trees saying, *Nihil, Nihil.*

We spend a long afternoon on the beach, naked, swimming, lying in the sun. Martin has brought a handful of wooden target arrows, and we shoot them at an old red flannel shirt filled with green leaves and twigs. I like the feel of the bow. I could shoot it for hours.

The sky is white and doesn't change. The afternoon is airless and damp. In the hot sun the water wears a corona of haze.

I lie on the beach and wonder about Martin, about the way he acted yesterday morning. It's easy for me to believe that he could be interested in Kate, and yet it doesn't seem to make that much sense. I watch him beside the water, his eyes and his hair and the way he moves, and I wonder if I trust him. When the girls are around, he looms and stares, and sometimes tries to intimidate them. Other times he is passive, and ignores them. He never seems solicitous of them. The way he looks, it would be easy for them to be interested in him—if he were different.

I listen to the birds and the gentle slap of the water against the shore; I listen to the whir of Carl's bowstring, and the soft crackle of the arrows when they sink into the shirt. I get up for a while and shoot my own bow. Carl is not as good a shot. Sometimes his arrows slide off the side and pile deep into the loamy soil. I like the feel of the bow in my hands. I like the potential of it.

I think of my father and our camping trips here years ago. In a way, because of how time feels today, I could look up and he would be here, same as he was then, before the evening law school classes, before the babysitters and the dark house.

Finally, when the afternoon begins to cool into evening, I get dressed and go into the woods to run.

I leave my bow by the cabin and head west. It is cooler in the trees than it was on the beach, and music comes almost immediately. Voices rise out of the trees, full and sonorous, drowning the crush of my feet in the rotting leaves. I pass the gully where I was with Kate, pass the wide, sweet expanse of ferns (it seems somehow that she should still be there, or some part of her) and I can almost taste her skin in the air. Everything goes out of me and when I close my eyes to feel the shudder of my body, the space is blank, clean, white. I wish it could always be this way, wrapped so deeply in the music and movement that there is nothing else.

The music stops suddenly, and I stop, blood flooding my head.

Above me, on a knoll about twenty-five yards away, a doe stands absolutely still, her head raised into the current of the air. Next to her is a speckled fawn. They stand there for a long time, the doe motionless, the fawn moving, eating. I try not to move, not to breathe. The light color of them, like creamed coffee or toast, surprises me. I stare. I stare so long that when they catch my scent and spring away to dissolve back into the forest, they become a conundrum of light, like a word repeated too many times.

I stand a while and look at the place where they were, and then I go back to the camp.

Kate sits on the edge of her porch in a white dress. I'm on the lawn, in the almost-darkness, watching her. It is hot and muggy, and she keeps her legs together as she eats a cherry popsicle. Langston feels strange to me after the woods, as though I carry some of the weight of the forest with me.

"God, what happened to spring?" she says. "It's already summer and it's not even June." She pushes her hair back over her shoulder, then takes the popsicle and rubs it across the inside of her wrist. The warmth of her skin causes droplets of frozen juice to come away and bead. "Sit down or something," she says, bringing her wrist to her mouth to lick. "You're making me uncomfortable just standing there."

"Sorry. I wasn't thinking. I mean I was thinking about my father." I look down, run my foot through the fineness of the grass beneath me. "You know."

"Yeah." She pulls a piece of the popsicle away with her teeth.

"And I was thinking about that day in the woods." I was not, but I say it and smile at her.

"I don't want to talk about that, if it's okay." She smiles back at me, but it's hard to make out the quality of it. "Let's just talk about normal things. Those woods are crazy."

She's right. There are a million possible things to say, but nothing seems to make sense. I say, "So," sitting down next to her, on a lower step, "how's the new piano teacher?"

She bites off another part of the popsicle, and then, when she speaks again, she rounds her mouth to keep the frozen juice from freezing her lips and teeth. "She's an absolute maniac for Bruckner, don't ask me why." She swallows. "Nothing against Bruckner, of course."

"Of course."

She finishes the popsicle and holds the sticks in one hand. "So," she says, mimicking me, "had any trouble with the track guys lately?"

I laugh through my nose, but it leaves me with the sensation of being hollow inside. "No," I say quietly, "not lately." I wonder vaguely what would happen if they came into the woods looking for me, whether we would hunt them. I almost wish they would try—just so we could scare them.

"Listen, Al," she says quietly, "I don't want to sound like a mother or anything, but I was just wondering—" She pauses.

"What?"

"If you just want to ignore me, then go ahead. I mean it's just curiosity."

"What?"

"Are you going to graduate?"

I look at her and she is looking out towards the street, not at me. "I don't know," I say. "I guess so."

"What'd Mrs. Schwartzmann say? I mean when you guys talked with her?"

"That I've got to pass English and government. She says I'll pass English with flying colors. Government I'm not so sure about."

"Have you done anything at all lately?" She gathers the loose fabric of her dress in one hand and holds it tightly over the apex of her knees.

"No," I say. Somehow when I say it to her it sounds stupid and thoughtless.

She gives an incredulous laugh. "Why, Al?" Her voice is soft, concerned. I want to throw my arms around her.

"I don't know," I say. "I just couldn't. I didn't know where to start. You know. And I was in the woods. I mean in the woods it just didn't seem relevant."

"So what are you going to do?" she says chidingly. "Live the rest of your life in the woods?" Her smile is ironic.

"I could. It wouldn't be impossible, you know. Martin and I, if we wanted to, could be completely self-sufficient." My shirt is wet with perspiration.

"Al," she says, then lowers her head. "What does your father say?"

"Not much. We don't see each other much. All he ever does when I'm around is watch television, anyway."

"Al," she says.

"Sure, if I flunk out, he's going to be upset. Sure."

"Don't be stupid, Albie. Don't make excuses for yourself."

When I look at her I am flooded with things to say. I want to tell her that she is beautiful, that her eyes are like jewels or like windows or like my mother's eyes. But I can't say anything. I don't know what the truth sounds like.

After a while, I say, "What about Mahler?"

"What about him?" she says, sighing, laying the popsicle sticks on the wooden step.

"Heard anything new lately?"

"Yeah." She hesitates a moment and looks at me as if sizing me up. "Something called 'Song of the Earth.'" She bites her lip. "But it's not new. I got the tape a couple of weeks ago."

"Do I get to hear it?"

"Sure," she says. That she sounds vaguely annoyed with me makes me wince.

She gets up and goes indoors. I sit on the porch and wait. The evening is too hot.

When Kate returns, she has a tape player. She puts it between us and pushes one of the buttons on the top. "The first part," she says, "is called, 'Drinking Song of Earth's Misery.'"

The tape crackles a moment. Then, the orchestra rolls out.

"The songs in the work go back and forth," she says. "Joy, sadness, and back again."

A man's voice, a tenor, moves out over the music, thick and lovely. He sounds full of turmoil.

"In Mahler's book," she says quietly, evenly, "sadness is the eventual product of joy—or vice versa."

She is quiet and we listen. We listen for I don't know how long. The man's voice gives way to a woman's, then returns. The turmoil of the music subsides into a beauty that is transfixing, here on the porch in the hot evening.

When it's over, we are silent for a long time. I can hear the music rebuilding and reconstituting itself over and over in my head.

"In a way," Kate says finally, "this is like Mahler's farewell to the earth. He died before it was performed."

The music is in the air and it brings up a million pictures in my head—Kate on the beach, Kate with her guitar, or beneath me in the soft, ferned gully; the shimmering of the woods in my running; and further back, things I can't identify.

"He loved life, but he had a hard time, according to the book

I was reading. Like he always felt there was a. . . a separation between himself—you know, between his physical and spiritual lives."

"God," I say.

My father sits in the television-illumined darkness of the living room, a glass of wine on the table, and the cutting board with cheese and crackers on his lap. The television squeals and yammers, the light flashes, changes color and intensity. I stand watching, afraid to disturb the spell.

"Hey," I say finally. "What's going on?"

Slowly—I can see he's slightly drunk—he puts the cutting board onto the coffee table and stands up. He's taller than me. With the remote control, he turns off the television.

The silence is harsh, as harsh as the darkness. We stand together like shadows, waiting for the movement of something outside of us to bring us to life. Or waiting for some kind of light to kill us.

"Hey," my father says. "I remem—Don't I know you? I know I've seen your face somewhere before. Just a minute. Don't tell me."

"Dad," I say.

"Wait a minute. Wait a minute. I know. It's all coming to me."

"Stop it, Dad, please," I say quietly, hating the darkness, hating him.

"Now I know. You're my son. You're the fellow that my ex-wife had. Listen," he says, coming forward, "I want to shake your hand."

He comes forward and takes my hand. His hand is limp and moist. I can smell the wine on his breath.

In a moment, when the joke is finished, he drops my hand and just stands there in the darkness staring at me.

"A guy named Ron Haverty called you this evening," he says. "When I told him you were out, he said you were probably out renting a tuxedo for the prom or something." There is nothing in his voice now but sarcasm. "You weren't out renting a tuxedo for the prom, were you, son?"

"Cut it out." Blood burns in my face.

"Anyway," he says, tossing one hand to the side, "he wants you to call back. He said something about congratulations." He walks away from me. "I thought, *my* son? Congratulations? Naw. But that's what he said. I know. I was amazed, too."

I look at him. I can barely see him in the darkness. For all it matters, he could be a ghost. "What about? What did he call about?"

"Gosh, son," my father says, slumping back down on the couch, "I don't know. What in the world could you have done to deserve congratulations?"

He turns the television back on.

"So call him," he says.

"I have no intention of calling him." I start to walk by him, to the kitchen, but he stands up, and with surprising force, grabs my arm and pulls me around.

"Call him," he says.

"No," I say.

He swings, catches me on the face open-handed.

Still holding onto my arm, he turns on the light. It surprises the both of us—me because of the paleness of his skin and the blood in his eyes. "Call him," he says again. His voice is quiet, cool. "Please just call him." In a funny way, it seems as if he is near tears. I turn away, I can't stand the sight of my father's face in the light.

"All right," I whisper, hating the waxy hand that holds my arm. "I'll call him and see what he wants."

When I pick up the phone and punch out the number written on the pad, I smooth out my voice, clean out the anger.

"This is Albert Santamoravia," I say when the voice comes onto the line. "My father said you called."

In frustration, like a man waist deep in water, my father moves from the living room to the kitchen, taking with him notebooks and thick black binders with *CCH* written on the spines. He gets a clean ashtray from the dishwasher and spreads everything out on the kitchen table.

"Did you hear me, Albert?" Haverty says. "Did you?"

My father puts on his glasses and sits down at the table, then gets up again. I can hear him rummaging for matches.

"I'm sorry," I say. "Yes."

"Well, congratulations."

"No," I say. "There has to be some kind of mistake. There must be. I'm not even—"

"No," he says, laughing at me. "Nope. Coach Shaddock gave me your name and number. And come on, how many Albert Santamoravias do you think there could be?"

I thank him, then hang up the phone.

My father has a cigarette in his mouth. He looks at me over the top of his glasses. "Well?"

"Why ask? You know what he wanted."

"Listen, Al, I know how you're going to react to this, and I just want you to think about it for a couple of minutes before you say you don't want any part of it." He takes the unlit cigarette and puts it on the table. "You've got to look at this as a chance to do something for yourself. Shaddock may be out to get your goat, but there's no reason you can't turn it to your own advantage."

It surprises me how clear his voice sounds. The drunkenness was just an act, something to embarrass me. I start to say something but he cuts me off.

"Can you just shut up for a second—just listen to me for a minute before you object?"

"I'm listening," I say.

"I know you don't like any of them, and I don't know if I'd look at things any differently if I were in your position. And I know how the idea of doing anything anyone else might consider worthwhile turns your stomach." He looks at me, waits for the sarcasm to sink in. When I refuse to react, he picks up the cigarette and lights it, then goes on. "What I'm getting at is that both of us know that your grades aren't anything to write home about. That's not a judgment, that's a fact. And both of us know that on the strength of them, and on the strength of your, ahem, participation in the community, you're not going to get into any colleges. That's another fact."

I hate my father when he's like this. It's almost as if he wants me to hate him. "Dad," I say, "You know I don't—"

"Will you just shut up for a minute and let me finish?" He drags on his cigarette. "Okay. You may think for the moment that you don't want to go to college. What exactly you're going to do if you don't escapes me, but for the moment, let's just put that aside. For argument's sake, let's just say that you've found a nice, cozy sinecure somewhere and they've promised to pay you for life to run and listen to Mahler or whoever it is this week."

I turn away from him, start to pace.

"Just what exactly is it going to hurt if you make this run?" He sucks on the cigarette and stubs it out in the ashtray. "Really? Your pride? I think you're old enough now to be able to have your pride dented a little bit without it becoming a terminal ailment."

"So what difference is it going to make one way or the other?"

"The difference it's going to make is that a college is going to make exceptions for a gifted athlete."

"So I'm supposed to whore myself?"

"Be a fool, Al, I expect that from you." His voice is as calm as water in a dish.

"Listen, why don't you save all of this wonderful sarcasm for somebody who appreciates it?" I turn and look at him. "I mean it's wonderful. It's really just great. But the thing is, it's not going to make me do it. Not for you, Not for Shaddock. Not for any of those other assholes. You want to know—you want to know—" I throw up my arms and whirl away from him.

"What, Al?"

"Nothing."

"What?" He stares at me. I was going to tell him who it was who beat me up, but I don't say anything. I won't give him the satisfaction.

"You know you really confound me sometimes," he says. "I mean most of the time I don't even know who this kid is who comes into my house and eats my food and sits upstairs in some kind of weird trance listening to music in his head. And then you're out running or camping or God knows where, and I think to myself, this is one hell of a capital outlay, and what am I getting out of the investment except a tax deduction?" He looks at me and his lips form a sarcastic smile. I know the look. He's stopped a moment to let his thoughts collect. Like a fish holding against the current until the moment comes to let go and take the momentum, he's listening, waiting, watching.

"All I mean to say is," he says, taking off his glasses and rubbing the dark circles beneath his eyes, "is that by doing this simple thing—running in some ten kilometer race—you can almost assure yourself of getting into a college. It's that simple."

"I'd have to win. Besides, it's a half-marathon, not a ten K."

"Everyone seems to think you're perfectly wonderful."

I want to laugh, but instead I lean over the counter and open and close the door on the toaster oven. I know it'll irritate him. "I've never run like that before, in competition."

"Well, you could try."

"You mean I could prostitute myself."

"Call it what you want."

"I'd be just like you. A whore."

He doesn't say anything.

I turn and leave the kitchen. "I'm going to Carl's," I say.

"Don't go out," he says.

"To hell with you," I say under my breath.

"You're gonna run," he shouts after me.

When Mrs. Rieger greets me at the door, she says brightly, "It's so very nice to see you, Albie."

"Hi," I say, nodding to Mr. Rieger, who sits in the living room, his dark head bent into a newspaper. "Is Carl around?" Mr. Rieger ignores me, and I hurry down the hall and up the stairs. Through the open door to the widow's walk, I hear Martin and Carl laughing.

When I open the door, Martin says, "Hey, Al, how are you?" He leans against the railing next to Carl.

"All right," I say. I had thought, on my way over here, that I would burst through the door and tell them immediately what Shaddock had done, and how my father was insisting that I go ahead with it, but now, as I close the door behind me and wander out onto the walk, the whole thing seems silly to me, like nothing at all.

"After you left today," Carl says, sitting up on the railing and hooking his feet around the bars, "Marty and I did some hunting. We went hunting for squirrels and rabbits." He sniffles and pushes at his nose. "You should have been there. We're standing in the woods and there's a squirrel in a tree, and Marty goes, 'Ssshh,' cocks his crossbow, and then fires. The arrow, the bolt, it went right into the tree, about two inches from the squirrel's face." Carl gives a look of mock surprise, and Martin laughs.

"He couldn't figure out what it was," Martin says, not looking at me. "Thought it grew right there. So I cocked and loaded again."

"And again he misses," Carl says. "Again the bolt goes right into the tree by the squirrel's face."

"He actually puts a paw out onto it to see if it's real." Both of them laugh together. "I guess he thought it grew there." Martin shakes his head and for a while there is silence.

I lean out over the railing and look at the lights of town. Langston. Even the name feels strange to me now.

Martin is next to me, big and stiff, with the vague scent of perspiration. Below us the lights spread out like some dirty galaxy, throwing a pale glow up against the low hang of the clouds. I watch the movements of headlights and taillights and something seems funny, like I'm outside of everything suddenly, as if without me they've made some kind of pact and I'm an intruder. I wait, looking at the lights, but nothing happens, and I imagine falling off the roof—how it might feel like to hit the sidewalk below.

"Look," I say, pointing to where I know the Baptist church is. There is a long trail of headlights, moving slowly. "It's a funeral." I look at the two of them. "Look at the lights."

"That's crazy," Martin says. "They never have funerals at night." Carl turns to look.

"I don't know," I say. "That's what it looks like." He's right, I guess. No one ever has funerals at night, but still there *is* a long trail of headlights, like the tail of a comet.

The three of us lean in silence against the railing. Martin, the tallest of us, is in the middle. Things swim up out of the darkness, filling the emptiness—Mrs. Schwartzmann, my father, myself. I wonder if that's what death is like, complete darkness, everything coming up from the outside to fill the emptiness.

"You guys know what?" I say finally. Somewhere off below us a lone woodpecker, wild with spring, hammers at a gutter. "Some guy from the Virginia State High School Track Commission called me tonight. He wanted to congratulate me. Can you believe it? Me. I told him I wasn't even on the team, but he wouldn't listen. They've selected me as one of West's representatives for the annual divisional half-marathon, whatever that is."

Martin claps his hands together. The sound stings. "That's great, that's fabulous. A myth in your own time." He laughs, and when he looks at me, I don't know what to make of it.

"What's that supposed to mean, Martin? You don't believe me?"

"They must think you're awful goddamned good. None of them has ever seen you run before, and they select you." He laughs again. "You must be something, Albie."

"Shaddock's seen me run. He follows me around in his goddamned car all the time. And he's the one who makes the selection."

"That's right," Carl says. "That's right."

"Come on, you don't honestly believe that he expects you to run? Come on."

"No," I say, shaking my head and staring at him. "No, I don't. He put my name down because he knew I wouldn't." I stand away from the railing. My skin feels hot.

"But he wouldn't have done it," Carl says, "unless he thought Albie *could* do it if he wanted to. I mean he wouldn't just sign up anybody. He knows Albie can do it if he wants." There's something in Carl's voice that I haven't heard since Martin showed up. "He knows Albie could beat anybody in the whole goddamned state."

"Well, either way he gets the best of you," Martin says. "If you do it, he wins. If you don't, he wins, too."

Angry, I watch him, but he doesn't pay attention to me. He looks out over the railing. For a moment, I wish the railing were rotten and I could just push him through it. But then I remember how he is in the woods, and I don't know.

"Maybe you're right," I say, not really meaning it. "Maybe he's done it just to see if I'm as fast as people think I am. But then I'm not sure I'd give him that much credit for intelligence."

"Me either," Carl says, drumming on the railing with the flat of his hands. "He's a dumb bastard." In a few moments he says, "You think you'll do it?"

"No," I say.

It is three weeks until June. I can hardly even imagine it.

I turn around and lean backward against the railing. Martin is smiling.

"I saw a deer yesterday," I say.

It is an offering.

"Where have you been?" my father says. He is still at the kitchen table when I come through the back door and let the metal storm door slam behind me. After his voice punctures the air, I stand a moment, looking at him. My father is surrounded by papers, as if some kind of wave has swept through and left him becalmed in a tidal pool of paper.

"I told you," I say, dragging into the middle of the room.

"I thought I asked you not to go out," he says. I smell the air, trying to think of what the combined scents of late coffee and burnt cigarettes reminds me of.

"You told me," I say. He doesn't look at me but at the whirl of papers. "You didn't ask. There's a difference, you know." I feel sleepy, angry. I wish I could vanish. He brings up a weariness in me that is overwhelming.

"All right then, I thought I *told* you not to go out." He pretends to look at his work, but I know that my standing behind him has blown his concentration. I want to unnerve him. I want to ruin his work.

He thumbs through a black notebook before slamming it shut and turning around. Quietly, he says, "Just what are you going to do if you flunk out of school?" His eyes are redder than they were before. Finally, though, he makes his glance fall away—ashamed, embarrassed. "It's hard enough to find a goddamned job in the world with a PhD," he whispers. "What are you going to do without a high school diploma?" He picks up his package of cigarettes and shakes it. One of them falls out onto the table and rolls, leaving a trail of dried tobacco. I stare at it, try to will it away from his hand, but he picks it up and lights it. The evenness of his voice, the absurd rationality of everything he does, irritates the hell out of me.

"What do you think I ought to do?" I say, mimicking his tone. For a moment he looks at me with something resembling hope. Then I say, "Maybe I should go to law school?" I think for a minute, and then tell him I'm sorry. In the bright light of the kitchen his features seem feminine, vulnerable.

"Well," he says, cigarette smoke leaking from his nostrils, "maybe you won't get a job. Maybe you'll—" He pauses for the effect, then blows smoke in a stream that fans out as it hits the table and skates across the papers. "I don't know. Maybe you'll run—but no, we wouldn't want to be competitive about it."

"Stop it," I say. The floor stands up. *The clock.* The refrigerator whirs. My head is too full of him. "I'm gonna go run. I'm gonna go run."

"Not now."

I wait for an explanation, some elaboration, but there is nothing. Behind us, beneath us, is the constant sound of the house —the refrigerator, the snot-sucking sigh of the coffee maker, the slow creak of the kitchen clock. If I could make the music come I'd bring it up like a psychosis to fill the house. I'd make it bleed down the walls and burst through the windows.

"Why not?"

"I don't really care right now why not." He looks at me for the first time. His eyes are yellow, and the color of his skin makes me picture him dead. "Just don't. If you need one, make up a reason. Pretend you're being punished. That should be fun. Pretend you're a fairy princess and you've been captured by an evil ogre. I don't give a damn." The coolness of his voice is finally gone, and as he speaks, it rises in pitch. "I don't care at all what you do. Just go up to your room and stay there." His voice gets coarse, his face gets red. "You're about the least thing I care about at this very moment, so just get the hell out of here."

I leave the room and listen as he starts to cough. My face stings with hatred. I can't believe how much I hate everything—him, his sarcasm, everything. But the coughing sounds painful, and I stay near the wall, listening, hoping that he won't cough his lungs out.

When it finally subsides, I go back into the kitchen. I don't know what I expect to happen. Even though everything in my head and chest and hands is jumbled and crazy, I know I have to make him understand, even if what comes out is nothing more than nonsense or tears. But when I cross through the kitchen door into the pale white light, I feel as if I've walked into a thick pane of glass. I stand there startled, looking at him.

"What?"

"I just . . . I just wanted you to know that things aren't like they are because I want them to be that way."

"Don't make excuses for yourself, Al."

"Listen, Dad, I—" He slides his chair backward and slumps his arms across his chest. "It's just—" I say, but nothing will come. I don't understand anything myself. Suddenly in my silence I can see myself as he must be seeing me: a boy, sun-burned, thin as a pole and incapable of doing anything but running, running, running. "What is it you want?" I say, things going rapidly in my head, changing from hate to anger to love to sorrow, clanging back and forth like the ball in a can of spray paint. "I mean it's not like I don't want to succeed in life. It's not. I do. I do. The thing is just that I want to do it honestly. Honestly." As I speak, I don't know whether what I'm saying is true, but I can't stop myself. "I don't want to whore myself to some idiot like Shaddock. I don't want to whore myself to a bunch of fascists who—"

"Stop it, Al," my father says. His face is red and puffy. I've misjudged him, misjudged his anger. There's something hard in his words, something sharp.

"*Listen. Listen to me!* You don't care about understanding at all. All you're interested in—"

"Go."

"Dad."

"Go."

"I wish you'd just goddamn listen to me once in a while. I wish you'd just—" But he's not listening. He's got his hands up over his face and ears. I stop, lash out, knock one of his notebooks off the table. Papers go everywhere and whirl around the kitchen so crazily that it makes me want to laugh. *"Listen!"*

"Get out." The calm is back. "Get your things and get out of my house."

I look at him for a minute, and then, knowing he means it, I turn around and run upstairs. For a long time, I wait in my room, crying like a child, waiting for the sound of his feet on the stairs, waiting for him to tell me he didn't mean it.

Finally, the kitchen door slams and the car starts. I go to the window and watch as the BMW pulls away from the garage and heads down the street. Then, angrily, I throw my things into my knapsack, put on my running clothes, and head out of the house. Not knowing what else to do, I go to Emily's because she has a car.

Emily drives like an old woman, her skinny frame hunched up to the steering wheel, her eyes fixed doggedly on some point just beyond the range of the headlights. The car moves smoothly, silently, and I watch the sweep of headlights along the road shoulders, watch the startled clouds of moths.

"Listen, Em," I say, touching her shoulder, ignoring the falseness in my voice, "I really appreciate your doing this. I really do."

She says nothing, only stares ahead of her, every ounce of her tense with concentration. After a long time, she says, "I still don't understand why you're doing this, you know. I honestly don't. And I don't understand why I'm helping you do it."

I look at her, and for a moment, I'm distracted by the fine

skin on her hands and arms. "You talk as if we're committing a crime," I say.

"It *is* criminal, Albie. Your father is the nicest, most reasonable guy on the planet. I don't see how you could—"

"That's just what he wants people to think. He's really a bastard. Besides, he kicked *me* out, and not the other way around."

"You really think he meant it?"

Suddenly more serious than I want to be, I say, "Yes," and go back to staring out the windshield.

Emily is quiet for a while. We're still five or so miles from the Outskirts, and the car goes slowly. This far outside Langston, the roads are narrow and canopied with trees. The air is full of insects, and we pass farms and ghostly white houses that materialize at the sides of the road, then recede back into darkness. There is a cat in the ditch, invisible except for the bright green glow of its eyes.

"Are you going to go to school tomorrow?" she says. She doesn't look at me. I can't tell whether it's because she's driving, or if it's because she's ashamed for me and doesn't want to look.

"No," I say, and look out the windshield and wait for the sound of my name in her mouth.

"Goddamn it, Albie," she says. Her teeth are together and she shakes her head. "I just don't understand. I just don't understand." Carefully, she takes one hand from the steering wheel and digs in her purse for cigarettes. The car slows perceptibly.

I start to say something, but she lights her cigarette and says, "Carl told me about this running thing. On the phone, tonight. He told me that Shaddock had signed you up for some kind of run."

"Yeah," I say.

"You want to know what I think? You want to know what I think about it?" Now she looks at me. I roll down the window a little to vent the smoke.

"Not really," I say, and smile at her. "No, not really."

"Well, you don't have any choice." She laughs a little, then coughs for a minute. "I think you ought to do it."

"Why did I know you were going to say that? Why?"

"Oh, shut up."

"Listen, Em, there's no way I can possibly win if I do it. None at all. Any way it goes, Shaddock wins."

"He wins if you don't do it, so what have you got to lose?"

She slows the car and makes the turn-off at the unmarked gravel road. I turn around and watch the dust rise off the road in the red glow of the taillights. "Okay," she says, "I'm gonna stop here and you can walk the rest of the way. I don't want to have to turn around in the dark."

"All right," I say, but for a moment, I don't move. I feel empty, hungry, and scared suddenly to be alone. But more than that, there's something I wish I could say to her, yet I have no idea what it is.

Trying to be funny, she says, "Do you want a goodbye kiss or something?" It makes both of us uncomfortable for a moment.

"Thanks," I say. "Maybe some other time. But I—"

"But what?"

"I don't know. Thanks, I guess. If you see Mrs. Schwartz-mann tomorrow, tell her I'll be in soon. I brought soap and clean clothes, you know."

"Good," she says. "If you want me to come pick you up, let me know."

"Yeah," I say. "I will."

Finally I get out of the car and shut the door. I watch as she backs away from me. The engine rushes. I watch her as she turns around, then strain my eyes and ears as she disappears.

When she's gone completely, I could be in a vacuum. The woods are completely silent, and my eyes are unaccustomed to the dark. After a while, I go through the thick of the woods to the water.

I take off my clothes, lay them with my knapsack, then get into the water and sit in the soft bottom silt. The night is dark, dark as the paint-black water that circles my chest, my lungs, my heart. All around the lake there are bullfrogs, lowing like useless old men.

I remember—for no particular reason but the blackness and peace of the water—being on a beach one summer with my father and mother. I could see my father at the edge of the water, his hair wet and black, his skin tanned. My mother was next to him, and in my memory I do not see her, I do not remember her face.

It was the height of the season and the beach was crowded. There were voices everywhere, gathered in a single chord of speaking that carried back and forth across the beach over the radios and towels and blankets and sand. The radio music bled into the sound, into the oily, fragrant air. I smelled cigarettes.

And suddenly I began to panic. I was surrounded by people and there was nothing I could do to get away from them. I pulled my towel over my head and gathered it to me. Still, the sunlight seeped through the fabric; still, the voices churned all around me. I knew I was going to be sick.

That afternoon on the beach with my parents was the first time I ever made the music come. I have no idea how, or why. Under my towel, at the height of everything, suddenly the panic stopped. I could hear music that was not a part of the shamble of the radios along the beach. It was jazz, and I recognized it because it was something my father had been listening to one evening that week. As soon as I understood that it was mine, that it originated inside my own head, I began to play with it. It was cool and wintry, and, slowly, I made it rise up all around me, smothering everything else.

I came out from beneath the towel and watched the sunlight in the waves. I watched the sailboats moving across the bay like jewels. I watched my father wading in the surf, watched the water and the sky, watched the moon in the day like a sliver of pearl against the blue, blue sky, and for the first time there was no sorrow, no joy, nothing at all but my mind and the music— rational, sane, a new language, a new way of defining everything.

Though the forest is black around me, the sky grows paler as my eyes get more and more used to the dark. It is full of stars. I imagine if the water were perfectly still, it would reflect the stars, and the sky in turn would reflect water, and then I would float in the sky, sunk to the chest in stars.

"We came back to keep you company," Carl says, standing in front of Martin at the edge of the clearing. "At least for tonight and tomorrow." He smiles and rubs his fist against his cheekbone. "We're going to cut school tomorrow."

I'm glad to see them. Last night and today were murder-ously boring. "That's great," I tell them. "But what about your mother?" I ask Carl, but then I look at Martin and realize that I could be asking the same question of him.

"That doesn't matter," Martin says. "Besides," he says, laugh-ing, "we didn't want you out here all by yourself hogging all of the wilderness." The edge of his voice makes me understand that Martin at least hasn't come back to the Outskirts on a Monday afternoon for anybody but himself.

* * *

In the early evening, before dusk, Carl digs clay at the edge of the lake, and when he slides back through the underbrush, the three of us, without shoes or shirts, rub the gray smooth mud on our arms and legs, then take turns rubbing it on each other's backs.

Martin daubs his fingers into the clay and drags them across his forehead and the ridges of his cheekbones, Indian-style, parting his fingers so that they slide above and below his ears. His face is still and serious. He pulls his thumb down the sharp angle of his nose. The wet mud gleams in the green-gray semidarkness.

Carl watches him studiously, then imitates him. I make my own pattern—vertical stripes on my forehead, like a cage, then arcs across my cheeks that go all the way back to my ears.

In a few moments, the clay begins to dry and contract. I can smell it—vaguely brassy, vaguely animal. The evening air, and the possibility that we could kill something tonight, makes my hands tremble.

"All right," Martin says when we've got everything together —bows, food, water, razorheads, knives. "Stay behind me and stay quiet."

"I want to wear my shoes," Carl says. "Can I wear my shoes?"

"Do what you want," Martin says.

I look at Martin but he doesn't smile; it's as if everything is deadly serious, and for a moment, beneath the drying clay, beneath the shock of dark, wildly curled hair, his face seems completely unreal. I try to remember what he looks like normally —at school or in the neighborhood—but I can't.

We range into the darkening woods, against the breeze, away from the direction of the new woods. Martin leads, and Carl and

I flank him widely. We go slowly, steadily. I want to laugh at how serious we are, how deadly, but there is nothing funny anymore.

Despite the cool, the forest seems like a jungle—damp, erotic, full of rot and death and growth, and moving around us like steam.

We go for a long time, feet quiet against the rotting leaves. It is like a ritual, the three of us walking, breathing, thinking in unison. I think of the doe I saw in the new woods, and I know that the others are thinking of her too.

The sky above the forest is rouge and orange, as if someone has taken fire and smeared it on a blue palette.

When we stop, I have no idea how long we have been going. Maybe an hour, maybe three. It is dark now; the forest is illumined only by the gray bleed of light from the moon and stars. We have not spoken for most of the way, and now, almost crazily, I feel like I'm in a trance—no longer thinking in a linear way but in washes, or colors, like musical notes and chords.

Martin says nothing when he stops, only stands looking. I can hear Carl's breathing, thick and impacted. Martin unshoulders his crossbow and knapsack, then begins to search around the area. "Stay where you are," he says. Carl and I look at each other, then watch Martin until he turns into a shadow and dissolves into the darkness.

We stand for a long time, waiting while Martin finds each of us a tree and marks off the area around it. We can hear him only now and again.

I stare at Carl. Before Martin came, the two of us would have laughed at this, standing so still and so serious and so full of the woods. We would have made it a joke, a game.

When Martin comes back, he swings up into a maple near us, and we hand him his gear. For a long time there's silence, then rustling, and then he slips back down again, quiet and slick as a mink.

"Come on," he whispers. In a straight line, we follow him to another maple. "Carl?" he says.

"Okay, give me a step up."

I put my hands together, interlocking the fingers, and his weight is intense, then gone. "This is great," comes the whisper.

"Shut up," Martin says. "Shut up and listen."

"Yeah."

"If you have to take a leak or anything, just stay right where you are. If you see a deer, just keep quiet, and for God's sake, keep still. Move only when you absolutely have to. And no shooting at rabbits and squirrels."

"Okay."

We cross away from Carl's tree, up a tiny incline to a point maybe twenty-five yards from either of the other trees. At the bottom of my tree, Martin stands close to me.

"If you want to fall asleep," he says, touching the dry clay on my shoulder, "just hook your belt to one of the limbs. Don't want anybody to break his neck." He looks at me for a moment, and I can see him clearly. I remember that night at his house, the faces on the walls of his room. I remember standing on the stairs with him, his voice and breath so close I could taste them in my own mouth. "You'll be able to tell when it's going to get light," he says. "Notch an arrow. Then, if you see a deer, you'll be able to make as little movement as possible." He stops a minute and thinks. "Oh, the markings are in fifteen yard increments. Don't shoot anything between fifteen and thirty yards. Leave it for someone else. And don't shoot randomly."

I nod.

"You with me, buddy?"

The tone of his voice is alluring. "Yeah," I say.

In a moment, alone in the darkness, I pull myself up on the low cross-branches, the bitter redolence of the bark in the air around me. I swing up, and the bow and rack of razorheads dangle from my neck, cutting off the circulation and sending a wave of lightheadedness through me. I get a leg up, catch my balance, and hang the bow on a broken branch.

I go higher up into the tree, looking for a place that will cradle me. I break a branch, pull my bow up and hang it near me. The honed edges of the arrowheads flash in the dark as the bow swings.

I put myself in a cavity between three limbs, then unloop my belt and hook it to one of the limbs. I try to get comfortable, but it is impossible. Instead, I close my eyes and think of Kate, try to fill my head with the feel of her skin, with the sound of her music, but I get nothing—nothing but confusion, worry, a high jumble of threads that winds through my ribs and pulls my shoulders together. I can't help but think of my father. *My father sits in the television-illumined darkness of the living room. The television squeals and yammers, the light flashes.*

And then there is Kate, *sitting on her porch in a white dress, with a red popsicle in her hand. I'm on the lawn, and I watch her lips, stained with the melting liquid.* It is music I want.

When I wake up, the air is cold, and my head is sharp. I can't remember having been asleep, yet I know I could not have remained in this position awake. My body is stiff, and the morning air makes me shiver. It is still dark, and the forest trills with insects. I have no idea what time it is.

I try to stand up, but I've forgotten about my belt, and it holds me against the tree. I reach behind me to undo it.

To take my mind off the cold, I start to search through the

trees for Martin and Carl. I stand up, let my eyes drift across the layers of leaves. The leaves stir lightly with the breeze.

When I see something glint, I force my eyes. Martin. I look harder. He's lower in his tree than I am, and he appears to be asleep. It surprises me how much I can see in the darkness; it surprises me too that the low moon is as huge and bright as it is. Everything has a hard, silvery brightness.

I stand for a long time in the tree, unwilling to go back to squatting. Then I hear something in the forest below. I freeze. Slowly, I go for my bow. I can't see anything, but I can hear it, right below my tree. As soon as I have the bow in hand, it stops. I wait and still there is nothing but the grind of insects. Maybe it was nothing. Maybe it was a squirrel. I close my eyes to listen, and I can feel the throb of my heart in my head.

Don't look down, a voice whispers. I open my eyes and whirl around, but there is nothing, and no one. My feet are raw from the bark of the tree. The tree seems to move yet of course it doesn't move. *Boy,* it says again, still a whisper. I bring my hand up close to my face and dust from the clay comes loose. I can smell it. *Listen to me.*

I hold close to the tree, then shake my head. I'm tired, I'm half into sleep in the worst possible way, and, cold as I am, I'm starting to sweat. I press my eyes closed and dream of music, any music. I want the death songs, the *Kindertotenlieder*, but there is nothing at first.

Dawn comes slowly—light high on the horizon, descending, then a smear of color fingering out over the trees. Without trying, I locate Carl. I watch him get up and piss from the tree. I can see all of the markings Martin made—torn cloth, broken branches. I lean against the bough of the tree and take one of the razorheads from the rack and notch it. I wave to Carl, but he hasn't seen me yet, so I watch him scanning the trees below and beyond him. And then, a voice says, *You could shoot him,* quite distinctly. I look around. He scrambles for his bow, then freezes. *Kill him, it would be easy.*

I smell the buck before I see it materialize from the trees. It's a big, musky odor, big as the giant, antlered head moving slowly along the edge of our triangle.

I steady myself against the tree, and slowly, one foot locked into the Y of the tree, one knee against the bough, I bring the bow up and draw the string back. The deer lifts his head and blinks. His eyes are huge, black as pitch. I look to Carl, and he's stopped, his string drawn, still as night. The deer is twenty, twenty-five yards from me. I think of what Martin said about aiming for the heart.

There's a whisper behind my head. *You won't do it. You're a coward.* I shake my head and the deer looks straight at me. Without moving, I look to Martin; he's up now, and has his crossbow ready.

My arms throb with the weight of my bowstring. My fingers burn with holding the arrow. The deer puts his head down and keeps wandering. Closer to me. I can feel every muscle, every nerve in my arms and chest. Blood is going in my head, ringing in my ears. *You won't,* you can't. I don't have a good shot. Then, Carl's arrow goes shrieking through the trees, whipping in the leaves and rushing over the top of the buck. He raises his head, quivers for a moment, and I think to myself, *Now! Now!* but the reflex won't work, and he bolts. Finally, a million years after I should have released it, I let my arrow go. It licks through the trees, then thunks dead deep in a tree trunk. My arm aches, and suddenly my head feels as though it will explode.

We stay up in the trees, waiting, waiting. I watch the sun come up in the air, first orange, then yellow, then white. I can feel the heat of the day begin to settle into the trees. My stomach is tight with hunger, and my arms and legs feel weak, feverish. A spell has settled into them.

Now my own doe is moving through the forest. The doe I saw on the hill the afternoon I was running. I can feel her, the way I felt her in the forest the day I was running. I can feel her thoughts crowding my own. I can feel her in my arms, feel the heat and sweat of her fur. I am looking down at the forest from above, but in my line of vision, I can also see my own eyes looking, sketching along her path as she slides through bramble and blackberry. I can feel her weariness. I can feel the scent of locust and birch and weeds. I can feel her eyes and her weight and the tired jangle of her legs, but she does not feel me. I notch another arrow, but my hands have lost all sensation. I know her breath and the clang of her blood and the sinew that crosses my chest when the string begins to tighten and the pulleys begin to move. *It is not your hand. You are absolved in guilt.* I feel her but I do not see her in the string at my ear and the notch of the arrow in my fingers at my cheek. *Wait, wait.* My blood is still, the forest is blue, my insides are burnt out. The death songs. The woman's voice curling out through the clean of the air, an object of sound, as palpable as the warming light. It moves in me, ringing in my chest and in the shadows of my head. Then she's in the clearing THERE and my shoulder rises. My eye moves down the shaft of the arrow beyond her head to the frame of her neck in the razor. Down. I look at my arm, at the ridge of the bone. *You won't.* And the arrow is gone, vanished like the deer vanished the last time I saw her.

My arrow makes a popping noise on impact, but I still cannot see it. Then, behind the deer's shoulder, there is a tiny bloom of red. One of Carl's arrows sings above her and dives into the deep woods.

She stays glued to the forest floor for a moment, her eyes gone to jelly. She quivers and her hind legs dip a little. She's already dead, but she hasn't learned it. She takes a step, as if relearning the movement of her legs, then bolts into the trees, out of sight.

A high, shrieking sound tears through the forest, making the trees and the earth and my body vibrate. I toss my bow to the ground and slide out of the tree, the bark scraping along the ridge of my spine. The shriek comes again, and the forest fills with sound.

Already I'm running through the trees, branches whipping wildly around me, my head full of the deer. There is blood on the leaves, bright and red, and I follow it, follow the tears her hooves have made in the ground. And I follow the sound of her thinking—the complex of panic and love and fear and picture. I run at top speed, bare feet going like light, ignoring the bramble and locust and the shred of stickers on my skin. My breathing burns my throat. I go down a long grade, stumbling through the rotten leaves and trees. More blood, bright and pink. I chase her like she's in season, following the smell of the blood, the vulnerability of it, but following without thinking, without knowing. I go down through marsh grass, over a tiny stream, the ground blurring beneath me. I follow her, hooked by some weird kind of magnetism. And then I stop. She is ten yards away from me, gulping from the stream. I can feel the breath like fire in her throat, in her chest. I can feel the water in her face. I can feel it lifting her off the ground.

Carl and Martin heave through the woods behind me, crashing, thudding down the incline. I stand next to her body, and I see a rippling reflection of myself in the stream, my face streaked with mud and sweat, my mouth wide, my head inflamed. I want to fall over and vomit, but my stomach is empty. I want to go into my own head and die.

"It's a good one," Martin says, standing next to me and leaning over her. "Is she dead?"

"She's dead," I say.

"Be careful of her hooves. If she's still alive, she can kick the hell out of you."

"Jesus Christ," Carl says, coming close, then kneeling down to prod her with one of his arrows. "Jesus goddamned Christ you killed a deer." He stops a moment, and his face lights. "You killed a deer." He starts to giggle, the wild giggle he had the afternoon he caught and killed the snake.

Martin touches my shoulder. "I've never seen anyone run so fast in my life," he says. He looks at me, and, shaking his head, slaps me on the back. "Goddamn," he says, as if I've done something wonderful and unusual, then he turns to Carl.

I stand away from them, staring. In their excitement, they begin talking crazily—about taking the deer back to camp and dressing it out, about hunting and becoming self-sufficient—and their voices begin to crowd up around me and blur. When I wonder about my father, things begin to spin. School couldn't be less real to me—like a bit of cellophane rising in a kaleidoscope.

The air is still and warm and bright, and the surface of the lake is smooth and unbroken. I take off my clothes and wade in. I go deeper and deeper, let the water lift the clay off my skin. Finally, I let my head go under and I stay there for a long time, my eyes open to the dull, blurred green light, the unbelievably blank peace. I wait until my lungs begin to burn, and then wait a little longer.

When I climb out, the clay is gone, and my welts and scrapes are bright pink in the sunlight. But the scent is still there. I know I will never get the scent out of me.

"Right there, right there," Martin says.

The deer hangs by its hind legs from a tree behind our clearing, its throat cut and its head bloody. Carl has Martin's bowie knife, and he stabs it, according to Martin's instructions, into the soft belly of the deer, between the gather of the hind legs.

"Easy," Martin says, hanging close. "You don't want to cut into the guts. It'll stink."

Carl slides the tip of the knife in between the skin and the muscle wall and draws the knife downward. Blood oozes onto his hands from the gutter of the knife. He puts his fingers into the flap of the belly and holds it, then pulls the knife against it. He grits his teeth. His eyes glisten. "God," he says.

"Well," Martin says, laughing, "what did you expect? It's leather."

"Yeah," Carl grunts, liking the feel and the stink of blood.

In a moment, the intestines, scored slightly but otherwise beautiful in their smooth, blue-pink and shiny perfection, fall out of the cavity. Carl reaches inside, makes a cut, and they flop against the deer's chest.

"What about the ribs?" he says. "Do I do the ribs?" His hands are covered in blood—up to his elbows like long red gloves. There's blood spattered on his chest, on his legs and face. It's on the ground, seeping into the soil. It's in the air.

Martin closes his eyes and rubs his head with his knuckles. "I'm thinking. I'm trying to remember how they did it." For a minute I wonder if he's ever really seen a deer field-dressed, or if he's just making it up as he goes along. "Yeah," he says finally,

"I guess go ahead. We've got to get rid of the rest of the guts so —No, wait." He swings around. "I guess the thing to do is just cut the head off and yank the lungs and stuff out afterward."

"All right, but what do I do with this stuff?" Carl says, laying the blade of the knife flat against the intestines.

"Just wait a second for that," he says.

I stand close, looking at Martin. It surprises me to see him indecisive. A light veil of nausea wings in my throat.

"All right, cut the head off. Wait until you do that to do anything with the entrails."

"Albie? Albie?" Carl looks to me. "Can you back this up for me?"

So I stand behind the hanging carcass and dig my fingers into the fur. Flies swarm on us, on the deer. I close my eyes, and I can feel the movement of the soft, still warm body as Carl saws at the neck.

When Martin and Carl go swimming, I come with them. I stand in the shallows. The sunlight hits hard on the water, and my stomach rings with hunger.

There is cigarette smoke in the air, and I look up. At first there is nothing, but I hear movement in the trees. Carl and Martin are oblivious to it. A moment later, a man comes crashing through the trees onto the beach.

The three of us stand together, Martin in the middle. The man is smaller than any of us, and has dark, longish hair that covers his ears, and seems to sprout as a corona from the slight, perfectly round bald spot on the top of his head. He looks at us, and doesn't say anything. He's startled by our nakedness—just as we are startled that he should materialize here.

He looks half-dead. His eyes are deep in his head, pushed deep by whatever caused the dark, hollow circles around them. His skin is pale and waxy as a cancer patient's.

"Who are you?" Carl says, threatening.

"Say," the old man mutters, backing away and gesturing, "don't I know you from somewhere?" It is unclear which of us he means.

"How'd you get back here?" Martin says.

The man smiles and moves his feet. "I didn't mean—" he says, and starts to cough. It's a deep, liquid cough, a smoker's cough. "I didn't mean to interrupt your skinny-dipping, fellas," he says, his voice unsteady, the coughing subsiding. He wipes the moisture from his eyes.

"Be that as it may," Martin says, "you're trespassing." He looks to Carl and me. "Isn't that what it looks like?" I back away a little. I want to get dressed.

"Oh?" the man says. "I'm sorry." The words seem to surprise him, as if they've just awakened him. "I didn't, didn't know this was private, private property."

"It is," Carl says. "But still you didn't say how you got back here."

I dodge out of the group and get our towels. I wrap mine around my waist, but Martin takes a long time to put his on. He stands holding it, glowering at the little man.

"I, I didn't mean to intrude, intrude on anything," he says. "I was just walk, just walking, and here I was. Here I am. You ever do that?"

Only now does it occur to me that he's drunk. I wonder why I didn't understand it before.

"Just turn around and go walking in the direction you came from," Carl says. "Go on."

"All right," he says, throwing up his hands and letting them flutter back down. "Fair enough. Fair enough." He sways and moves toward us. "Say, uh," he says, his eyes narrowing a little, "you boys wouldn't have a little bit to drink, would you? I mean a group of fellas like yourselves have probably got a six-pack or something like that up here in the woods—" He sort of trails off, one hand out as if leaning against something invisible. He wears a dull green blazer with green, plaid pants.

"No," Martin says. "Now get out." I'm surprised by the sharpness of his words.

"None of us drinks," I say, vaguely surprised by the childish sound of my voice. "There's water if you're thirsty."

The man starts to laugh. "Water," he says. "Water." But he stops laughing suddenly. "People's got a right to live the way they want to live, and I'd never be the one to stand in their way." He nods at us dramatically. "I understand that. I do." I watch him, watch the rhythm of his body—like a rag hanging in a breeze.

"Did you hear him?" Carl says. "Get out. Go on."

"I'm on my way, young man. I'm on my way. All I got to do is get turned around and pointed in the right direction and I'll just walk right out of here." He laughs a little. "You know I'm a walker from way back," he mutters. "I'm a hell of a walker. When I used to live in the capital of this great nation —Washington, D.C., you know—I used to walk everywhere. Never took a bus. Didn't need to, no sir." He breathes deeply and the air whistles in his throat. He gets a crumpled pack of cigarettes out of his pocket and slides one from the pack. His mouth is gray and his teeth are the color of copper.

"What's your name?" Martin says, turning away from the man, turning away from all of us. When the man says nothing, Martin repeats himself, this time loudly, sharply, as if he suspects the man of being deaf.

"Meckler," the drunk says finally. He grins broadly, smoke

drifts from his face. "John Meckler." He thrusts out his hand and Martin shakes it.

"Nice to meet you, Meckler," Martin says.

"Goddamned nice to meet you boys," he says. When he extends his hand to me to shake, I refuse. I turn away. He's disgusting; the last thing I want to do is touch him.

"That's Al," Martin says, pointing at me. "Don't pay any attention to him."

Meckler steps back from me and looks at Martin.

"And this is Carl." Carl shakes the guy's hand.

"Good to meet you," Meckler says. "Good to meet you."

"You come out here alone?" Martin says. He stands very close to the drunk now. His size is threatening.

"No," Meckler says. "No. I got my cat here someplace." For some crazy reason, the sound of his voice makes me want to cry. "Hey," he shouts, and his voice carries wetly on the water, in the trees. He starts to cough, then, "Where are you, Pepper? Pep?" He whirls around and I'm certain he'll fall over. "Goddamn it," he says. "Never was such a thing as a cat that would come when you called it. Never."

"What kind of cat is it?" Martin says. I look away, toward the water. The surface is still again, as flat as a razor. In Martin's voice I hear a million things, but most of all I can hear the current of this thing—the woods, the short world—sweeping along. I stare at the burning, glassy reflection of the sun on the surface of the water.

"Just a cat," Meckler says. "She's red, or red as any cat can be. That's why I call her Pepper. Red Pepper. Been stupider cats, but not many." He coughs and spits into the dirt.

"You hungry?" Martin says. "We got fresh meat up at the cabin." I look at Martin. I have no idea why he's inviting the drunk to our cabin, but it makes me angry. It's Carl's and my place, not his. Not his.

"Well, goddamn," Meckler says when he sees the cabin. "Goddamn." He shakes his head, then stamps a little. "Jesus Christ will you look at this. It's nice. It's nice."

I look at him. With its uncaulked walls and crude, open doorway, only a drunk could think it was nice.

"Let's get a fire going and get some meat cooked," Martin says.

When Martin goes into the trees toward the deer, I follow after him, and stop him by the hanging carcass. "What are you doing, man?" I stare at him. "Why did you bring that drunk up here?"

Carl comes into the little clearing behind us. He has Martin's bowie knife in his hand. I wait a moment, and Martin says nothing to me, only glares.

"Come here," he says to Carl.

The entrails of the deer are still on the ground. They're all covered with flies. Finally, angrily, I turn around and go back to the cabin.

"Bury that stuff," I hear Martin say to Carl.

Emily sits on the dusty hood of her car with her legs crossed. It's afternoon and the sunlight hangs brightly on the dust and cigarette smoke in the air. She pats the filter of her cigarette against her closed lips and frowns. "Have you talked to your father in the last couple of days?" she says after a while. We are at the Outskirts, but at the very edge of the preserve, where the paved road meets the gravel road. It's Wednesday already.

I avoid looking at her. "No. I haven't talked to him. I don't know. I almost think it's better for me to stay out here." I can tell she doesn't understand. Still, I want to tell her about the drunk.

"Why?" she says. "Al, how could it possibly be better for you to stay here in the woods?"

"Don't, Em."

"Right, sure, no problem. You can just stay out here in the woods running around naked, shooting the wildlife God knows why and living the idyllic, romantic life of no responsibilities. Right."

"Em."

"No, I just want to get this straight." She hesitates a moment. "I saw Mrs. Schwartzmann today. I *went* to see her. I asked her if she'd talked to you. She hasn't. Guess what. Nobody has. Do you talk to anyone, Albie? Or is it just the animals?"

"For Christ's sake, Emily, I talk to you."

"Do you? Do you? When was the last time you talked to me?" She hops off the car and comes close. "When? What have you said to me lately besides 'Yes, Em,' 'No, Em,' 'Thanks, Em,' 'No thanks, Em,'?" She pushes me. "That's not talking, that's nothing. That's crap."

I look at her, then frown and look away. We stay silent for a long time. I concentrate on my heartbeat and the way I can feel it move my body.

"You used to talk," she says. "You used to have the goddamned biggest mouth in the neighborhood. I remember when we were little, you used to tell stories all the time. We could never shut you up. You used to keep Carl laughing all the time."

I hesitate a little bit. "Maybe I just don't know how to talk any more. Maybe there's nothing to talk about. Maybe I'm so sick of words and trying to make sense of things that I don't like to talk."

"That's crap, too."

I laugh. "Yeah, probably."

She looks at her feet. "What about Kate?" She gets another cigarette out of her purse but doesn't light it. "You expect her to wear a loincloth and run around in the woods, too?"

"Em, come on."

"And when the movers bring her piano, what are you going to say? 'Just stick it over there, fellas, by the lake'?"

There is silence for a moment. "How is she?" I say.

"No different from what she was the last time you saw her." She fiddles with the cigarette for a moment, then lights it. "If I had told her I was coming back out here, she'd have come along."

"Why didn't you?"

"You'd have no reason to go back home. And besides you smell awful."

"Well," I say, wincing a little, "I'll probably be home before too long. Martin came out here the day after I did. He's not going home."

"He's nuts," she says, spraying smoke. "He's worse than you. I just hope you get along."

"Oh, sure, yeah. We don't agree all the time, but we get along fine." I think of Martin's hand on my shoulder after I chased the deer.

"What about Carl?"

"You know Carl. All he ever wants to do is follow."

She nods. "But is he going to stay here?"

"God, no. He wants to. He comes every afternoon, but he's still going to school."

"Oh," she says. And after a while, "Oh well, I guess I'll see you later." She turns and opens the car door.

"Say hello to Kate for me."

"If you've got messages for her, you'll have to deliver them yourself. I'll be a cab driver—I mean I'll take you home when-ever you want to go—but I'm not going to be a messenger." She gets into the car. Smiling, she says, "Just let me know."

Before she leaves I want to stop her and tell her about the deer. I want to tell her how I can't get the thought of it out of my head. Every step I took in the woods after it, the brush of every leaf, the feel of the water on my skin afterward. I want to tell her about the drunk. I want to tell her about a million things. Instead, I just wave as she turns the car around.

When Meckler talks, his teeth slide beneath the hood of his lips as if they have no real relationship with his mouth. His teeth are dark and discolored from smoking and from God knows what else, and when he talks the gleam is deep, like moss on a wet rock.

"I lived everywhere," he says, leaning against the wall of the cabin with the cat in his arms, staring at the fire. We all stare at the fire. It's as transfixing as a television set. "When I was a boy," he says, his fingers working against the grain of the cat's hair, "we was in North Carolina—my mother and me, don't you know. We lived in a trailer park, in a double-wide, in the same trailer as another woman and her little girl." He stops for a moment to think, to drink from the bottle Carl drove him into town to get. In the growing dusk, the only sound is the pop of the fire.

"Summers were hot. Sometimes we would go out onto the beach—Nag's Head, don't you know—and it was so hot you couldn't walk on the sand in bare feet." He pulls at his chin as if he is going to pull the trailer and the state and the woman and child they had lived with from the gristle of his chin. "And

I remember one summer I had chicken pox, or measles, and I remember lying in bed. The only way you could get away from the heat was to sleep."

Carl stands up and puts more wood on the fire.

"Then one summer I met the governor of North Carolina, yes sir." His mouth moves from side to side as if he is chewing. "His name was Jimmy Earl Cummings. I walked right up to him and shook his hand. Never was a nicer fella. It was in a little country store where my ma and I went on Saturday mornings to buy taffy and soda. He was smoking a big cigar like Huey Long when I met him, and I said to myself, 'John, you're gonna be just like that man.' And I wanted to be, too. He was handsome, as big as a tree. Stood right there and shook my hand pretty as you please." The cat struggles a little, then jumps out of his arms. He watches it go, then looks up over the fire to the rise of sparks and ash. His eyes are wet and shiny as his teeth. "Said to me," he says, almost like he is in a trance, "said to me, 'Pleasure to meet you, John.' Called me by my first name."

"You're a liar," Martin says, then laughs. Carl and I look at him. "There wasn't any governor of North Carolina named Cummings."

"Ha, boy," Meckler says, then opens his bottle. "Ha."

Carl watches the cat sashay through the clearing, then throws a stick at it. It jerks to the side and races into the trees, into the darkness. Carl pulls Martin's knife from the log where it's stuck and starts carving a sliver of wood.

"Then later, I lived in the capital of this great nation, Washington, D.C. That's how I got to be such a walker. Almost wanted to change my name to Walker, you know." He laughs at this, but none of us do. "Well," he says, and his head lolls dreamily to one side before he snaps it up again. "Where's Pepper?" He blinks. He seems surprised by something. The knife flashes in Carl's hand. "Pepper!"

"He's in the woods," Carl says. The knife goes *thupp, thupp.*

"Did you meet the president?" Martin says. "Did you shake his hand, too?" If you didn't know Martin, if you had only walked into the clearing this minute and overheard his question, you would probably think he was serious, and wouldn't detect the sneer concealed below the surface of his voice. He looks, at this moment, just like his mother.

"You're a clever boy," Meckler says. His voice is soft, sad, like rotting wood. "You're a clever, clever boy." Not only in the drunk's words, but in Martin's too, there is something concealed, something only the two of them understand.

"Don't pay any attention to him," I say, sad and disgusted. "Go ahead, talk. At least I'm listening." I don't really want to be sympathetic to him. I don't really want anything more than for him to leave. I look at Martin, but he seems to look across me, through me, as if I'm made of glass.

"Isn't really nothing to talk about," the drunk says. "Just lived there, is all." He looks at Martin, then away. "I did see the funeral of Mr. John F. Kennedy. I did see that. It broke my heart to see the caissons going down the avenue that way in the sunshine. And I stood there at the Arlington Cemetery and watched as they lit the eternal flame." He laughs and bows his head, and for a moment, I think he's going to cry.

"I went to Washington," I say. It's only about two hundred miles away but it seems like a lifetime. "We went to the top of the Washington Monument and my mother lifted me up to the window to look down. That's all I remember." I wonder, suddenly, if my mother knows anything at all about my life at the moment—flunking out of school, fighting with my father like he is a stranger, and now, living in the woods. If she does, I wonder what she thinks.

"Have you ever been hunting?" Martin says to Meckler. Martin is standing now, on the opposite side of the fire from the drunk and from me. Color comes up into his face from the flame.

"Used to hunt. Went a few times. Many years ago. Before the war, when I lived in Pennsylvania, I used to do some trapping." He lights a cigarette and makes love to it the same way he has been making love to the bottle. The cigarette smoke makes me think of my father, of the summers we camped together; then I think of the deer hanging in the woods.

"Liar," Martin says again.

Meckler looks at Martin and shakes his head.

"You said that you grew up with your mother in a trailer in North Carolina where the summers were hot."

"I'm older than you, boy."

Martin kicks dirt into the fire with his bare feet. Bits of loam sizzle in the flames. "You haven't told us a single thing that's true. Why don't you tell us the truth? Why? Why don't you tell us about how your mother was a whore, about how you never knew who your daddy was, and how that's the reason you are like you are, a lousy, stinking drunk? Or why don't you tell us how your father was a dog and how you were raised by wild bicycles in the African bush? Or maybe you did go hunting with your father once—and you killed him." He laughs through his nose, and moves like he is flying through the air at high speed and using his arms to slow himself. Carl laughs too.

"Go to hell, Martin," I say through my teeth.

"You're going to defend him?" He is still laughing. "You're going to stand up for a drunk and a liar? Look at him. Look. Can't you smell him?"

"Smell yourself," I say, staring at him blankly. "Just shut up, you sound like a lunatic."

"Don't call me a lunatic," Martin snaps.

Ignoring all of it, Meckler says, "You who will sing my praises shall be my shepherd." He laughs, then drinks from his bottle. It makes a low, throaty sound when he takes his mouth away from it.

"Listen to him," Martin says. "Just listen to *him*."

"You're the fool who invited him back here," I say. I stand up, look into the irregular pattern of light that the fire throws on the old man. I think of leaving—but I'm stuck. I try to remember Kate in the music room, I try to remember what she looked like in the white light. For a moment, I close my eyes and try to make the music come.

Martin walks over and kicks the drunk's leg. "Hey drunk," he says, "Hey drunk."

"Leave him alone," I say, and push Martin back. "Bully someone else."

"Drop dead," Martin says sharply, and pushes me away. "Have you ever been hunting, drunk? Have you ever been hunted? Maybe we ought to hunt him."

"Yeah," Carl says, giggling. I know he's not serious. I look at Martin.

Meckler puts his bottle against the wall of the cabin and tries to stand, but as soon as he's up, he stumbles forward and falls toward the fire. Before he can land in the coals, he catches himself with one arm and rolls toward Martin's feet. Martin looks at him and backs away. Finally, the drunk stands up. "You'd hunt a man?" he says.

"I was only kidding," Martin says, suddenly contrite. "I was only kidding." He laughs uncomfortably for a moment, then dips his head and puts his hands together. "I'm sorry if I scared you," he says, extending a hand and putting it on Meckler's shoulder. "You can take a joke, can't you?" He smiles, offers Meckler his other hand to shake. The drunk laughs and shakes his hand uneasily. "Sit down," Martin says. "Sit down and have another drink."

I take the wood from the stack Carl made and put it on the fire. Meckler's wet laugh blends with the sound of the fire. He is here, and there is nowhere else to go.

"You're a clever boy," he says to Martin, settling back against the cabin wall. I wonder why he says it. "I knew you were clever the moment I saw you."

After a few minutes, Martin says, "I used to work with homeless people, you know. I did." He comes over to where Meckler sits and squats down. "I used to work with alcoholics. Do you consider yourself an alcoholic?"

What is going on between the two of them seems to me at this moment like some sad ballet—inevitable, both awkward and graceful, with a knowledge that neither of them seems to understand. They are waiting, only moving in the footsteps that have been laid out for them. It goes on, and it goes on, and the sound of the fire rises like water in my ears.

Meckler shrugs and ignores the question. Carl comes out of the woods with more firewood and dumps it on his pile. "I have to go soon," he says, and the firelight gleams on his chest and face. I wonder what would happen if I went to school tomorrow.

I wonder what would happen with Shaddock and my father. I wonder if my father notices that I'm gone.

"What's it like?" Martin says, rising away from the drunk slowly. "I mean what's it like to be completely dependent on something to live?"

Slyly, Meckler says, "You come over here and take a swallow from this bottle and you'll find out soon enough what it's like."

Carl grins at the drunk, and the drunk grins back. The cat wanders through the clearing, and Martin tries to grab it, but it swings off again into the trees.

Later, when Meckler falls asleep, Carl and Martin talk. I stare at the fire, at the changing orange shapes in the coals. I imagine a million things in the fire—I imagine Martin and Carl's voices are moths fluttering in the darkness. Half asleep myself, I watch as Carl comes over to where the drunk lies. Martin watches too; I can see his eyes at the edge of the clearing. Carl unzips his pants and pisses on Meckler. The drunk doesn't stir.

"You're disgusting," I say sleepily, fighting to focus my eyes.

"Yeah, Albie," he says. "You may be one of my best friends and everything, but you act like a coward, and you sound like Emily." For a while he stands staring at me in the darkness. My eyes do not work: it is a dream, a shape from the fire. "*He's* the one who's disgusting."

I run deep into the woods, away from the lake, away from the cabin and Martin and Carl and Meckler and the Outskirts. I go toward where the forest preserve butts up against the mountains miles and miles away. I go toward the elevated horizon, where the stone cuts the late afternoon sunlight to orange spray, then snuffs it like a hand cupped over a candle. I wait for the sweat to wash everything out of me. Again, it is like fever. And then,

finally, music. Mahler's "Song of the Earth." *Kate on the porch.*
The tenor rolls out through the trees, the forest itself the skeleton
of the sound.

The forest could be endless. One solid mass of trees extending
from one edge of the world to the other, itself a kind of ocean,
and like my dream, a good place for drowning.

Two or three miles in, when I turn around, the music has come
up full, the two voices in their joy and sorrow and adoration
filling the woods cleanly, purely, *her hands on my skin* as though
they and a thousand voices just like them were in the trees, in the
sky, singing, letting the depth and heft of the forest flow through
their bodies, letting it fill their heads and minds with the quiet
damp and gathered warmth of the day. I run and the music grows.

And then, mirroring the sound, a picture starts to open up.
I'm still in the forest, but I'm in two places at once, not only
where I am, but following the deer again. The voices, swelling,
carry me. *It is just out of sight; I can see the fluttering leaves.
I can smell it, smell the blood. Then it stops, but it is not the
deer. It's Shaddock. In his red sweat suit he whirls around in the
clearing, and when he whirls I can see the shaft of the arrow,
the feathers buried deep in his chest, the razorhead reaching,
clawing out behind him. Then he is on his knees. Blood coughs
from his mouth. There is blood everywhere.* And yet I am still
running, the tenor and the soprano are still singing, pulling back
and forth between them.

Almost back, I am lost. I stop but the music will not. *Shaddock's head falls backward and blood rockets from his opened
mouth and as it rises it begins to burn.* All around, the woods
are sudden, concealing. No path anymore, just brambles and spider webs and deep brush. I stop, wander, the music going and
going. Sweat comes and burns in my eyes. Always I have sensed

the right direction. *Now, now*. But the music is too loud, and I can't think. *Here, boy*. I start to get scared, to tremble. I go in one direction, but it's wrong. *Here, boy, here. It's your*—I close my eyes, try to think. There's a wild sensation of blurred shapes, of movement beyond my eyelids. I feel like I'm drowning, and suddenly the music stops. There is nothing. No movement, no sound, nothing but the long green shade and the quiet stretch of trees. *Coward*.

My legs cool and begin to stiffen. I start to walk, zigzagging through the brush. I walk for a long time, out of the arc of the sun. Eventually I come to water, and there are boats in the distance. Though I am completely still, I feel as if I am swaying, moving on the inside, and for a moment, I have no idea where I am, or what I am doing. It makes me panic again, and I take hold of a tree and wait for the fluttering in my ears to subside.

I sit in the leaves and the swarm of the insects, and for the first time or the millionth time, I wonder if coming here was the wrong thing to do. But I can't think. There is music, or there is blood in my ears, or there is panic coming like a voice through the woods. I know nothing—not past not future not truth. The only thing I know is now. I try to think about the fall, or the wild possibility of going to college, and it is unimaginable. I can't even imagine the fall. There is nothing but this crazy spring, the heat and the insects and the sweat that's growing like a virus all over me.

Finally, I figure out where I am, and head toward the cabin. I can hear Martin and Carl arguing with Meckler, and at once, with hunger humming all along my arms and legs, I hate them. I trip over something hard and it goes through me like electrical current. The doe's head. Eyes gone, skin dried back away

from the mouth, bits of skull showing through the blackened fur.
Coward.

"During your death moment—during the moment just before
your death, your thinking becomes fantastically clear. Imagine.
Out of desperation, out of horror, knowing that it can't ever think
again, your mind suddenly works the way it ought to have worked
all of your life. Suddenly it's so charged that everything inside
and outside your head lies down around you with utter clarity.
You understand. For the first time in your life, except maybe
for the moment of your birth, you understand. Things you saw
years ago, things that happened, everything in your life appears
to you and you see it as if it were happening now. It makes sense.
Everything. The infinite order of the planets, the whirl of the
stars, the logic of humans and animals, the slow march of plants
or clouds—of anything you can imagine. Suddenly the order of
it all is perfect. Perhaps even so perfect that just before you die,
just before you never see again, you see the unseeable. God,
standing right there, participating in your death."

"God?"

"Think of your deer. In the moment before she died, right
after you chased her through the woods—there was probably a
moment right there by the stream. She probably saw her reflection for the first time, and she probably understood that it was
herself that she was looking at. She probably understood the
shape of her face and everything around her. Anything she had
ever known was there in the eyes that stared back at her. Think
of it. What she saw in her own eyes—what she saw right then
because she had never needed to see that way before, was the
only thing she needed to see. God."

"Martin, I—"

"Think of it for a minute. When you were chasing her in the woods, you knew that she was dying. Didn't you? You knew exactly what was going through her head. Didn't you?"

"I had shot her. I knew because I had shot her."

"Did you see the arrow hit her? Did you see it go into her?"

"I never even saw the arrow leave my hand. I never saw it after I drew the string back."

"Then how did you know? How did you know to chase her like that?"

"I saw the blood. I saw it like a flower on her side."

"But what did you feel when you were running through the woods?"

"I don't know. I'd slept in a tree, for Christ's sake. I hadn't eaten anything in hours. I wasn't thinking at all. I don't remember thinking."

"But you followed her, probably faster than you'd ever run before. And you knew where she was going."

"That was easy. I could smell her in the trees. It was like she was in heat or something, like her blood was female blood. I couldn't have *not* known where she was."

"But you were part of her death moment. You didn't stop her. She stopped herself. And she wasn't dead. Not yet. That's just what you said."

"No."

"She was dying and she looked up and she saw you and you were God."

"That's silly."

"It's not. No, it's not. Just listen to me. She saw it in your face, she could sense it all around her. She looked up. I know she did."

"She did. But she didn't see me. She couldn't have. Her eyes weren't even working by then. They were like jelly. They were nothing."

"She knew you were God. You didn't know it, but she saw it in your face, in your eyes. You were the instrument of God."

"I don't know what you're talking about. It sounds crazy."

"That's because you're not listening. That's because you're not listening. You were the instrument of God. As godly or God-like or as full of God as the Bible, as an angel, as Christ Himself —for that one moment. She saw in your face her own history, every moment of her life as if you had pulled it out of her and smeared it like blood on your skin. You were her death."

"People got a right to talk how they—"

"Shut up, old man."

"People got a right to talk how they like, but to my mind, that kind of talk is sacrilegious."

"You shut up. Listen, Albie, think of it. Just think of it. The possibility that death—certain kinds of it—might be worthwhile. Think of it. Sudden, brief, absolute knowledge."

"Absolute knowledge is God's alone."

"Shut up. You don't know anything. Just shut up."

"Even if it is true, what difference does it make?"

"It makes every difference in the world. Every difference. Isn't it crazy that anyone's alive? Isn't it? Humans are the only creatures that know they are going to die, and know that there's no possible way around it. Why don't we just do it and get it over with? That's all there really is to look forward to, and all of the rest in between is just agony and suffering over what's going to happen, when it's going to be, and how it's going to be, what's going to come after. So suppose that your death moment is the only moment you get to see God. Suppose that in terms of the universe, humans are such a tiny tiny worry to God that He only has time for that one glimpse. And suppose you go on living, denying the truth of what has to happen to you. Suppose you just go on living."

"Well?"

"Suppose then that there's a nuclear exchange."

"I don't see what that's got to do—"

"It has a lot. It has a lot. Just listen."

"All right, I'm listening."

"With nuclear weapons, there is no death moment. POOF. People are extinguished immediately. Immediately. There's no moment, nothing. There's no looking up at the edge of the stream and seeing God. There's no seeing the instrument of your death. There's no looking into your own eyes at the edge of the water before you take your last drink and knowing that you were alive and that everything around you is living, and connected by a crazy living poetry, a poetry you can see in the trees and in the soil and the water. There's nothing. Instantly. No God. It's the negation of God."

"You're crazy, boy. You're crazy. You oughtn't to talk like that."

"And you shut up. Shut up. You goddamned piece of living shit. You're dead. You're dead, old man.

"Martin."

"You're just as dead as you look. You don't know anything at all but what you drink. You've narrowed your life down to that. That's God. That bottle's killed you. That's God right there in your hand."

"Martin, I don't see the relationship between the original—"

"Of course you don't, Albie. Of course you don't. You see nothing. For you there's nothing ahead or behind you. There's nothing but your body. You know what it's like to be alive, but you don't, not really. It's not real for you. Nothing's real for you but your own body, and what's happening right now. You didn't understand your relationship to the deer's death because you couldn't see it dying. You saw it dying, but look. Right now, you can smell it rotting there in the trees, but that means nothing to you. You don't know what decay is."

"You're talking like a lunatic."

"Don't you ever call me that again."

"I'm going to sleep."

"The moon, the stars, everything. I know nothing. I talk as I know, and I know what I say, yet I say nothing, because the world is all there is."

"I'm going to sleep."

"You're already asleep. Tell me you're going to wake up and that will be some news. Then we'll have something to talk about."

"Maybe I should be like you, then. Maybe I should be self-sufficient. Maybe I should have contempt for everything but myself."

"Listen to me. Listen to me. I know what it's like to live and what it's like to die. I know what a psychotic sees, and what a genius sees. I understand the connection between living things. I see it go through everything like electricity. But the one thing I understand most is how alone everything is. How alone, how apart we are from one another. You'll never know, no matter how long you live, what it's like to be someone else. You'll read books and see movies, and you'll say that you understand, but you'll never know. This is it. You stand there and I stand here, and that's the closest we'll ever come. And we might as well be a million years or miles away from each other. You'll never know if I love or hate you, you'll know nothing at all. You'll be cold and desolate as the moon."

"I know a lot about you, Martin. I know more than you think."

"You know nothing. You know nothing at all. You don't even know if *you* love or hate me."

The rabbit is on the ground, motionless, looking at us, both ears pulled in close to the arch of its back. The notch and feathers of the arrow burn in my fingers. I let go and listen for the hum of the string. The arrow catches the rabbit in the soft, pale-haired underbelly, then drives into the loose loam beyond the body.

There's a scream. I've never heard a rabbit scream before, and it's startling, like a baby's scream, but higher, colder, abject, and I can feel it in my teeth, under my skin. I can feel it in my spine.

Martin's bolt catches the rabbit behind the ear, whipping it around and making it go suddenly silent and still. He says nothing, but gets the arrows, wipes the blood in the leaves, then gives me mine and puts the rabbit in his bag.

When he bends down to cock the crossbow, he says, "Do you ever think about the guys on the track team anymore?"

The scream hasn't bothered him, and I try not to let on that I can still feel it in the air. I look at the back of his head, at the scruff of hair on his neck. "No," I say softly, pressing my finger to my teeth to stop the vibration. "I thought about revenge for a while, but the more I thought of it, the less real it became."

"Do you hate them?"

"No."

He says nothing, but seems to want more.

"I've got no feeling at all toward them." I say this but it isn't completely true. I hate Shaddock. But I think I know what Martin has in mind, and it makes me uneasy. "Like I said, they're not really very real to me, not as long as I'm here."

We are walking toward the new woods, side by side, scanning the trees for anything at all. In the close, narrow pines, the hunting will be easier. There's very little underbrush.

"How do you mean?"

"I don't know exactly. It's the woods, I guess. I just don't feel convinced about it. As if I weren't there at all."

"And Shaddock?"

When I look at him, I wonder if he knows what I'm thinking. "Abstractly," I say, "I probably hate him. At least for all the garbage he's gotten me into, but it really doesn't make sense to me."

He leans close to me. "That's easy," he says. "He eats souls. Any soul he can get. And he keeps score. But the ones that taste sweetest are the ones that are hardest to get. It's the way Satan works."

I watch him. When I first met Martin, I thought that, like my father, he was a person of endless patience. But where my father has always been, beneath his sarcasm, a truly gentle person, Martin roils and seethes beneath the surface.

"Why abstractly?" he says in a few moments.

"What?"

"Why do you hate Shaddock in the abstract? What do you mean?"

Why is he compiling this information—relentlessly asking questions, relentlessly watching? One day all the information will surface—and then what?

"That I don't care about him, mainly. But at the same time, he doesn't seem very real to me. Only once in a while does he seem real to me." Suddenly I can see Shaddock on his knees in the woods by the stream, his head falling backward and blood shooting from his mouth. "I mean I think if he were dead right now I wouldn't know the difference." As I say it, I know it's a lie.

He gets in front of me and blocks my way. "You're always saying that things don't seem real to you. I want to know what you mean."

I look at him, then let my eyes focus away from the bitter darkness of his eyes to the soft browns of the woods, of the pine needles and boughs. I start to speak, to tell him that even he doesn't seem real to me unless I'm looking directly at him—again, it's a lie—but I stop myself. There's a flash of movement just beyond us. Another rabbit careers out of the trees, then stops and stands utterly still. Slowly, Martin turns, and slowly, I slide an arrow across the bow and into the string. The rabbit holds. I bring the bow up and take back the string. Martin starts to bring up the crossbow, but the rabbit takes off, dodging in and out among the trees. I loosen the bowstring, but Martin whips off a shot. The bolt streaks white and high, and skims over the carpet of pine needles before it thunks into a tree.

"Good shot," I say.

Martin says nothing. Then, as we go toward the place where the bolt stuck, I say, "What about Meckler? Do you hate Meckler?"

He turns around and looks at me. It occurs to me at first that the question was a mistake, but his voice is soft, even. "No," he says, "why should I?"

"I just wondered, is all. I don't know." For a moment, I think I hear music, and I turn, scan the woods. But it is gone as quickly as it comes. I think for a while, listen to the sound of our feet, and to the sound of the wind moving in the trees. When Martin says nothing, I say, "How long do you think he'll stay?"

"As long as he wants—or until we tell him to go." He bends down to take his bolt out of the tree. "So far, he has no reason to leave."

Then, not thinking, I say, "I just don't want him to ruin what we've got out here. I don't even see why you invited him to stay."

"Let me worry about that, okay?" His voice has sharpened, but he doesn't raise it. "I'll take care of him." After a moment: "And no, I don't hate him."

"We need more food," Martin says, circling around behind our backs. Carl turns and looks at him, but I do not. I just stare at the black pit of the fire. "One goddamned rabbit isn't going to feed the four of us."

Meckler stands up. He is filthy. He says, "Yeah, food," and puts a hand on the side of his head. He looks at Carl and me. His eyes look like they could fall out of his head. "What do you boys say?" he asks, eyebrows floating. "What do you say? Get some food?"

Martin watches him, and then, angrily, shouts, "Shut up," and kicks the drunk's legs out from under him. Slowly, crazily, both of his legs rise beneath him and he goes sprawling, rolling toward the cabin.

"You didn't have to do that," he whines, rubbing his hip.

"All right," I say. "Fine. We'll go into town. We'll get more food." I stand up and stare away at Martin. I haven't been into town all week, and the idea appeals to me even if I can't imagine it. I stare at the edge of the cabin's plywood roof. In the moisture, the layers of wood have swollen and separated. *Decay. Decay.* "Carl?"

"No," Martin says.

"No? No what?" I stare at him. My own hunger, the stink of the rotting deer—everything makes me edgy, angry.

"No buying food."

"And what are we supposed to do? We did a goddamned fine job of hunting. One squirrel and three trees. You want to plant a garden?"

"Just shut up and listen. There are people at the campground now. All we've got to do is steal a cooler."

"Jesus."

Carl lights up. "Hey," he says, "that's a good idea."

"That's the stupidest thing I ever heard."

"Why, Albie? Why is it stupid? It seems logical to me. Aren't you with us? What's the matter?"

"It's stupid because you've got money, Carl's got money. I have money. Even if none of us had money, we could get food from Carl's refrigerator." I watch as Meckler's cat wanders through the clearing and stops, sniffing, at the fire place.

"But it's not self-sufficient."

"Oh, Jesus," I say, wanting to hit something, to break something. "How is stealing from campers any more self-sufficient than stealing from Carl's mother? I don't see that, Martin. Maybe you can explain that to me."

"Relax, Al. Don't be so obstinate." Quietly, suddenly, he sits down. The cat turns to him, then noses close. Martin scoops it up and holds it in his arms. His hand goes over the cat's skull, then down the ridge of its spine. The cat raises its head to meet the return of Martin's hand.

"Listen," I say.

"No," Martin says, "You listen." His voice is firm but calm.

"Are you going to desert us? Or are you with us, part of the group?"

"What?" Everyone looks at me. "It's got nothing to do with anything like that."

"Then you're afraid of stealing a little bit of food from a bunch of fat campers? Tell me, Al. I think it's important that this gets out into the open."

I roll my head. Frustration wants to rise up into my head, but I'm too tired, too hungry. Once again everything is moving away from me, and I feel helpless.

"Listen," Martin says, his voice smoothing out the knots in the air, mirroring the movements of his hands on the cat's body, "We're like a family here. Like a tribe or something. We have to think about each other, the group. We have to keep that in mind." He avoids looking at Meckler, and for some reason, a wave of sorrow for the old man comes up in me. "We know these woods. We know things about them that no one else does, that no one else could. We don't ask anything of anybody. We don't pollute. Those people—" He looks at me. "Those people in the campground that you're so worried about, they're takers. They'd be the first to chase us out of here. Look at their campers and their television sets and radios. And look at us. We don't even have electricity here. And we don't want it."

My arms and legs have begun to tremble a little with edginess. "So what happens if we do it? What happens if they come after us?"

"They won't," he says, smiling. "The two of us will go. We'll take the motorcycle. No one will follow us."

"Fine," I say. "Fine."

"You and me. It'll have to be you and me."

"Of course."

"I'm not asking you to do anything I'm not prepared to do," he says. He drops the cat and stands up. The cat rubs against Martin's leg, but he nudges it away. "It has to be you. You're the fastest." This echoes in my head.

"What about me?" Carl says. His face reminds me of the Cro-Magnon faces in the pictures hanging on the library walls at school—his forehead stupid as a block of stone or ice. The thickness of his face is mirrored in his arms and chest.

"Can't get three on a motorcycle," Martin says.

"If Albie doesn't want to do it, why in the hell—"

Martin puts his arm around my bare shoulder the way my father used to. He smells like lemon, like ginger. His hand is smooth and dry. I look at him, at the side of his smiling, smiling face. I look at the dry speckle of whiskers on his cheeks, and at the cut of his chin.

But it rains, and the four of us sit in the damp cabin listening to the rain on the roof and in the trees as it picks up and dies away, as it rakes across the surface of the forest like sleet.

Meckler stays to himself and quiet. It's easy to see that he expects Martin to throw him out into the wet if he says the wrong thing.

The walls bleed moisture through the cracks between the logs, and everything smells of mildew and decay. I sleep on and off, on and off, the sound of the water carrying me down inside myself, into the rhythm of my thinking. When I wake up, it is still raining, and cold and dull as evening.

When it lets up some, Carl goes up to his car to see if there is anything to eat. He comes back empty-handed, but he says that Emily is up on the road, and wants to talk to me. "She's not going to come down here," he says, "not even if the sun comes out and the whole place dries up."

"God," I say, and get up. I try to remember what day it is, but I can't. Thursday, maybe. Friday.

I put on my shoes and shirt, and, while it's still a drizzle, I run up through the trees toward the road. It starts to pour again halfway there, but I'm already soaked.

The back door opens, and I jump in and slam it behind me. Kate is there, and I stare at her a moment in surprise. The whole car reeks with a near-asphyxiating mixture of perfume and cigarette smoke, and my eyes begin to burn. "Hi," I say. Kate sits in the front seat, on the passenger side, and I lean up and try to kiss her hello, but she turns her face away from me. I sit back quickly in embarrassment.

"God, Albie," Emily says, "you really stink."

"I don't see how you can tell with all of this. And besides, I just had a shower."

Kate turns around on the seat and laughs. The sound makes me uneasy. "That's what you get," she says, "if you're going to play Tarzan."

We're silent for a while. The stuffiness of the car is almost unbearable. The rain rattles on the roof and pours over the windows. I feel like I'm hanging in an air bubble.

Finally, Emily says, "I just came out to tell you that I'm coming by to pick you up to go to school. I'm coming Sunday night, and you're going to go back home. You've got an appointment with Mrs. Schwartzmann first period Monday morning."

I try to imagine it, but it doesn't connect. "You mean I haven't been expelled."

"I want you to take this seriously, Albie. I do. I've gone to a lot of trouble to work this out. This is a chance for you."

"All right, I'm sorry. I'm sorry. It just seems impossible, if you know what I mean."

I can't help but look at Kate. She's wearing a raincoat, and her hair is matted with the dampness and bunched up around her shoulders, yet there is something about her—if only the color of her skin or the way the dull, cloudy light strikes her—that draws my eyes. When I look at her, when I think of her, I wish I hadn't come out here. I wish I were like everybody else in the world. I wish I were able to accept everything. I want to lean forward and kiss her. I want to take her face in my hands and taste her mouth.

"Listen," she says after a minute, "I came out here for a reason, love. Emily almost didn't let me come, but I've got something to tell you and I wanted you to get it from me, not through the grapevine, or whatever vines it is you guys are swinging on. And I don't want you to get all excited about it either." She reaches over the back of the seat and puts a finger on my mouth. It has a smoky taste, and I open my mouth and run the ridge of my teeth along it.

"Sure," I say. "No problem."

"Al, now don't look at me like that. Come on. It's not that big of a deal. It's nothing like what you're thinking. I just got asked to the prom is all."

"The prom. The prom. You got asked to the prom a month ago. What's the goddamned big deal about the prom. It's silly. It's—"

"Albie, I know. I know how you feel but this is different. This time I think I'm going to go."

"Oh," I say. I don't look at her, but at the rings of dirt in my fingernails. I look at my legs, at the dirt and bits of grass stuck in the hair. I want to get up. I want to get out of the car.

"It's not like I'm leaving you or anything. I'm not breaking up, Albie."

"Listen, listen. Do we have to discuss, to discuss this in public?" I open the door of the car and start to climb out into the torrent of rain. "Do you mind if we just climb out of the car or something and talk about this in private?"

"Albie," Emily says, "get back into the car." But it makes me climb all the way out of the car and shut the door.

"Will you please just get out of the car and talk to me about this?"

She rolls down the window partway, and then, in anger or frustration, pushes the door of the car open and climbs out. "There's nothing to talk about, really, Al. It's not like I'm going to marry him. It's not. I just want to go to the goddamned prom is all. Is that such a big deal? When I get old and look back on my life I want to have a prom memory. Okay, so it's a generic one. Okay, it's with someone I don't even like all that much. At least I will have gone. At least I will have gone." She stops a moment and looks away from me. "I can't get that from you," she says quietly, "not while you're out here playing Tarzan with Carl and crazy Martin Willman." It seems for a moment that she is close to tears. It would serve her right. But she just moves her hand across her face and whatever it was is gone.

"Listen—no, that's just fine. Really. If you want to, then by all means." I wait. Rain streams down my face and through my clothes. The silence between us is big and wild as a migraine. "Who, um, you know. Who is it going to be?"

"What difference does it make?"

"It doesn't. You're right. It doesn't." *Who is it? Tell me who it is.*

"Al, don't take it this way," she says, her hands in her raincoat pockets, her arms pulled in tight to her body. "It's not like that."

"What time did you say, Em?" I shout. "Sunday night?" I stare straight at Kate. I look right through her. "I'll be up here waiting."

"Your father says to tell you he misses you," she shouts as Kate gets in and closes the door.

I turn into the current of the rain, give the side of the car a knock, and then, unable to tell whether I am crying or not, run back into the woods.

The motorcycle knocks back and forth through the trees, jumping, lurching, braking, chewing up the underbrush and rattling out a trail of sweet blue smoke. It will be dark soon. I am watching the color of the remaining sunlight—cool from the west like light reflected on water, like the color of tangerines—but I do not feel quiet inside, I do not feel real.

We keep our heads down and dodge the low branches that whip past, sometimes tearing at our hair or beating our arms and legs. For me, the huddling into the bike, into the closeness of Martin's back, is like a prayer—but for what I couldn't say.

We have painted ourselves—for disguise, for concealment in the darkness, for the crazy, inhuman look it gives us. I wear Martin's crossbow over my shoulder, and once in a while branches catch in it and shred, leaving bits of green in the corners of the bow. It bounces with the sway and jar of the bike.

We go three, maybe four miles through the woods, along a stream, then through marsh grass and up into the thick of the woods. We stop about a hundred yards from the edge of the campground and lean the bike in the trees. The silence is sudden, like stepping off the edge of a cliff.

I give Martin his crossbow and we go toward the campground without speaking. There is an understanding between us of movement, of sense. Like people who have lived together for a long time, we don't need to speak.

The long cascade of woods ends in a stand of high, heavy grass. Beyond it is mowed grass that spreads away from the trees in long, smooth terraces that fall from the forest toward the lake. Each terrace is lined, like a drive-in theater, with electrical outlets for campers. On the first one, just up from the lake, from the developed beach and boat-launch point, there is a cabin where there is a little store and an office for the rangers. I know because when my father and Carl and I used to camp here we would go into the store to buy candy or fishbait or talk to the rangers. I can remember standing in the little aisles looking at the fishing lures, the colored taffy and licorice and hard candy. I remember looking into the tanks full of blue water where they kept the minnows.

Still, the broad expanse of green is startling after leaving the cover, the sanctity of the woods. I feel naked, crazy, foolish— as if I am in a dream and about to commit murder and can't turn around, can't take control, can't do anything but follow the momentum of things toward whatever happens.

There are voices, but the only people in sight are way down the slope near the office. A fat man smokes at the edge of the lake. A boy throws stones. We move along the grass, crouched close to the ground.

There are campers—Winnebagos, Jetstream trailers—up and down the terraces, but it's early in the year, not yet Memorial Day, and it isn't crowded.

Maybe it's because of the hunger, but everything that happens —the way Martin and I crouch and run toward the nearest trailer, the way our breathing is gone beneath the breeze, the way the accumulated warmth of the day rises out of the broad green exactly as the insects rise (as if they have come from the same timeless beginning)—seems as if it is etched into the air ahead of us, as if it is part of the curvature of space. We were here before. We are here now, and we will always be here, in the half-evening, sweating and running toward an aluminum Jetstream camper. When I follow Martin's signals and move toward the back of the camper, it isn't me who is moving at all, but the breeze, the tide, the world, the relentless momentum of things.

Martin slides along the driver's side and I go down the other. There's an awning and a picnic table beneath. In the rising darkness, I can't see anything worth taking. There are toys, plates and a stove, but no cooler. When Martin rounds the edge of the camper I shake my head. Hunkered low, he nods and waves in the direction of the next one.

We go over the grass, down one terrace and toward a small, squarish, green and white camper. My hunger makes me nervous, and I wish there were music, but there is none. I look again, and everything is still.

We run together, and I can feel Martin's closeness—I can smell the sweat and warmth and movement.

Both of us see the cooler at the same time. There's a folding table by the camper door, and the cooler, a big aluminum thing with metal handles on the sides, sits on it next to a picnic kit. There's a light on inside the trailer, but the door is shut. We ease around to the back of the camper, and wait a moment, catching our breath and gauging the distance back to the trees. I can hear low voices in the camper. I look at the crossbow, at the razorheads and the bits of leaf stuck in them. "Ready?" he says. I blink, and we rush for the cooler. We each take a handle and whip it off the table. The goddamned thing is monstrously heavy, and two steps away from the trailer, the hollow metal table and picnic kit go clattering like thunder to the ground. We tear for the woods. The trailer rumbles and a man comes out. In a moment, he is shouting. His voice bolts up, each word standing above him in the damp air. We go up the terrace, past the first trailer, and up the long stretch toward the woods. My heart screams. Then there is a woman's voice. "Come on," I say. Martin is slower. "They're following us." Fear scrapes my face and arms like sandpaper.

There are other voices now, like a crazy music, one layering over another and jumbling. Ahead of us, the forest shouts too. *Hurry, hurry.*

I look at my feet against the gray reflectionless grass, and the weight of the cooler burns my arm. I want to drop it where it is and run, but my hand does not let go. Nausea and dread lap against my sides; it's the hunger, the flavor of the deer in my teeth. The forest is laughing. *You won't make it. You'll drown halfway.*

The woods waver like a curtain in the unsteady, colorless light, and then, finally, we hit the high grass. But we can't stop. With the voices coming after us, we burst through the curtain of the trees, branches tearing our chests and arms, beating us as if willfully *the wild hush of BIRDS and insects and chattering squirrels. Watch OUT!*

"Where's the bike? Where's the bike?"

"Up there, straight ahead. Straight ahead."

Ten, twenty yards in—the darkness is almost full and complete because of the overhang of the trees—we put the cooler down and rest. My head feels light and my hand and arm are frozen stiff from the weight of the cooler. We listen, and the forest is quiet.

There are three or four people at the edge of the trees, probably at the edge of the high grass. They're talking, but what they're saying is lost to us. The trees swallow it. The only thing I can make out is "goddamned savages." Then, in a moment, "Ranger."

"Come on," Martin says, and we get up again and take the cooler deeper, toward the bike, but we stop when there's crashing at the edge of the trees.

"Come out of there you goddamned cowards," comes a man's voice.

Martin looks at me and grins. I can see the light of his eyes in the darkness.

"Come out of there!"

Crouching down next to the cooler, Martin unshoulders his bow, cocks it, and takes a razorhead from the rack. *Where's the line?* Martin lies down and pushes the bow ahead of him. The safety is on.

The man is in the woods now—I can hear him moving around. He stops and then he's silent. I can sense the apprehension building in him. I can feel it when he strains to look into the slashes of gray and black silence that make up the forest. I wait for the sound of the crossbow's trigger. *Where's the line?* But something startles him—something from inside of him, probably—and suddenly he retreats through the curtain of trees.

After a moment, we get up again and pull the cooler back to the motorcycle. Martin gets on the bike and kicks down on the starter. Nothing. "Goddamn it," he hisses. He kicks down again. The engine flutters.

"What are we going to do with the cooler?"

"I don't know, I don't know." He kicks down again. I can feel my own gnawing hunger and anxiety in his words, in his movements. He kicks down again. Again there is nothing.

There is a commotion at the edge of the woods. The voices go like a flock of birds. Dogs bark, and the dark splotchy sound of them gets closer.

"Can we get it on the back?"

"It's not going to make a hell of a lot of difference if the goddamned thing won't start." He jumps down on the starter again and again, and finally, the bike catches, sputters, and fills the air around us with noise and heavy smoke.

"Strap it to the back. It's the only way. I'll stay here with the crossbow and run back later."

"You can't do that. It's a couple of miles. It's dark."

"I can find the way. Two miles, three—it's nothing. The only other choice we have is to leave it behind."

Both of us shiver in the dark. Everything is exaggerated by the sound of the bike, by the darkness, by the baying of the dogs.

He hands me the still-cocked crossbow. I take it and lean it against a tree.

"Okay," he says, "lift," and we strap the cooler into place on the back of the seat. "They've heard the bike," he shouts. "They'll think we're gone." He looks at me a moment, then yanks the throttle and the engine screams. "Okay," he shouts, then turns on the headlight and lets the bike carry him away into the thick of the trees. For a minute I watch the splash of the light —it turns the trees to bright, crisp spiderwebs in the darkness.

In a few minutes, the sound of the bike begins to fade. I wait where I am, quiet, surprised by the druglike calm that has suffused my hands, my chest and my head. I can hear the people at the edge of the woods.

"They had a motorcycle back there," one says.

I look for a tree to climb, and uncock the crossbow, then shoulder it when I swing up into a knotty beech tree. I still can't

see anyone, but in the increasing darkness, it is difficult to make
out anything but shapes.

"I think you ought to let the goddamned dogs go in there."

"You heard, sir. They're gone."

I hear the warble of a woman's voice and the sound of a dog
baying. I sit in the tree for a long time and nothing happens. I
wonder about Martin, if he really would have shot the man—or
if I would have. And I wonder about the people at the edge of the
woods. I wonder about the power of the darkness and the trees.

I wait and wait and wait, but the silence becomes deeper, and
eventually the people dissolve away. The darkness doesn't scare
me anymore. Being alone doesn't scare me anymore. In the trees
I close my eyes, and it's almost like a movie—my father and
Shaddock and Decker, the principal of my school. I can feel the
stifling, killing mix of aftershave and cigarette smoke. I can see
the dull, aged, man-skin—foreheads and knuckles and baggy
eyes, chests gone slack and womanly with age—the crisp fabric
of laundered shirts and snug ties, and all of it makes me afraid.
You're dead, or you're them, or you're Meckler.

I slide down out of the hard tree, and, fabulously, there's music
in the dark woods. "Song Of The Earth." And as I hold the
crossbow close to my chest and run back toward the cabin, I
wonder about myself. I feel like a stone, blind to the current, but
rolling toward the falls.

"Good to see you made it," Martin says, standing in the clearing, the firelight flickering crazily, painting the foliage around us
orange.

"Where's Carl?" I try to remember what day it is. If it is
Friday, then Carl will stay the night.

"He and Meckler went into town."

"Oh," I say, and then, turning, confused by hunger and weariness, "We've got to do something. They're going to come look-ing for us."

"Who?" He seems preoccupied, and unconcerned. I want to shake him, tell him what he already knows—that I just ran two or three miles through the woods, in complete darkness, so he could steal a cooler.

"The rangers. I heard them. We've got to do something." I can't think. Things go back and forth in my head but do not connect.

"They'll never find us," he says, tossing it off and turning away from me. "They were probably just telling the poor bastard who lost his cooler that to make him happy. They won't come."

"Please. Take this seriously. It was stupid of us to use the motorcycle. They could follow the path blindfolded. That's how I got here so fast. Even in the dark."

"If they come, we'll go deeper into the woods. We know the woods. We can live off the woods. It doesn't matter."

I turn away from him. I don't know whether to be angry or confused or to believe him. "If they come—"

"If they come, what?" He turns and glares at me. A bright blade of flame jumps in the fire. "If they come, what?"

"I don't know. Maybe we ought to leave for a while. We could leave Meckler here and let him take the blame."

"Don't be stupid, Al. They're not going to come all the way back here just for some old man's cooler. They're not. Particu-larly if they saw the crossbow."

I let the breath go out of me and turn away in silence. The fire crackles. "What are you going to do?" I say under my breath. "Kill someone?"

Then, his voice a measure gentler, "Let's not worry about it, Al. Let's cross that bridge when it comes."

I stand there for a long time, as if caught in the flickering campfire. I just look, and nothing is resolved. Finally, I say, "What'd we get?"

"What we got," he says, smiling broadly, "is an absolutely wonderful specimen of the camping mentality. Basically, steaks, beer and potatoes. The beer made Meckler happy, but he and Carl went into town for cigarettes. The poor man would die without his cigarettes."

"I just hope he doesn't burn everything down."

"Maybe that would be for the best," Martin says, not looking at me, but folding his arms and staring at the fire.

"Why does Carl do it?" I say, but I don't mean the question to be answered.

"He does it because I ask him to." There is a way that Martin can look that is perfectly arrogant and haughty. When he turns to me, the dull, shadowy light of the fire uneven on his face, I feel a rush of hatred for him. Maybe it isn't hatred. I don't know. I breathe deeply and look away from him—ashamed to have to hate him. "Milk," he says slowly. "There's some orange juice and milk. Just like home."

"God," I say softly, my head full and empty all at once. When I came through the woods away from the campground, I felt glad to be in the woods, and glad to be concealed by them. Yet now I feel as if I could drown in them, as if they would swallow—or are swallowing me—whole.

"Did you guys eat?" I ask.

"Yeah," he says. "Cooked some steaks. There's a whole box in the cooler."

In a while, he whispers, "Fat bastards." I don't know who he's talking about.

The drunk kneels in front of the fire and tosses wood onto it. Swaying, he takes a beer from the cooler and sits in his usual place against the cabin wall. He is singing softly, and it surprises me that his voice is melodic, sweet. But then he coughs, and lights a cigarette from a burning twig, and the sound of the cough kills the melody. For a long time he stares at the fire, completely and perfectly entranced.

His hair is long and oily. His eyes are sunk so deep into his head they look like they've been ground there the way you'd grind a cigarette butt into pavement. The cat is cleaner than he is.

I keep waiting for him to say something that will make him into a real person for me. I think about it as I watch him—that the thing that makes a man different from an animal is what he can say about himself that rings true—and I want to hear him tell something true about his life. I suspect that Martin is right, that everything he says is a lie, that the one true thing in his life is the bottle, but that doesn't make him human. Maybe if I could hear him talk about the bottle, tell how he loves it.

After a while, I get up and roll out my sleeping bag in the leaves. Martin is in the cabin, and Carl, next to the fire, does not speak. As soon as I lie down I start to drift off.

I don't know how long I've been asleep when Meckler, on his way to piss, trips over me and kicks me in the head. I wake up as angry and clear-headed as ice. He stumbles away from me, muttering to himself. "Goddamn it," I say, and jump up and grab him. I shake him, lift him off the ground. I'm perfectly ready to kill him. "Why are you here, goddamn it?" I hiss into his face. "What good do you do anyone at all? What? Tell me that. Why the hell are you here? You eat our food, you make Carl drive you around. What good are you?"

Startled, he tries to shrink away from me. This minute, my own head smarting and ringing where he kicked me, I could crash his head in. Because of the anger, I see him more clearly than I have before. Holding onto his arm, I realize just how weak his is, just how frail and worthless. And suddenly the anger is gone and it is replaced by shame. I release him and push him away.

And suddenly Martin is there. "Leave him alone," he says. "Go back to sleep."

"Kill him, why don't you?" Carl giggles.

Carl drapes bacon from the cooler over a stick and hangs it over the fire. Immediately, the fat begins to drip onto the coals and burn. The smell of the meat cooking fills the air, and I wonder if the rangers and their dogs are already on their way through the woods toward us.

"Listen," I say when Martin comes back into the clearing, "I think we ought to decide what to do."

"What to do about what?" Carl says, looking up. His face is blank and huge, white as a grub.

"Last night when Martin left me in the woods, I heard the ranger say that they would come looking for us. I heard him say it. I think we need to do something."

"And I told *you*," Martin says, "that he was probably just *saying* that so the guy would get off his back. What's he going to do, *anyway*? Walk a couple of miles into the woods?"

"That's what they do, you know," I say, my voice becoming acid to match his. "They're here to protect the goddamned pre-serve."

"They could hunt us down easy," Meckler says, standing, squinting his eyes and swaying a little. He's not drunk, but he's not steady either. "When I was in the Philippine Islands during the Korean conflict, stationed at Subic Bay, don't you know, that was one of the exercises we had to do. We hunted one another.

Sometimes you got the feeling looking at those little Philippine men that you couldn't take them seriously. They was so small they looked no bigger than boys, well the same thing was true of the greyhounds, which was what we used to hunt one another. You seen them in the dog races in Florida, skinny and brittle and lanky, and you just couldn't take them seriously, except they was good hunting dogs. Fast as deer. Chased down those goddamned little Filipino communist son of a bitches, treed them and then it was up to us to blast the little goddamned—"

"Shut up, old man," Martin says. He picks up a burning stick while the drunk is talking and throws it at him. The drunk dodges it, but it has him off balance and he fights the air for a minute, as if he has walked into a giant spider web. I turn away from him and pick up the burning stick, put it back into the fire.

"I just think we ought to stay on guard," I say. "I think we ought to have a lookout. We find out if they're coming, and then we can do something."

"Like what?" Martin sneers. "Like what, *Albert*? Shoot a ranger?"

"Don't be stupid. We'll leave. We'll come back later when they've given up."

"Don't call me stupid," he says. "Don't call me stupid." Then, coming forward, he pushes me backward.

"Listen," I tell him, almost shouting, "this is my place. I found it and it was my idea to build the cabin. You just came along from God knows where, and I say we do something. This is my place. I need it."

"I think I'm going to be moved to tears," Carl says. I know he's said it because he wants to be funny, because he wants to lighten the situation, but it doesn't have that effect. Martin laughs. Carl laughs with him foolishly.

"Funny. Right. It's all very funny. If they find us back here they'll at least kick us out, but they'll probably send us to jail for the deer and the cooler and the fires and everything else."

"God," Martin says, turning away, "you sound like an old woman."

"I think the boy is right," Meckler says, sort of rolling his head. It surprises me that he is as resilient as he seems to be. "It's a nice place, a good place. No sense," he says, spitting, "in getting it ruined all to hell just because the rest of us is too lazy to put up a sentry."

"That," Martin says, standing and stepping to the center of the clearing, "certainly settles my mind." He extends a hand in Meckler's direction. "Certainly this is the voice of experience talking to us. Certainly this is the voice of wisdom." He paces, hands in the air, hands moving, voice getting a little more shrill each time he speaks. He looks at Carl and me, looks at Meckler and makes the old man hang his head. There is a kind of power that comes from him, but I don't understand it. It's a kind of blackness that hangs in his words and in his eyes and right now I get the feeling I could look right down into his soul and find it filled with a kind of power deeper and more asphyxiating than pitch. "We can listen to this man and know we're listening to someone who truly knows." Violently, he whirls around and kicks the drunk's legs. Meckler screams—a liquid ugliness— and gathers his legs close to him. He begins to cry. He looks like a stunned pile of laundry, gathered and pinned by a haphazard arrangement of bones. His eyes are huge and wet, and I want to kill Martin now.

"So you think this is your place?" he says, his voice sliding and clawing. "You think it's yours?" He laughs. "Think again. I count four people here, not just one." He comes close to me and looks down. I'm on my guard. My hands tingle with nerves. His eyes are white, as if they are illuminated from within.

"That's not what I meant," I say, and even as I say it I want it to sound different, not as if I'm backing down. "That's not what I meant and you know it."

"Oh," he says, his voice suddenly quiet and elegant. "Is that so? Sorry for the misunderstanding."

"I mean we've all put a lot of work into this. Every one of us, even Meckler." I look at the drunk, then at my hands. "I love this place. I've been coming here since I was a little kid, and for now, it's the only place I've got to go." I look down at the fire, appreciate the colored, crackling silence of it, appreciate the hypnotizing movement of shadow and flame. I feel the sensation of a tide within me, a long throating in an endless system of tubes. "I just thought we ought to—" but my voice weakens.

"It's silly to worry," Martin says, covering our silence. "The forest is huge. They'd never find us. And if they do, then we'll just go deeper. We'll go back into the mountains."

"They've got dogs," I say quietly, staring at the fire.

"He's right. I think he's right," Carl says. "We've been back here for how long? How long? That's why we picked this spot, isn't it, Albie?"

I look at him and try to think.

"I mean that's why we put the cabin against the hill, down here in the hollow. So no one would see the fire." Carl's eyes are wide. His mouth hangs open.

"All right. All right." I look back and forth between them. When I look at Meckler, he averts his eyes. It occurs to me now that I might have wanted a lot from the Outskirts. Maybe once I had an idea of what it would be like. Perhaps I would have cleared a space and built a garden the way my father used to do at home. Maybe I might have done a million things, but just this minute I can't remember wanting to do anything but keep my head above water. "Forget it," I say.

Meckler gets up and hunts for his cigarettes, making a growling noise under his breath. Martin watches him for a few minutes, then stares into the fire and sits down, his jaw set, his face impossibly long and stony.

"When I lived in Washington, D.C.," Meckler says, swaying, pressing his dull, rounded fingers into the mouth of the cigarette package, "I was just out of the army. I was on disability, don't you know. Getting treatment out of the VA hospital there." He opens his eyes suddenly, as if surprised by something he sees in the cigarette pack. "I had yellow fever."

"That's a lie."

"You don't know nothing about it," Meckler says, far enough away from Martin to be certain that his legs won't be kicked out from under him. He lights a cigarette, and as he exhales smoke, he swings his hair back. For a moment, because of the shape of his face and the climb of his forehead, I can see his skull precisely outlined in his skin.

"What I know," Martin says, "is that you're a liar."

"I got the yellow fever in Okinawa, fighting the Japanese. About a hundred of the men in my company got it."

"Just shut up, will you? You're driving me crazy," Martin says.

Meckler looks at him sadly, then looks at me. Leaving the cigarette in his mouth, he puts his hands into his pockets and stares at Martin. "Maybe I ain't talking to you," he says. "Maybe I'm talking to Albert here. Maybe what I'm saying isn't none of your business anyhow." He laughs a little, then looks at me. "I was talking to you, wasn't I? We were having a conversation."

Though I feel sorrow for him, he disgusts me. I say nothing.

"Wasn't I? Wasn't we?"

I look away.

"Tell him. *Tell* him."

I look at the wild orange leap of the fire. I can't say anything.

The drunk laughs. "Maybe I was talking to myself," he says quietly. "Maybe I was talking to myself." And then his face grows serious and old, and he sits down again. "Before this day is through," he mutters into the fire, "one of you will betray me." He laughs.

"All of us will," Martin says, and throws a piece of wood at him.

"Oh, Christ, Albie," Martin says. It's early in the morning, and the air is cool.

"I'm not asking you to go, but I'm going. If they're coming, then we'll know that much in advance."

"Do what you want," he says, turning away from me. He says it as though he's the leader—the reluctant leader—and I'm one of his subjects.

"I will."

When I leave, I don't turn around. I go first to the edge of the lake and smear my face and chest with clay, then I shoulder the bow and arrows and head into the woods.

I pick up the path that the motorcycle made outside of the cabin hollow, near the car, then follow it toward the campground. The sun is high and bright, and the sky is as blue as the anxiety that suffuses my hands and fissures out through my arms and legs, like through cracks in glass. My lungs feel huge, like they are half my body, like I could keep breathing inward and never exhale, but be subsumed and carried away by the air.

My feet move quietly over the leaves and loam, and without willing it, I start to pick up speed and run. The breeze rushes like water in the trees, and music starts to come up from the sound of my feet and the rhythm of the breeze and the flush of my breath. It sings in and out of the trees, no song I have ever heard before, at least no song I remember. It builds itself in the air, winding in and out in the breeze and the leaves like a trail of silk.

I go in a mile and a half, two miles, deep enough so that I know the campground is not far, deep enough so that I know the rangers will have to pass me if they come. The music follows. I find a tree and mark off the distance the way Martin did when we hunted the deer—ten yards, then fifteen, then thirty. Then I climb the tree. It's a maple. I sit high up, and the maple seeds auger downward in the breeze, auger around me like birdless wings, brown and green and perfect. I wait, and the music is loud. It careens in and out of the trees, echoing, rebounding on the thin blue shell of the sky.

The branch is hard, and the breeze becomes a wind. Clouds scuttle across the sky. I wait for the sound of footsteps, for the sound of barking dogs. I watch the shadows of the clouds drift across the trees. My back and seat begin to numb. The music fades in the trees. Around me some blue jays chatter; the sound goes along the wire of the trees like a small glitter of gossip. Finally, from the monotony, I fall asleep.

I dream that I am surrounded by dogs. The forest is white. Everything is white. I can feel the heat of their bodies as they jump at the tree. I can feel them suspended in the air.

I dream too that Carl comes and stands next to me. He holds a box in his hands, and in it is the deer's head. But he closes the box, and when he opens it again, in it is the snake he killed. I wait for him to speak or move, but he doesn't speak. When he moves, it is as smoothly as a shadow. He opens the box again, and in it is Shaddock's head.

I wake in the late afternoon. There has been a scream. I don't know if it is real or how long I have been asleep. The woods, now, seem fabulously silent, yet they seem to breathe, and it is as if I am inside a living, breathing thing.

I wait and listen. There is nothing. The scream doesn't come again.

There is movement below. I blink hard and look. It is nearly dark. At first I see nothing but heavy foliage, but then a buck wanders into the clear, near my thirty-yard marker. His head is enormous with horns; I am still, breathless. He looks straight at me, his eyes big and soft as water. He picks his way along, his hooves silent in the leaves, but as quickly as he has appeared, he disappears, apparently startled by something.

Again there is movement. A dog barking. I see nothing. I crouch on stiff legs, and take out my bow and notch an arrow. Then flashlights stab into the dusk. There are voices—two men at least. The dogs—one German shepherd and one Doberman— are ahead of them, and their flashlights spray over the trees and the backs of the dogs. I tense the arrow against the string. The dogs move skittishly, in and out, dancing, back and forth. They unnerve one another, and the men, who appear to be about fifty yards away, keep them close with their voices. One of the dogs stops outside of my markers and stands as still as a ghost. His nose is in the air. I raise the bow and draw the string back.

The forest is colorless in the evening light. The shepherd bays. The Doberman circles around him. They have gotten some kind of scent. I have no way of knowing if it is mine.

I tense the string. There is a tight red line of pain in my legs, and as I hold the bowstring, it travels into my arms and chest too. The Doberman moves out in front, skittling in the leaves, the fabulous arch of its back and abdomen as perfect as the deer.

He moves past my outer marker and quickens his pace toward where I am. I still don't know what scent he's got. His movements are liquid and perfect. His gait is sidelong, silent. His mouth is open, and I imagine his tongue as a slick pink snake. My arm begins to numb. The bow string is cutting into my fingers. He moves closer, sliding through the foliage like a big black fish. He closes up the space between us, running from side to side—twenty, fifteen, ten. He has *my* scent and is heading for *my* tree. I let the arrow go.

There is a humming in my ear, as gentle as a hummingbird, then a vibration in the leaves. I've missed. I notch another arrow. The Doberman, black as hell, stands still, then his hind legs quiver and he lets out a sound that is more scream than howl. The German shepherd stops near him and sniffs. Then I see the mark. It is difficult to see, but the arrow has hit him in the soft midsection, just in front of his hind legs. There is a mark where the feathers stick out on the glossy coat. The shepherd turns around and runs toward the men, yelping as he goes. The men call out the Doberman's name, but it doesn't move. He tries to wheel around, but he cannot, and the sound comes from him again, abject, at a pitch like an oboe, and holding, so that long after the sound has stopped it is still in the air, wet as blood. The arrow has him pinned to a tree. Whenever he moves, he screams. I draw back the second arrow to finish him, to stop the sound, but the rangers close up fast, their dull, water-green uniforms silver in the light. They stop and look at him in confusion, and I can hear it come into their voices when they realize what has happened.

The beams of their flashlights bound through the trees, and then, in unison, shut off.

Whispers. The sudden beam of a flashlight stabs through the trees, then goes off again.

He wags his stub of a tail, and tries to collapse, but the arrow holds him up. Again the sound, up and down the forest, now like a woman's voice.

"Jesus, God," one of them says. The sound spooks them. So does my own silence. They know I am watching. I know they sense me, and yet they do not understand. "Get it out and let's get out of here." I see the pale flash of his face as he turns to let his eyes sketch through the trees—for me, for anything. The spray of his flashlight crosses me once, twice, and the tips of my razorheads glint, but they don't see me.

"Dirk," one of them calls after the shepherd. "Dirk."

I can feel my own breath, feel the tightening of my lungs. The Doberman has broken into a sobbing whine. I want them to move. I want to kill the dog. What is wrong with them?

"Dirk," the man calls, "come."

"God," the one who is over the Doberman says, pulling the arrow out. "Will you look at this thing? What kind of a cruel son of a bitch—" And I wonder what Martin would do if he were where I am, the arrow stiff in his hand, the bowstring like a musical instrument. Quite suddenly, the music comes. I don't hear another word; it drowns out everything.

I sit in the tree for a long time, frozen, afraid of making noise, waiting out the music, waiting out the emptiness the rangers leave in their wake. Once they are gone, once the thrumming in my chest goes away, I know it is over. The Outskirts, and whatever unnameable thing I wanted from it, is finished.

The red wire of pain in my legs goes to blue. The surface of the forest eddies with the motion the rangers left. The forest whispers, *Murderer. Look at him. Murderer.*

I hold the bow up close under my arm and slide out of the tree. I start to run. I have to warn the others.

I can see them in the clearing long before I come up. The fire, just now, is as big as a bonfire, and despite the hollow where the cabin is, I can see the bright orange mound from the next hill as clear as a flag. Martin and Meckler are talking heatedly, and their voices carry easily through the trees, but the sense has gone out of the voices by the time they reach me. For a long time as I walk, the fire appears and disappears, and sometimes, when it appears, it seems to have risen, like a second moon, all of the rest of the forest made utterly black by it.

When I get close enough to hear the flame, to see the sparks that rise off of it and whirl in the air, I stop and wait. In a way, I feel as if I ought not to go back, as if I ought to go up to the road and wait for Emily when she comes tomorrow night. Or simply begin walking the narrow, canopied roads home. But the fire is there and warm, and the color of it, and the smell of cooking meat, coats the forest.

Quietly, I lie down in the leaves on the hill that forms the back of the hollow and watch. A month ago, I couldn't have done this. The foliage would have been too thick, and I wouldn't have known how, but I have begun to understand the woods in a way I had not expected. Now, because of our comings and goings, because of our indiscriminate cutting of branches and trees for one purpose or another, the immediate forest has thinned.

(I understand now, I think, why the rangers decided to wait

until dusk to come. Even with dogs, it would be easier to find a campsite at night, and easier to surprise its occupants.)

Martin sits by the fire with a long, sharpened stick in his hands. A half-cooked piece of meat dangles from it, and fat drips into the soft bark of the wood, darkening it. The flash of the fire brings it into and out of darkness, and as the fire slows, he moves closer to it, holding the meat near the coals. In a moment, I can't see his face any longer for the shadows. I can see his eyes, dark and pocked in his head like chestnuts. The hollows of his face are blocked out by shadow, and his chin and eyebrows and nose throw long shadows.

. Meckler is next to him, gray as ash. His face is round and as wrinkled as his clothing. He is crouched on the ground with his filthy cat next to him. He too has a stick in the fire—his is draped with bacon, and the meat, burnt and black at the ends, gleams with fat. He watches vacantly, as if unaware of the cooking, unaware of anything but the crack of the flame. He sways. They are still talking, now warmly, as if they are old friends, talking about old times.

Carl is almost completely in darkness as he circles around the edges of the clearing searching for scraps of wood to put on the fire. But the area around the cabin and into the woods is almost completely devoid of firewood. Slowly, talking quietly to Martin and the drunk, he goes farther out of the clearing. I can't hear what he's saying. His voice is as light as the flame. Martin and Meckler laugh about something, and when they laugh, suddenly both faces look astonishingly like one another.

There is something about the way the clearing looks without me—as though I simply do not exist—that makes me anxious, and I get up, pick up my bow, and circle around in the direction that Carl has gone. I'm surprised how quiet I am, surprised that I can come within a couple of feet of him without his knowing it.

I wait. I follow him farther into the dark. Martin's and Meckler's voices flutter in the air. The fire pops. When we are in complete darkness, and when my eyes become accustomed to it, I say, "Carl," in a loud whisper.

He whirls around and drops the sticks he's holding. Before he can say anything, I stand close to him and say, "Ssshh."

"Jesus," he whispers, "what are you doing?"

"I want to talk to you," I say. "I want to do it before I talk to you know, Martin." I look back toward the clearing, and suddenly I feel very weak and insubstantial. "They were coming with dogs. They'll come again. We've got to leave. We've got to get out of here. We've got to do *some*thing." My voice sounds vaguely desperate, and for a second, it affects him. Then, his face changing, he squats down to pick up his firewood. "Who was?"

"The rangers," I say. "I guess I stopped them temporarily. I shot one of their dogs." When I say it, I realize how foolish it was. It will only guarantee their return.

"Stop it, Albie," he says. He smells like sour milk. "Marty said you might do something like this."

"I was out there, I saw them."

"What's the matter with you?" he says, his voice no longer a whisper. "You've been acting like a crazy man for the past couple of days, going against the group and stuff. Why don't you listen to Martin? Why don't you? He knows what's going on."

I look at him but in the darkness I can no longer see his face. I thought he would listen to me, but I feel as though I've completely missed something, that something important has gone by me. I had thought—"What's the matter with *me*? Why don't you *listen* to me?"

"Carl?" comes Martin's voice from the clearing. "What's going on?"

"Albie's back," he says before I have the chance to stop him. Then he turns and heads toward the clearing. I stay in the darkness before he turns to me and says, "You coming or are you just going to stand there in the dark?"

When I tell them what happened, Martin laughs. It is a big laugh—a laugh predestined to be that way, and to conceal the current of falseness that rides beneath it.

"Now what'd you go and do that for?" Meckler says, standing, hitching his pants, rubbing his greasy fingers on the grimy fabric. "You oughtn't to have killed no doggy." He laughs. Carl laughs with him.

"I don't know if I killed the dog or not—it doesn't make any difference. They'll be back."

I cannot feel my voice—it is not real. It is like the air, it is like a thing that trills up and down, repeating itself incessantly.

"Listen," I say, but it makes no impression on the flatness of the silence. "We've got to do something. If we just sit around doing nothing, they'll find us."

Martin laughs again. "You're a liar," he says, stabbing the long end of his stick into the ground and getting up. "You're a liar. If they were going to come looking for us, they'd do it in the daylight, not at night." He brushes off his pants and stares at me.

"They did. They could have spotted the fire from a mile off at night," I say. The breeze changes and smoke drifts between us. My eyes smart.

No one looks at me. Even Martin turns away and sits back

down. Carl looks like an animal in the sleepy, idiotic droop of his eyes. I try to remember him like he used to be, but I can't. Martin and the drunk sit together by the fire like some crazy kind of lovers, bound by responsibility or guilt to something as inevitable as the doberman screaming in the darkness, as inevitable as the wind in the leaves.

Martin runs his hand through his hair, then rolls his steak on the stick so that it flops the other way. The coals of the fire are covered now with a thin patina of white ash. The heat makes everything waver.

"I'm leaving," I say, but they could be frozen, or only as real as something on a television screen.

"Oh, shut up and sit down," Martin says, his voice threatening. "Don't go throwing a temper tantrum."

Carl laughs.

Furious from hunger and weariness, I throw my bow into the trees; the arrows come loose and clatter against it. "Listen to me, goddamnit. You haven't listened to a thing I've said." I come close to where he sits and look down on him. I'm so angry I want to kick him. "They're coming. They came tonight. The only reason they're not here right now arresting us is because I killed one of their dogs and scared the hell out of them. And the way I see it, it's all your fault, wanting to go out and steal from the campground with your stupid goddamn idea of self-sufficiency. Well, there's not much that's goddamned self-sufficient—"

I turn away and pick up my knapsack. Everything is trembling —my hands, my eyes, the leaves above us. I start to rummage through everything, pulling out my clothes and tools and books and all that I have accumulated here in the million trips back and forth. "You guys stay," I say, going into the musty cabin and throwing things around. "You can wait and wait and the goddamned world can end for all I care. I'm leaving, I'm going." From staying in the woods so long, my voice has gotten shrill, crazy—even my thinking shrills in my head. My heart feels as if the valves and chambers have gone thin and brittle. It could shatter with a word.

Martin gets up and comes to me. I don't even see him until, like an angel, he appears next to me. I look at him, then at the hypnosis of the steak hanging next to the fire, and then back at him, utterly dark but for the corona the fire makes around his body. Suddenly, I want to cry, to throw my head against his chest.

"Sit down," he says. "Have something to eat." His voice is like age and anger and peace and nothing. He puts his hand on my neck, and it is coarse and hot from the fire. Crazily, I duck from beneath its warmth and bat it away.

"Go to hell."

It's sudden as a flash of light, like something has burst inside of him and its flood hurls him toward me. His hands take my back and neck and my legs bend beneath me. I'm surprised by the strength of him. He throws me toward the fire, and the earth rises toward me. Dust comes up; the fire sparks and cracks. I can taste ash and dirt. I roll away and catch my balance. Without thinking, I hurl myself toward him.

Long before it hits me, long before I can recoil and do something to protect myself, I can see his fist; or I imagine it. I can sense the darkness of it, the ash and dirt and sleep and bark and hollow of the forest and fragrance of trees on his knuckles. I can feel the inertia of it, and yet I can do nothing. My head flashes white, and for a moment, the whole forest is illuminated, and I am moving, reeling off balance—a long plane of weightlessness, backward, floating like water thrown in the air.

"Get up," he says. "Sit down." He kicks me in the hip. The

pain is dull, and knots the muscle. I look at him and the fire exaggerates the redness of his face. He kicks again.

"Hey," Meckler says, standing unsteadily, "you ain't got to treat the boy like that. If he wants to leave, let him leave."

Martin turns to the drunk and moves forward. Meckler backs away, one hand searching the air behind him. While he has his head turned, I get up and dive toward Martin, and my weight carries both of us into the dirt. Carl stands up and stares, unsure what to do. We roll, and Martin comes up on top. He hits me in the mouth. I push at him and he grabs my hair and hits me in the face again and again. I hit once, twice, aimlessly, like hitting a pillow in a dream. I want to kill him, but it won't work. Nothing happens. He pins me. He sits on my stomach and pins my shoulders to the ground with his knees. I close my eyes. I can't stand to look at his face, can't stand the smell and the taste of the hatred in my mouth. He could kill me now, and I wait for it. I wait for it.

"Well, now," he says, breathing long and heavy.

"You guys ought to cut it out," Carl says. "You're too close to the fire. Somebody's going to get burned."

"You're a wicked boy," Meckler says.

"Well, now," Martin says again, ignoring everything but me, "what's it going to be, Al? You going to cut it out and be reasonable, or what?"

I keep my eyes closed and say nothing. He shifts his weight to his knees and they drive into my shoulders like fire. I can't feel anything in my hands.

"Apologize," he says.

I say nothing.

He grabs my face with his hands and digs his fingers into my cheeks as though by forming my face he can form words.

"What's it going to be, Albert?" he says, spitting on my face as he speaks. I start to struggle again, try to kick my legs up and grab his shoulders, but it won't work. He hits me again, this time on the jaw, and I feel blood in my mouth. My face is raw and hot.

"Martin, stop it," Carl says, too stupid, too stopped by whatever it is he feels for Martin, to move.

"Shut up," Martin says. It is like a shot.

"The boy's right," Meckler says. "You let him up right now." I can't see Meckler but I can feel in his voice a weak attempt to take charge, to assume a place he hasn't had with us. And then Martin's knees are gone, and his hand is gone. I watch him move toward Meckler, straightening his shirt. Surprised and scared, the drunk stands his ground. "I'm sorry," Martin says. His voice is maniacally gentle, and as I get up, I watch, knowing something is going to happen. Yet nothing does happen. He just stands there, looking down on the broken little drunk, his breath going in and out, in and out. "I didn't mean to hurt him," he says, almost apologetically. Meckler straightens some. "He just ought to do what I say. All of you ought to listen to what I say." Meckler turns and sits again, his face looking proud, satisfied. Martin stands there, breathing and staring.

Finally, I brush myself off, and go into the woods, toward the lake, to wash myself.

"Where are you going?" Martin says abstractly.

"*Go to hell,*" I scream. My voice stands UP in the forest and rips a hole in the air, but I feel like a fool, like a miserable child, no better than, no different from the drunk.

When I come back, my right eye is closing. The three of them sit around the fire like they did before, entranced, still. The darkness outside of the clearing is liquid and full. The fire hollows a space in it, cancelling everything that is outside the circle. I stand away from them for a while, exhausted and confused, and then, caught by the inertia, I sit down too, in my usual place. The only sound is the fire.

"We're all friends again," Martin says after a long time. "We're all friends again." He doesn't take his eyes off the fire. There is something odd about his voice, something odd in his breathing. If I could take the last two days and erase them, I would. Something feels broken and bleeding.

No one says anything. After another long silence, Martin continues.

"None of this is going to happen again, all right? Good, good. We're all going to be doing the things we ought to be doing, and not wandering around the woods, making up stories. You know one of the stories I heard—well, that's not necessarily true. We're all a family, right? Really, we are. Really, we're a family." He doesn't look at anybody. Carl puts some wood on the fire, and the new light and shadows just make everything more hypnotic. "It's a crazy family. I'd be the first to admit that. Three boys and one crazy old drunk. But look at us, just look at us. We do love each other. You love me, don't you Al? I know you do. And Meckler, Mr. John. Mr. John Meckler. You love me, don't you?" He rocks a little, and stares up at the round black dome of the sky. "It's all love," he says. "We are all lovers, intertwined with ourselves and with the woods. We love the woods, we love each other. That's our way."

I want to say: Hypocrisy. Lies. But I don't speak. The silence hangs close and waits.

The cat picks itself up from where it has lain next to Meckler, then drags its body across Meckler's knee. I watch it through the uneven curtain of flame as it stretches and stands next to the fire to soak up the heat.

Martin reaches forward and takes hold of the cat, then pulls it onto his lap. I try to think whether the cat is male or female. I know; or I knew. But I can't remember. Martin talks to the cat, holding his face close to its neck and mumbling, but as far as I can tell, it's nonsense. When he strokes it—his fingers roughing the fur on its neck and back, then smoothing it out again—his hands move like some quiet desperation, and Meckler watches him, warily, his eyes sharp and quick.

Finally, unable to keep myself awake any longer, I unroll my sleeping bag and climb into it. In a moment, Carl goes into the cabin. Martin and Meckler stay where they are. The drunk says, in an absurdly loving and avuncular voice, "Pleasant dreams, boys."

I dream the forest is on fire. Miles and miles of flame, like a new planet, or like the sun. An ocean of flame. The flames grow hotter, and the fire grows whiter. Cinders fly up like spume and whirl in the white sky. Things begin to disappear—first Meckler, then Carl. Then, the only thing left is the tiny, unburnt patch where the cabin is. And Martin sits on top of it, riding it as if the forest were flooding instead of burning. The everything is black again except the fighting in my ear.

"Come on, Red," Meckler says, his voice pitched up, his hands shaking. "You come over here, Red."

"He's fine here," Martin says. "He wants to stay here with me. He loves me." I would expect his voice to be mocking, but it sounds utterly convinced. I can't tell whether it is a joke. Martin crouches over the cat, gathering it into himself, stroking it crazily.

"Don't you mistreat that cat, boy," Meckler says, beginning to stand.

"Don't you tell me what to do, you disgusting old faggot," Martin says, his hand moving in a circle, back and forth around the cat's neck. "Know what he told me?" Martin says, his eyes looking in my direction, but not looking at me. "He said he killed his daddy. He said he shot him through the heart with a bow and arrow."

"Don't you hurt him, now. He's the only goddamned thing I got left in this world."

"He won't hurt him," Carl says, smiling, watching. I sit up and look around. Carl stands outside the cabin, blinking. I look at him and wonder. Something has evaporated in him. I don't know who he is anymore. "Just leave him alone. They're all right."

Angry, but visibly worried, Meckler stands up and steadies himself, then starts toward Martin. Martin stands too, and holds the cat close from beneath the front legs. Its rear legs walk the air.

"Give him to me," Meckler says.

"He's all right," Martin says. "Let me hold him. Let me." He sounds like a child, but I don't want to believe him.

"Just let me have him back, please."

One hand beneath the cat's ribs and the other on the scruff of the cat's neck, Martin lifts him forward, toward the drunk. Meckler reaches out, but before he can touch the cat, Martin's hands change. There's a crack and a squeak; the cat's legs whip violently at the air.

Meckler staggers. "God damn you," he says slowly, "I pray God damn you," and he throws himself forward. Martin turns and pushes him to the side.

I am standing now, out of my sleeping bag, but I can't move. The drunk reels toward the fire, and Martin throws the dangling cat at him. It slaps him in the face and chest, then falls into the leaves.

The drunk kneels down and takes the cat to himself and holds it to his chest. He is crying and I can see the sobs like green vegetation rolling in a wave. They color the forest with an olive darkness that rings and will not stop. Martin kicks out and catches Meckler on the arm. Off-balance anyway, the old man rolls over in the leaves. The cat falls away. I yell for him to stop, but the noise is blunt in the air, and it is like the roll of sputum from the drunk, like nothing. "Stop!" I shout, and as if spurred by my words, he kicks the drunk again. Meckler coughs. He is like a baby reduced to wet face and dirt and clinging hands as small and perfect and human as a mole's hands if he could only burrow away from the flashing feet. If only any of us could do something. He howls and coughs and it is like waves and waves, rolling away from him, rolling up out of the forest. Dirt is in his face and in his hair, and Martin screams wildly, kicking, kicking, and the forest stares and stares and I am in the trees, myself a TREE, solid and fixed in place *He helped you* the sky comes close in disbelief *why couldn't you help him* the stars throb but the screaming is stopped and the trees whisper to the sky *Murderers* Martin picks up the cat and throws it into the woods. Meckler is still, and Martin kicks him in the head.

And then there is silence. Martin stands away from the cabin. Martin stands away from the idiot transfixtures of Carl and me.

It's a long time before Carl says, "I think he's dead." The air is cold. The fire is gone.

"Congratulations," I say, the utter impotence of my voice, my words, apparent to me. "You've killed him." But I don't believe it.

"He's not dead," Martin says. "He's a *liar,*" he shouts. "He's an actor. He's not dead at all." He kneels down and turns the drunk over. Meckler's eyes are open. "Get up, John. Get up. I'm sorry." The drunk does not move. "Get up now. It's not funny. Get up." Martin sings the words. "This is not a funny joke." He nudges the drunk with his foot, and Meckler moves, but settles again into stillness. Martin turns and walks toward the darkness of the woods, then stops abruptly and comes back. He kneels down. "Get up, John," he says. He claps his hands. "Get up, John." He looks at me, then at Carl. The fire is almost gone. I can feel the cold of the dark seeping in. The drunk does not move. "John, this is not a funny joke."

In the cool, cloudy, static morning, the body still lies in the clearing, face up, sunken eyes half opened, clothes rumpled with dirt and leaves. Whatever was unapparent in last night's darkness is apparent now. It lies there in silence, a look of surprise on its mouth. It stays there, unmoving, throughout the morning and into the early afternoon. We do not speak. We can hardly move.

I finish putting my things into my bag, then squat next to the drunk in disbelief. Nothing has ever been like this. Nothing. I have never seen a dead man before. I have never even been to a funeral.

Flies sound against the flat of the air. They come and rest on his face, touch the film of his eyeballs. I imagine them to tickle, even though I know it can't be true; and I expect him to move. He is nothing now, not even the long-haired, sunken-eyed drunk. He is nothing—less now in his stillness than he was last night or a week ago.

"We've got to bury him," Martin says, standing in precisely the same place he has stood for the past two hours, staring off into the trees. He does not look at the drunk. Instead, he seems to gather energy from the dull sunlight, from the wild lush green of the forest.

"I'm not having any part of it," I say. "I'm leaving. It's your fault. You did it. You bury him." I look at him hard, trying to will him to turn around and look at the body. My face is swollen from the fight last night but I feel empty-headed. I haven't thought for hours—too tired, too hungry, too amazed.

"You're involved. You are," he says. "You're just as involved as Carl or me." The way he talks is as if he is miles away and curious, involved only inasmuch as he can see himself and control the mechanics of his body.

"You killed him. I'm not involved. Not with that." I wait for my words to congeal in the air. I wait for some sort of conviction to move me.

"He's just going to lie there and rot." Carl says, moving toward the body, looking down on it. "You've got to help, Albie, it's the decent thing to do."

No one talks about the legality of it. No one seems to believe that his death is any different from that of the deer, or the rabbits.

"Decent for who?" I look at him. "Who is it the decent thing for? For Martin or for him? It's really great that we start doing decent things for him now. Great."

"Shut up, Albie." Martin turns. It's as if he's just awakened. "What's the matter? Weak stomach? Coward—oh, that's right. We've already established that."

"See you later," I say. For the first time in weeks, my voice sounds real to me.

"You can't go," Martin says.

I try to remember exactly where I threw my bow.

"You can't, Albie," Carl says. Strangely, it is almost a plea. "You've got to help. Once we bury him, we'll all leave." They are both serious. They stand together now, the cabin beyond them, and behind that, the rise of the wooded hill, and beyond that, the trees and the sky. I swallow against the weight and emptiness of my body, wait for the sudden wave of fear to subside.

"I'm leaving."

Martin says something about the three of us, about family, about how regardless of everything, we have to do just this one last thing. Carl nods in agreement. *You see? You can't leave.* But I'm not really listening. I'm moving out of the stillness, out of the clearing, toward the place where I threw my bow, toward the movement of the woods. I'm watching as I turn, watching their faces, watching the body and the cabin—watching all of it turn and wheel around and away from me as I go—taking the flash of color from the sky and wood and foliage as a signal. Then it breaks. They see me pick up the bow (only one arrow still attached) and the moment of jumble in silence, the moment of lyric motion, is gone and I am going through the woods, bag in one hand, bow in the other, running like I was born in fear, taking the slap of leaves and swipe of branches like a penance, hearing the wild call of birds overhead, hearing the red voices and flurry behind me. I go faster, not trying to run, but moving like some kind of magic. Then one of them shoots an arrow at me. It is a line of light, a laser moving over me, whistling in silence like an open-mouthed snake. It stops in a tree ahead of me as if it has grown there, as startling to the tree, to the forest, as it is to me. I turn, duck and tear for the new woods, for the gully of ferns, and for the road. The woods are a riot of sound. My own feet crash in the underbrush. Without looking I go through bramble, through sassafras, through blackberries and honeysuckle. My breathing is knotted, and every scent and sight brings up some bright memory

—each vivid and brilliant and temporary. My heart goes smooth, then breaks, then goes smooth again, like a stream moving in and out of rapids. I stop, gulping air, and look around. They're still behind me, but I've gained ground. I can't remember where I am. At the edge of panic, I choose a direction and take it, then push myself faster and faster, and let the sweat come down into my eyes and burn.

At the top of a small hill, another arrow comes. This one is from the crossbow, and I watch it disappear into the leaves like a needle in thick carpet. I know that he'll have to stop to cock it again, so I pick up speed and turn again.

And in a moment I am at the gully where I lay with Kate.

I dive down and crawl along the ridge of it, then into the moist of the leaves at the bottom, beneath the heavy tangle of the mountain laurel. Everything is pounding red. I hold myself still, try to quiet my breathing, but I am still shaking.

Listen, use the bow. I look at the sky and the sky is only a jumble of gray resting on the tips of the trees.

They are coming. I can feel them the way I felt the rangers, and before that, the deer. I get to my knees and move deeper along the gully. I want to see Kate—the swell of her body, the sweet kink of her hair. But I only see Meckler in the clearing, eyes open, blackened. Then, Martin and Carl, crashing in the woods. CLOSER: a slipping in the leaves. I know there will be copperheads, moving beneath the leaves like mercury on a plate. Nothing CONFUSION. I move farther along.

"Albie!" one of them calls.

I listen, and the only sound is my heart, wild, drowning out everything.

"Albie," he says, "come on, man, this is silly. We need you, man. We have to stick together."

I roll over, notch the single arrow, then hold my bow against me, my fingers raw against the string.

"Albie." This time it is Carl's voice. *The cat's mouth opens, showing teeth, showing the bright pink, textured tongue.*

I want it to stop. I want the rush of things to stop. I want to stand up and say that it is all a mistake, that nothing has really happened. But I know that the drunk is still dead in the clearing. I know the smell of Martin's hands, the bruises his knees left on my shoulders. (Still I can see him in his room that evening weeks ago, looking at the posters, the whites of his eyes and his teeth perfect and bluish as he spoke.) *Kill him.* It will not go away.

I can feel them fanned out against me, moving through the woods, waiting for some kind of movement. They know I have stopped. They know I am waiting.

"What's going to happen?" Martin shouts. "What's going to happen to all of us, Albie?" He waits, then: "It's easy," he says, his voice growing softer, more difficult for me to hear. "We just dig up the deer and put him underneath. No one will miss him. No one will be the wiser. Let's not make it any worse than it already is." He gets closer and closer.

I roll to my side and bring the bowstring back. Pain begins in my shoulders and spreads across my chest.

"Are we all going to jail for murder, just because of you? Don't be so weak."

I bring up my knees beneath me. There is mud beneath the scatter of leaves in the gully, thick and alive as blood.

"Are you going to spoil everything for us? Are you?"

"*You spoiled it,*" I shriek. It's the reaction he's wanted, but panic and anger flood my head and hands. "You spoiled the whole goddamned thing with your stupid philosophy."

Thrum. There is a vibration in the air, and one of his crossbow bolts sings overhead. He knows where I am now, but not exactly.

"You're going to die, Al," he says. "You're going to make us all die here."

I bring myself up, bring my head out of the gully and fire the arrow at the nearest flesh-colored shape. It's twenty, perhaps thirty yards away, and with the quickness of the motion, I don't take any time to aim, or even to focus on the target. Instead I duck back into the gully, drop the bow, and crawl deeper.

The scream that comes next is shrill and unsettling. I can't tell whether it's faked. I wait. There is a fury of movement, of words. I can't understand any of it. I go farther, deeper into the laurel.

Then Martin's voice: "You've killed Carl."

"You're a liar."

There are more voices, another scream. This time there is a long wail. There is a flurry of movement, then silence, the natural silence of the forest.

I lie on my stomach, my face in the leaves. I leave the bow where it is and wait for the sound of the motorcycle. I wait for the sound of footsteps, or the sound of Carl's car in the distance. The leaves move around me. The sun dips away from the trees and the shadows elongate. My body echoes with hunger, with a million things. The emptiness makes my vision go odd—funny shapes, dots of color as bright and clear as cellophane held up to the sun. I imagine smoke—cigarette smoke—and I imagine Meckler's voice, but there is nothing. I close my eyes against the movement of things, close them against the rush of evening. I imagine I hear the woman singing the death songs. But it is not like the music should be. It is empty, without accompaniment, and whirling and whirling around. And then I imagine the earth songs, my father singing the tenor parts, his thin, beautiful voice like some Sunday morning a hundred years ago in a church I don't remember. Mrs. Schwartzmann sings the soprano. Still, there is no orchestra. My hands tremble, my legs are weak.

When I awake, it is dark. The moon is high and the sky is clear. The light seeps into the forest. The trees are colorless, the leaves like stainless steel. I get out of the gully slowly and try to walk in the direction of the arrow I shot. I can't remember. I try to look for blood, but I can see nothing. My head seems clear, almost too clear. I begin to cry. The forest is silent.

I work along the little ridges of the forest, running with my hands in front of my face to protect my swollen eye and bruised cheeks. My crying will not stop; it bucks in my chest with a weird kind of pleasure.

I don't know how long it takes, but I find my way out to the road and run along the edge of it, in the high bracket of grass. My heart is as skittish as a rabbit in the open, and I search along the silver roll of the road for the first trace of headlights. I smell smoke again, this time wood smoke, but I know it is an hallucination. I think of the doe and of Meckler, and suddenly I hear his voice, *Hey boy,* strong and clear as the first time he came stumbling out of the trees. I look at the woods, at the long row of trees, as even as fencing, but there is nothing at all save the low dull hush of night. *Run, boy, run.* And I do. I go along the grass and gravel.

And then there's a long low spray of yellow light skimming along the power lines, along the tips of the trees. Then it comes closer, throwing color into the trees. I fall into the weeds and wait for it to pass. It moves like a giant manta, slow, black, deadly. The lights bring up insects, and they hover in the road, stunned with the chance of light. An owl hoots somewhere off in the woods and suddenly I see that it is Emily skinny Emily driving hunched up to the steering wheel and staring out at the slow road ahead of her. I get out of the spiny grass and run for the car, hollering like a flock of crows, then banging on the car.

And then I realize, suddenly, stopping, that it is not Emily. The woman looks through the windshield at me—wild, terrified at the ghost that's appeared out of nowhere.

"Goddamn it, Albie, one of these days you're really going to make me pee my pants," she shouts. I go around to the passenger side of the car and throw it open. The car is full of cigarette smoke and warm as breath. I get in and collapse in the front seat. "Turn around, Em," I say. "Turn around." I can feel everything going out of me.

"Jesus Christ," she says, pulling over onto the soft shoulder and wheeling the big car around. "You scared the hell out of me."

I look at her and she seems a little odd to me—not precisely as I remember her, the wrong color, or the wrong shape.

"We're leaving now, right? Okay? No excuses?" She stops the car in the middle of the road to look at me. I try to smile at her, but my face is sore.

"You know you look like you got put through a goddamned blender." Her voice is low and hoarse from smoking; she sounds old. I roll down the window for air. "I talked to your dad again," she says.

"Listen," I say, and the word goes around in my head like a whisper, like the sound of my feet on the road, "I don't know

exactly what's happened, not yet." I look out the windshield at
the road, at the slow push of the headlights through the darkness
beneath the canopy of trees. I listen to the sound of the radio, to
the hum of the engine, and all of it combines around me, working
me down. "If you want to know," I tell her, "I don't know what's
going on." When I say it, I'm not at all sure what I'm talking
about.

"Hey," she says, "why don't you just relax? Just shut up or
something for now. Just lie down on the seat. Put your head on
my lap." She reaches up and shakes a cigarette out of the pack
on the dash and pushes in the lighter. "Come on," she says,
cigarette in mouth, slapping her bare thigh. When the lighter
clicks, she pulls it out and presses it to the tip of the cigarette.
"Put your head on my lap."

I look at her and my body rises from the seat, rises in the tiny
space of the car and hovers over the seat. Suddenly it feels like
I am in warm water. I *want* to be in water. I am floating, not
thinking, not moving, and the water's hush drowns out everything. Her hand is on my neck and warm, and its warmth sends
a signal of sleep through me.

I wake again in Langston. The glassiness of town as the houses
and lights slide by is startling, frightening, after so long in the
woods. Everything is *real*. I shake my head and get up. "Emily,"
I say, fighting back the muddiness whirling at the bottom of my
skull, "I want to go to Carl's. I have to go to Carl's."

"Albie," she says quietly, "It's late, go home. You need to
rest. I mean it. You don't need to see Carl. Not this minute."

"Stop, Em, please. You don't understand and I can't explain."
I hold her arm; despite its bony appearance, it is soft, womanly.
It is vaguely surprising.

"All right," she says. "All right. But listen. Listen to me, Albie. I'm taking you to see Mrs. Schwartzmann first thing tomorrow morning. All right? All right?" She looks away from the road at me, and suddenly I want to stay here in the car with her. I want to sleep forever.

She swings the car around, away from my house, and heads back up the street to Carl's. I say nothing but look at her in silence as the car slides along. "Why?" I say to her finally. There are other words in my head, but that's the only one that can materialize.

"Why what?" she says. "Why am I going to take you to see Mrs. Schwartzmann? Why what?"

"Nothing," I say, closing my eyes, trying to pull energy up inside of me. "Why anything."

Without looking at me, she reaches over and gives me a quick, embarrassed pat on the leg.

When I tell her, she lets me out of the car, half a block from the Rieger's. I get out unsteadily, then duck back in for a minute to thank her. Absurdly, I want to kiss her. "Don't go back out to the lake," she says, her hand trailing along the seat where I lay. I shake my head.

"I won't, Em, I won't."

I watch the car pull away, and once it has turned the corner, I walk up the street in the dark. It feels like time has collapsed a little, because everything is the way I remember Langston being when I was a child.

When I get to the Rieger's house, I sit down on the lawn in the damp grass. There aren't any lights on. I have no idea what time it is. When I lie down to go to sleep, the town is quieter than the woods.

* * *

By the time Mrs. Rieger comes to the door, the early morning sky has grown overcast and dark. When she turns on the light, her head bobs for a moment in the yellow wash. When she sees who it is, she smiles and pulls the door open.

It is raining, and the house has already begun to fill with water. The door sucks in it, and sends a low, whirling current out and splashing onto the steps. I look at Mrs. Rieger's face, then her feet. "Hello, Albert," she says roundly. "It's so very nice to see you this morning."

"Is Carl here?" I say, but my voice sounds peculiar in their house, as if it too is a liquid thing. I step into the water and the door swishes closed behind me.

The water moves over the hardwood floors, turning them bright as glass. It moves in and out of the legs of the mahogany highboy in the hall. Its warmth seeps into my shoes, into the bones of my feet and legs, sucking, pulling itself up on me, and on Mrs. Rieger, who seems oblivious to it.

"Carl's not here right now," she says. "I imagine he's gone to school." She seems to think for a moment, a trace of a smile on her broad lips. She is drifting. She doesn't notice the water, she doesn't notice the bruises on my face or the dried blood or the shirt torn from running through brambles and blackberries. "Come in," she says, "come in," and motions me through the entranceway into the aquarium. I hear water rushing through the house—from every faucet, every drain, coming through the roof and the windows from the torrents of rain—cascading down the stairs and across the floors in ice-thick rivulets. It works into the closets and behind the doors, skating over the carpets, swelling the wood and turning every color darker, deeper. The carpets loosen from the floor as the fibers fill with water and swell. Willingly, I follow her, fascinated by the glimmer of it all in the dull morning light. The warm water eases the tension in my legs, suffuses me with a kind of numbness like sleep that works its way up through my veins and bones and radiates through my muscles.

"Would you like some coffee or tea?" Mrs. Rieger says, and I smell toast in the house, dusky and sweet. I want to sleep. The water is warm. "Or some orange juice perhaps." The water rises slowly, surrounds her thick calves and darkens and lifts the hem of her skirt. "I was just going to have some tea myself."

"Whatever you're going to have," I say, caught by the inertia of the house. Speaking is difficult, and the quality of the words in the damp air is peculiar, like the images of fish on the picture window.

I feel sleepy, and I sink into a chair. When she leaves the room, she hardly seems to move at all. She's like a buoy on calm water.

The water seethes. In the dull morning sunlight, the fish decals throw bands of light that float across the room. The fish move and swim, and I sit watching, unable to keep my eyes open, unable to pull myself up from the rising warmth, almost ready to let myself drown, to sink down out of the chair and become one of them, brightly blue and yellow and red, skimming along the floor of this house where I have played since the moment when I first crossed through into the open porch and got onto the jumping mattress with the flying Carl. *Where is Carl?* someone says, and I shake my head. Carl is not here. "I don't know," I say aloud, turning, trying to pull myself up out of the dimness, the rain, the confusion.

"What is it, Albert?" Mrs. Rieger says as she comes back, pushing through the rising water, a tray with a tea service in her outstretched arms.

"Oh," I say, dreaming the word, "I don't know." My voice is like something I have heard in the distance, not mine, but wanting to be mine.

"Well," she says, sitting down and arranging herself in the chair, "would you like some sugar? Milk? I'm sorry I don't have any lemon."

I shake my head. "No," I say. Something huge and dark slides through the water. Mrs. Rieger is oblivious to it, oblivious to the water, to everything. After the dark thing there is a wake, an insuck of current. Mrs. Rieger smiles and pours tea. It is soundless going into the cup—the sound is subsumed by the water running everywhere in the house, in the world.

It rises steadily, exponentially, first to our knees, then to the level of the furniture. I try to pretend I don't feel it, that I don't see it, but it swirls over my lap, soaking the seat of the chair, soaking my pants; it turns the gray fabric green. It rises over the coffee table and into the tea service. The tea seeps from the cups and rises away from them. The tea rises from the pot. I stand up, fighting it, but I can't move. Mrs. Rieger stays seated, watching me. The water covers her lap and begins to rise up her stout torso. The wrinkles of her neck begin to move, to undulate, and suddenly I recognize them as gills. The chairs rise off the floor and float. Everything floats. The water inches up the window glass, and as it covers the fish decals, they are freed from their stillness and swim away. The water goes higher. Finally the water covers Mrs. Rieger's sitting form, and her hair drifts like a dead woman's. Her skin is white and dull. Her mouth opens and closes, speaking something only she knows. I try to move, but the current picks up and whirls against me, a crazy inertia, as if the water is holding me here, keeping me from getting out, trying to drown me because it knows that I am not a fish, will never be a fish, that I will not swim but run run run run. It tries to push me back deeper into the house, and I am borne back by it, struggling, beating. Everything is quiet but the water. My body weighs nothing. It wants sleep. Memories come up in my head. Now and again I can hear Carl's voice the way it used to be—the way it was when I first met him. I fight and fight, but there is nothing to fight against anymore. The water says this. *Stop fighting.* The fish look at me, the green membranes of their eyes shining in the refracted light. Sucking air, desperate, I beat against the water, push toward the door. And suddenly I am outside, but it isn't just the house, it is the whole world, and the water fills my lungs.

JUNE

My father edges the BMW through traffic. It is the first day of June and the bright sunlight charges everything with a nimbus of electricity. Everything around us gleams—the festive, bannered street, the wildly colored crowd, the black tarmac and white lines of the street. In the car we are silent, and I look out at the crowd. My father knows I am alone, and says nothing except when it is necessary.

I know nothing of racing.

When we park the car and get out—me in my new, school-colored track suit, my father in jeans and a polo shirt—the jump of voices from the crowd is as hard as the sunlight. The road where I will run with the others gleams like idiot glass.

On the grass that rises away from the road toward the stadium, there are canopies laid out, each a different color, each struck with an insignia for its school. The boys and girls who will run pace now, talking anxiously and stretching on the grass. It is as crowded and colorful as a beach in summer.

My father walks beside me, and there is some comfort in his presence, like a warm red blotch on closed eyes. It seems as if he's the only person here I know.

We go through the crowd. Girls selling baked goods and doughnuts sit at a folding table. There is another table with a seeps from his face and for a moment—because he looks embarrassed, because he seems terrifically out of place—he reminds me of Meckler.

More cars arrive, gleaming and crawling through the throng of spectators. Big-bellied men in sweaters shout at one another, and clap each other on the back. Women talk about the race, and carry their coffee and purses close. After a while, my father walks over and strikes up a conversation with Shaddock. I stay where I am. I can tell the coach is busy and my father is bothering him. Shaddock points across the grass, and my father cranes. He points again, and my father looks the other way. I wish to be in the deep woods, alone. I wish for music. But there is nothing but the sound of voices and radios and automobiles.

Nervousness, light as helium, creeps along my bones. I want to sit down and dream myself away, or shake it out of my body.

The man who called a month ago and told me I had been selected to run in this extravaganza gets up on the reviewing stand .and welcomes the crowd over the PA system. His voice bounds off the brick walls of the school and reverberates in the neighborhoods. He introduces himself—Ron Haverty is his name. The crowd gradually hushes. In the warm sunlight, the crackle of his voice is just the texture of the pavement. He makes announcements, introduces officials, all of whom are dressed in white. He explains where the first aid station is, and then directs everyone's attention to the red, white, and blue flag hanging in the still air from a pole by the stadium. "Let's all put our voices together," he says, and my father stands next to me again, "and sing 'The Star Spangled Banner.'" Then he leans over and the speakers crackle. All around me people line up together in silence and put their hands on their breasts. When the music begins—the record sounds old and worn—people begin to sing, as they stare at the flag. My father sings in an uneven, unsteady voice, as though the act of singing is unnatural to him. A woman near us with red hair sings in an operatic voice that swells out over everyone else's. It's a beautiful voice. I try to sing, but nothing will come. I bow my head and drop my arms to my sides. I feel ashamed for my father, ashamed for the crowd, and ashamed of myself for being here. I don't know why. I honestly don't. I'm just so filled with shame I want to shrink away. My father's voice wavers and cracks. People turn their heads and stare at the woman with the beautiful voice but she ignores them and sings stronger.

When the song is done, everyone turns away from the flag, back to the reviewing stand. The man announces the events in the order they will take place, and then calls out the names of the participants of the first event and tells them to report to the clerk of the course.

I wait on the grass, hungry and nervous, as alone as I ever was in the woods. The sun is hot on my shoulders, but it feels good. The events go by one by one, and each time the starting gun cracks, I think the sky will split.

My father sits down next to me and claps me on the shoulder. "Don't look so miserable," he says. "It's a sport. It's supposed to be fun. The thrill of competition. Enjoy yourself."

"I'm going to do it," I say. "Just how about letting me do it whatever way I want?"

He shrugs. "Mr. Shaddock pointed out a couple of scouts from colleges to me," he offers.

"Just sport, huh?" I say, and then I wish I hadn't. Still, as long as I run, it doesn't make any difference what I say.

"Albie," he says, and then he gets up and wanders to the starting line.

I wish Kate were here, and I wish Carl and Emily were here, too. In another life, perhaps they might have been right here, standing next to the road and cheering me on. Before Martin. It would have been different before Martin.

I stand up and look around. Kids from my school team look at me. Some of them point and turn away. I hate them, all of them.

It is almost two hours before my event is called, and my name resounds on the loud speakers. My father comes over, and together we go to the desk of the clerk of the course. She's a woman from the neighborhood, and my father smiles and says hello. Other boys line up. She smiles and checks off my name, then gives me a number to put on over my jersey. I shake my legs and my arms, then move into a clear space of tarmac. I take off my sweatpants and start to stretch. There is a light veil of panic, of claustrophobia, as I sit in the middle of the crowd. I try to make music come. The voices rumble around me. I think I hear my name, but the voices swell and fall, and everything is indistinct.

"Hey, Albie, hey handsome," someone says, and it is Emily. She fights her way through the crowd, then stands next to where I am and looks at me. "I came to see you run," she says. I nod. My nerves are jangled. I can't really see her face, I can't really concentrate on it. Behind me, to the sides of me, are the boys I'll run against. One of them is very tall and lanky. Another is a short and stocky kid with tremendously muscular legs.

"Thanks," I call out, and I can hear the nerves affecting my voice. I look at her, but she wavers in the bright sunlight, like a mirage.

"Good luck," she says, holding her purse in front of her, her skin bright and clear, her mouth a clear red, her teeth white and beautiful.

"What about Kate?" I say, but my voice is swallowed by the starter's. I'm just as glad the question couldn't be answered.

"All right," the man in the white suit with the pistol in his hand says. All the boys look at him. The crowd spreads back, away from the starting line. I'm trembling all over as I listen to him tell us the course. We all know it, but the formality is necessary, he says. We'll go down the street to Division Highway and turn right, then go as far as Grant Park. At Grant Park, we turn off onto the footpath, go around it once, head up Parsons, and back to the highway. There will be various checkpoints along the way, and our numbers will be checked off at each. He asks if there are any questions. I look at Emily, then back at the bright white suit. I want to run, but I feel more like vomiting. Some kid—a small, pale, blond-haired boy—asks a stupid question about the rules, and the starter, happy to have charge, happy to be the center of attention, answers him with a long, repetitive explanation. I start to move, to take my place on the starting line. I shake my arms and legs, try to quiet my insides. I move toward Emily. "Em," I say. "Em."

She seems startled—by me, by the sunlight, by the look on my face.

"Em, give me your lipstick."

"What?"

"Just give it to me, please."

"All right," she says, flustered. She opens her purse and digs through it. "Albie, what . . . ." There are whispers around, but I don't pay attention. The starter is still talking, his voice a monochromatic yellow. In the crowd I can hear my name. I take the lipstick when she digs it out and move the silky, fragrant paint across my forehead. It has a strong odor. Someone says, "Psych out." I move it across my cheeks in parallel lines, then down the bridge of my nose.

"God, Al," Emily says. All around us people have begun to talk.

My heartbeat begins to quiet.

"Take your marks," the man in white says. I give Emily her lipstick and take my place along the line. A hole opens up in the crowd, and we can look down the road into the sunlight and black pavement. One boy whispers to another, "It's all a bunch of crap they've made up to psych us out." "Well, look at him." I see Mrs. Schwartzmann at the edge of the crowd in slacks, her look concerned, surprised. The man in white orders us up to the line and raises the gun. The lipstick has confused him, slowed him. I watch the gleam of his uniform, and I watch the other boys. Some are small, some are large, but most are as skinny as me. The tall, lanky boy next to me crouches on his legs like a praying mantis. I look at my father, but he will not look at me. I can feel his shame. His lips are pressed together and his cheeks are knotted. But there is the report of the pistol and my father is subsumed by movement, by the quick scent of sulphur, by the surge of my heart and the surge of the crowd. Everything swirls with noise as we are lifted away from the starting place, as if being thrown forward by a wave.

Excited by the crowd and the noise, some of the boys jump off the line and start sprinting up the road toward the highway. Others start out too slowly and drop back instantly. I'm in the thick of the crowd, and I cannot breathe. My muscles are cold, and the pavement comes with a dull shock through my bones. A boy with dark hair and a long, flat nose pushes me, and I push him back, send him sprawling into his teammate. I work toward the right, toward the outside. I try to get myself warm, to establish a rhythm.

We run close to one another, and when we get away from the crowd and up the incline toward the highway, the air begins to quiet a little. Some of the boys watch me because of the lipstick, but most ignore me. Soon the only worry for any of us is the slap of our feet.

The crowd loosens some when we sway around the corner onto Division Highway. My fingers have begun to dampen and warm in the bright sunlight, but I'm still cold, and my breathing hasn't settled yet. I want music, and there isn't any.

It was envy, Martin, at least for me. When I think of it all, when I think of the way you held Meckler's cat, the way he lay across your lap while you ranted like a man walking about in his own head like going from room to room, I think I envied you. The way the cat's mouth opened when you turned his neck, the way it sounded like a caught fish croaking, and the way its teeth showed —this keeps playing again and again, and what I know is that I envied you. Not for the killing, not for hating. I envied you— and still do—for not being compelled by guilt or circumstance or whatever it is that compels me now through this idiotic race and compels the rest of us through life, to do anything but what you wanted to do. You said contempt. Was it contempt? Or something different? Right now, as I listen to the whisper and pound of my own feet, as I feel the obscenely thrilled blood in my head and chest, my head full of violence and so many things, it is not the howling of the drunk I hear, but your own voice CONTEMPT and it's the cracking of the cat's neck, the croak of its scaly tongue NIHILISM and the strain of its claws against nothing, against NOTHING at all.

There are two other entries from my school besides me. One, a dark-haired kid who stutters, is one of those who left the line sprinting, and he has dropped back now, and probably won't catch up. The other, a narrow-featured boy with a thin face and pale, colorless lips, was one of those who ambushed me that afternoon in the neighborhood. I can remember his face, the broken-looking ridge of his nose, and the way he dove through the clump of boys to get at me. In the few team practices I went to before this race, he made no secret of his dislike for me, but I tried to ignore him. Now, as the crowd lengthens still more, he is on the other side, to the left, and just slightly behind me. I watch him, and something like hatred for him comes up in me.

When I tell you that I envy you for disappearing, for taking Carl, for taking my woods, my Outskirts, and making them all yours, I will say it with envy, but not admiration. Because when I tell you how I came back here, and how I know you would have killed me that afternoon and tried, then you will understand that it was your fault that I had to leave. I couldn't have killed you. I couldn't have found that kind of contempt in me. I couldn't have hunted you down the way I would have had to if I had wanted to stay. I couldn't do anything but come back.

It's four miles up Division Highway to the turnoff at Highland Street. As we go, things start falling into place. I watch the blacktop, but do not see it.

I went to Carl's house to see if he was dead the way you told me, and I spent the night on the wet lawn, half out of my mind with hunger and exhaustion. I woke to rain. Carl wasn't there. I went inside. Water lifted Mrs. Rieger's dress and the spines of fins came out of her skin.

Of course I was starving. Of course I was hallucinating. Carl was dead. Was Carl dead, or had he come with you? Things swim up at me, memories of the two of us. Now and again, I can hear his voice the way it used to be, as if once it originated in my own head.

I threw myself against the door, again and again. But the water that filled their house was too deep. It coiled around me and slowed me, dulled my head. It ran into my nose and ears.

And for the fifth or sixth time in two days, I was asleep again. I dreamt I was in the gully. I could smell the dirt. Then I dreamt I was in my father's house. I dreamt Meckler owned the house next door, and on the inside, it looked just like the cabin—cluttered with clothing and trash and stinking of mildew and rot. And I dreamt that after Meckler was asleep, you sent Carl into the house with a can of gasoline, and he doused the clothing, he doused the wood, and then set fire to it all, including Meckler. But then he didn't come out, and I could smell skin burning, I could smell hair. And then the screaming started. It came up and it stayed so hard against the air that it stopped being sound and became a solid red beam up the side of my head, and the gasoline smell was thick and sweet and the fire lit up the whole neighborhood. My father came out, and so did your mother, and then Carl's mother and father. I ran away.

When I awoke again, I was in the hospital. They had tubes that went in my nose and down my throat, and my throat was dry and raw. They had me strapped down to the bed. My head felt like it had been exploded. I don't know why they bothered to tie me down. I was too weak for anything. There was a man in the room with me, in another bed. He was asleep, but his skin was as white and translucent as candlewax. He needed a shave. I watched him as he slept. There was nothing else to do. The room smelled like urine and disinfectant. I didn't know where I'd been, but I knew that the man was dying of cancer. Maybe *it wasn't true, but that's the way I imagined it. I imagined his whole history—his wife, his mother and father. I listened to him breathe, and I knew that he wouldn't breathe much longer, and I wondered how it felt, being sentenced like that, being forced to confront your death every moment. And then I became suddenly terrified, because I could see my own death. I knew they had put him in the room with me so I could understand death, so I could see it up close and I looked down at myself, the fragile meat and bone, and it made me shudder. I tried to look away. But every time I turned my head, the look of his skin pulled my eyes back. I wondered if the man was dreaming of death. I watched him for a long time, helpless not to. Finally, when he awoke, he looked at me. I wondered if the warmth of my eyes had awakened him. His eyes were yellow and his face was completely vulnerable, like an infant's, and I looked up at the tangle of instrumentation around us. When I looked back at him, I came out of myself for a moment. I was in the middle of the room between us, and then I was him, or as much him as I was myself. I became terrified because I could see it all, could see too much. I shrank back, looked away. He said hello. It was like death saying hello.*

When I went home—it was days; I think there was some speculation that I might try to kill myself, or that I already had tried—the police came to our house. I was in bed, and my father came and made me talk to them. I didn't feel sleepy, so I got dressed and sat with them in the living room. I knew they knew about you and Meckler, I knew they knew about everything—the Outskirts, the dog, the rangers, the cabin, the deer and Meckler. I could see Meckler in my mind when he lay through that whole day in the middle of the clearing. I could see him perfectly. I could make out every crease in his face, every wrinkle, every whisker, every fine, baby-black hair on his head. All around him there were flies, and his eyes had begun to go black and hard. The words were in my head.

They were taller than me, and their uniforms were deep blue and starched clean and sharp, and we sat on the couch and armchairs, chatting like old, formal friends. They asked me about the two of you. They seemed never to have heard of Meckler, and I didn't say his name. Why? Maybe because I really couldn't believe in him, or in what you did to him. But that's not true. Maybe in another life that becomes true. I said nothing because I was frightened, because I had done nothing to help him. I was as much an instrument of his death as you were. I told them we had gone camping, that the two of you had disappeared. I told them that I had gone looking for you but had gotten lost myself. And that's how I got sick from exposure.

They said you were both adults, both eighteen, and legally you could do what you wanted. But your mothers were worried. I thought of your mother, her black eyes and white tremulous hands. If I heard from you they wanted to know. I said I'd tell them. At that moment I knew I would. I sat and watched their clean-shaven faces so antiseptic and unreal that they could have been robots.

But later I began to wonder if I would tell. I could see from my father's expression that there was a lot he wanted to know.

I wanted to go back to the Outskirts to see what had happened. If anyone could have found you it would have been me. I told Emily everything, and she said not to go. She made me promise not to go. But what I wanted was to see the cabin once more, to destroy it in my mind, or see how you had destroyed it for me.

You'd laugh, but I went back to school the next day. I never thought I would. People had heard rumors about what we were doing, or they'd heard something. Maybe through Emily and Kate. Maybe through the three of us before we left for good. When I went down the hallway the first day back, people said things under their breath and people started crowding around to look at me like I was something feral.

That first afternoon—I think it was a Thursday—my father and I were supposed to have a meeting with Mrs. Schwartzmann to try to straighten things out. All that day, everywhere I went, there were crowds of people—by the doors of my classes, by the lunchroom, and finally, by Mrs. Schwartzmann's office. I don't know what happened, what they'd heard, but it made things all the more difficult.

My father was as nervous and pale as the man in the hospital. Out in the hallway he took out a cigarette to smoke and I had to stop him. There was a crescent of people by the administration offices. I couldn't understand it. Everybody was looking, some wanting to look at the wild man, others wanting to see what the others wanted to see. Nobody said anything. They just looked. They just looked. There were boys from the track team, and one of them, the red-haired kid, said, "Hey, track star," and it was that as much as anything that made me go down to Shaddock's office later that afternoon after we had left Mrs. Schwartzmann's.

Even my father and Mrs. Schwartzmann treated me gingerly, like a wild animal. All I could think about was putting things behind me, mainly the look on my father's face when he saw my cuts and bruises and my miserably swollen face. He cried. Mainly, I think, because he had kicked me out of the house.

They talked to me about finishing school. I might have to go in the summer, but I shouldn't think about that now, Mrs. Schwartzmann said. What I should think about now are the colleges I might like to attend in the fall. I almost spat. God. I wanted to tell them *about the music, and about how easy it is to die. I wanted to tell them that the future, the fall and college seemed about as real to me right then as the face of God, or the opposite end of the universe. I wanted to tell them that if the fall ever came, and if I was still alive, I'd be glad to go to college. Any college. I said, because I didn't know the names of any other colleges right off, "Harvard."*

"That's very charming, Albie," Mrs. Schwartzmann said.

I looked at her, at the darkness of her eyes, and she was beautiful to me. Not the way the forest was beautiful, or even the way that Kate was beautiful. Her eyes were soft as rotten wood, and the smell of her was a good smell. It filled the room and seeped along the edges of the table and my hands. My father tossed out the names of some colleges, and I watched her, suddenly dazed, and as her hands and her eyes moved, as the sound of her voice moved along the air, I knew things about her that I shouldn't have known. I knew what she had been like as a girl, and I could see the way her mind worked. I knew instantly that the things she said, she believed, and I wanted to believe them too, to have that kind of certainty. Her thinking was good. It was logical and linear, but most of all it was full of faith, full of trust, and I thought to myself if I could be like anyone, then I would be like her. I understood that she was not a coward. Even if she died centimeter by centimeter from some horrible disease, I knew she'd still be cheerful, that she would still have faith in God and in the people around her. I started to cry. It was embarrassing, and, as far as they were concerned, completely out of the blue. They didn't have any idea why, and I couldn't tell them. I think they thought I was losing my mind. But I couldn't stop myself. I kept wondering why. I kept wondering why she would take the trouble and the time.

She said: "I'll check around and see what kind of feelers some of these people have out, and then I'll help you put together a few applications." She smiled, and my father nodded and smiled. I listened, or only half-listened, because I realized that they were talking about running again. About my joining a college team. I thought to myself that the world was a goddamned perverse place. That stopped my crying. No matter how much faith she had, she knew I had to run. No question of grades, really. No question of academic ability. Just legs. God, if I'd only known before how easy the world is. If I'd only had the contempt. I could have gotten away with any kind of crap in the world as long as I ran for someone. Even murder.

I didn't want things to be that way, but I just nodded my head along with them. I'll run. When I left the Outskirts, I had made up my mind that I wouldn't think, that I'd do what they wanted. It was the only way.

When we got out of Mrs. Schwartzmann's office, I made my father leave. In the empty hallway—classes were going on—I went down to the gym, and then to the athletic department lounge. Shaddock was in there alone, looking bald and cool and little, and he had the air conditioner going and was reading a running magazine. I stuck my head in the door, and my heart was all water and wings. I asked him if he had a minute. I went inside and my hands and feet got cold quickly. I started to tremble. Like a dog, he could sense it. What I really wanted to do, Martin, was leave. What I really wanted to do was spit in his face and tell him that I wanted no part of anything he was involved in as long as I lived. It was humiliating. I looked at the yellow-painted cinderblock walls and they reminded me of the walls of the cabin, I don't know why. I rubbed my hands and looked at him and finally I told him I wanted to be on his team.

"It's a little late in the year," he said, drawing the words out,

"don't you think?" He didn't look at me, but at some point just above my head. I knew I had it coming, but still it made me want to split his skull.

"Do you want me or not?" I said flatly, turning.

He stayed silent for a long time. I stood at the door, my head against the wood. He got up and walked back and forth between the hard plastic couch and the table, and I waited, and the coolness of the room made me hold my arms close to my body.

Then one of the track boys came into the room with a stack of towels in his arms. It was one of the boys who'd ambushed me, the one with a bad case of acne. Right then, I wished I had listened to you, I wished I had gotten some kind of revenge.

Shaddock turned to me, and then to the boy. "What do you think, Ron? Should we let Santamoravia onto the team?"

The boy was surprised by me. He was smaller than me, and I think he was a little scared too. Still, Shaddock was there, and he wanted to appear clever. "How much does he want it?" he said, not looking at me, but at Shaddock.

Shaddock looked at me, and then the boy looked at me, his eyes going like nerves, and if it had gone on a moment longer, I would have walked out.

"I think he wants it pretty bad," Shaddock said. The tone of his voice surprised me. Then, he said, "You want it pretty bad, don't you, Santamoravia?"

I nodded my head. I didn't care.

The boy smiled. "I guess we could use a half-marathoner."

"Sure. We can always use an extra."

"It's okay, then?" I waited.

"Yeah. But wait a minute while I get your stuff," he said, and I stood looking at the boy Ron while he got me a sweat suit, a jersey and a pair of trunks in the school's red-and-white pattern.

Martin, after the first day, after all that had gone on, Kate came to my house. It was cool out, evening. She wore jeans and high boots that I hated. I hadn't seen her since that day of torrential rain when she came to the Outskirts in Emily's car to tell me that she was going to the prom. We sat on the front lawn. I didn't want my father to hear. She said she wanted to stop seeing me, she said that she thought it would be the wisest thing for me, considering, and really, the wisest thing for both of us. At least until things blew over. I wanted to say, "Things have already blown over," but I knew it was just a figure of speech. I wanted to cry, Martin, if only to show her how cruel she was being, but it was all gone. All of it. I watched the texture of her skin, I watched her face, and I wanted to put my arms around her, I wanted to kiss her. And finally I just wanted her to be gone.

The world is a goddamned crazy place, Martin. The past couple of months have felt like years to me. If I died right now, I'd feel as if I'd lived almost forever. I try to imagine college. I try to imagine the fall. But I can't even see the end of this race, much less the end of this season.

When Kate sat on the lawn with her boots tucked beneath her, when she told me that she wanted it to stop, it didn't surprise me.

What did surprise me was that I knew that it was coming. In almost everything that ever happened between us, I always had the feeling that it had happened before, that it was all only laid out before us and we were walking through it like actors walking through lines. It's stupid to say, I guess. I wanted to tell you. I thought you'd help me to understand.

The day we made love, Kate and me, I was outside of myself. Like at the hospital when I looked at the man next to me, or like at the Outskirts when I sat in the trees, waiting to kill the dog. I never felt like it was real, because it was too real. It wasn't me, I kept thinking, but it's my hands. I don't know. I wanted to understand.

All that morning Kate had felt strange to me. Even the god-damned air at the Outskirts felt strange. And when she said that she wanted to go running with me, it came to me instantly what would happen, where and how. I felt it in the trees. I could see it in the humidity. It was a kind of poetry that ran through everything like electricity. And then when we went, I wanted to remember everything in every possible way.

All morning I'd imagined her eating grapes with Emily. They had brought them from town. I watched as she popped them into her mouth, then tongued them a moment before biting in and sucking out the juice. I could feel it in my own mouth, the texture, the tang. Later, when we were in the forest, and I was convinced we were being watched—was it you, or Carl, or Meckler? or maybe the forest itself?—I could taste the grapes in her mouth. There was a human taste too, the way I remember my mother's breath tasting. But there was still the grapes, and still the feeling we were being watched. When I put my mouth against hers, when I was covered with sweat and leaves and broken fern, I felt as if she were toying with me a moment before biting in and sucking out my life my soul my heart. Silly. I felt real and I didn't feel real. I wasn't even there. I was so thrilled I could hardly breathe; I was bored. I sat above us, watching, trying to impress upon my skull each sensation, each texture, as it came. When she took off her clothes I could smell her body and see it all, but I watched apart, the dissolution of myself, of any sense of being or of person I had ever had. In that sense it was like running—nothing but pure sense. But then we were being watched, and I was on top of her, my teeth on her skin, my hands desperate—like in a torrent of water and trying to hold onto something. It was one moment a perfect existence, and the next, a disease.

What I want to say, Martin, is that the world makes no sense to me. One moment this thing was true. She was naked and perfect and with me. In the next moment, another thing completely was true. She was sitting on the lawn, telling me what the wisest thing was. I was trying to remember how she smelled, and what she looked like, so later I could read those things back in my head—like music.

I hurried her. I said, "Say it." And when she did say it, I got up and asked her to leave.

It was not until later that I cared, or that I thought to care. I sat in my room and the death songs came to me, and they played the woman's voice fine as china in the air, and I listened over and over, the way it went up and down and came like a real thing. I could smell her hair, I could taste her skin, and in the woman's voice I could see her. But then I could smell the acrid scent of wood burning, and then I saw the drunk lying on the ground, his body utterly still. Kate was gone.

And my life was simplifying itself as it went along.

In the halls at school, I looked for you and Carl—the way I used to look for the two of you before we left. I waited for you, hoping somehow that you would come and take me out. I wanted to say, I will say nothing, but you never came. In two days the crowds that came to look at me disappeared, and I was alone again. I liked it that way. Maybe that's another way of being self-sufficient, being alone. Emily was the only person who talked to me, and I went to her house every afternoon. Then she got a job as a waitress at a little restaurant in the Crossland shopping center, three or four doors down from the store where you and I stole the tools. A couple of times I went in, to look at the people, to get the feel of the tools in their racks—the potential of them. No one recognized me.

Emily was going to save money. I went every day for two weeks

*and sat at a table. The man who owned the restaurant was a
sleazy little guy, and he made Emily and the other girls who
worked there wear skimpy little skirts that were hardly like skirts
at all but like some kind of obscene upside-down flower. She hated
the skirt. I hated the man. I went there with some lingering idea
of protecting her. I wanted to make her quit and get another job
someplace where she'd be treated like a human being, but she
just put her hand on mine and told me it was all right. Before, I
probably would have beat the guy up. Now I just closed my eyes
and listened to the sound of her voice.*

*I waited for you. I thought you would come. Either to kill me
or to take me back. I felt that there was something unfinished,
and I waited for it to end. In the evenings I would sit on the front
lawn, watching the cars. More than once I felt like crying, just
because of the way the evening was beautiful. I waited in the dark
for the sound of your motorcycle, for the bob of the headlight
up the street. I waited, at night, for the sound of your fingers on
my windows. I almost went back to the Outskirts to look for you,
but I couldn't. Time went by. It got to be June. I thought about
Meckler, about decay, and once, I almost told my father. The
thoughts kept circling around in my head, wanting to get out. But
I knew he wouldn't understand.*

We go by the checkpoint at the corner of Highland and Division, and head down through the houses and parked cars. The
sunlight angles in, everything bright and sweet and clear. The
lanky boy and the boy from my school are in the lead along with
me. Behind us, at a distance farther than shadows, is the little
blond kid who asked the stupid question at the starting line. I'm
warm enough now that the running feels good, but there is something—in the air, maybe—that makes me feel uncomfortable, as

if something isn't quite right. The sight of the woods approaching makes me feel wary, but I hurry toward them—toward the scent of the trees and dirt and wild vegetation.

All along the edge of the forest the grass is high, the way it was at the edge of the campground at the Outskirts. The path is dark and shiny, and skirted by heavy weeds. Over the top there is a canopy of hanging grape vines and honeysuckle.

We pass the man sitting at the check-table and he reads off our numbers, then we file into the shade. The lanky boy is in front. I'm second, and the boy from my school is third. I watch the lanky boy—he's gaunt, but bigger-boned than I am, and awkward. Up close like this, I can see how each step he takes tires him. Already he looks flushed, and I know that in a mile or two, the ungainliness of his stride will start to pull him back.

Directly behind me, following almost like a shadow, is the kid from my team. I can't remember his name, if I ever knew it. All I can remember is that he is a friend of the red-haired boy, Roger. I can remember them together at practice, running together, talking together in the locker room, and together this morning at our team canopy. I don't trust him, and I try to keep him in sight.

Since the last time I ran through here a month or two ago, the trees are fuller, the skunk cabbage is gone, but still the floor of the forest off the path is thick with weeds and brambles and rotting wood. The sunlight strains through the heavy leaf-ceiling. Everything is hushed—even the sound of our feet is swallowed by the echoless green.

We go uphill, then down, over a grassy clearing, then down a place where the hill is stepped off with railroad ties. The lanky boy falters, and when we go down, pound across the wooden footbridge and come out on damp, stiff, marshy grass, he falls back. The boy from my school is directly behind me. He's close enough to touch me.

Deeper into the woods, the silence becomes greater. It's just breath and feet. The lanky boy drops back farther, and when I turn, I see the blond kid—his glasses strapped around the back of his head, his face utterly without expression—pass him. The air is cool and dry, and I'm covered with sweat. I try to make myself more comfortable, to take away the edge that keeps my thinking from dropping completely into rhythm, but it won't work. *Watch out.* I want music and it won't come.

The boy from my school hovers behind me, drafting. I try to keep a mental picture of where he is, but he moves back and forth, bobbing in and out, taking my stride for his and shadowing me. He obviously knows more about racing than I do. I start to worry and wonder. I look up ahead of me and comb through the trees, looking for snatches of color. It wouldn't surprise me now to see Martin, or to run into another ambush. I wasn't supposed to run this race—no one, not even me, believed I would.

Despite my inability to drop completely in, I feel better than I have since running at the Outskirts. The woods are lush, fabulous, and the sunlight that streams through the trees is as brilliant and hard as mercury.

I can smell the lipstick on my face. Sweet and heavy. I would have forgotten it but for the smell, but for the look on my father's face, the look on Mrs. Schwartzmann's face. I feel sad for them that they didn't understand why I needed to do it, but I couldn't have explained. It makes no difference. I am here, and they are in the schoolyard, miles away. I needed something.

Deeper into the woods, the boy from my school picks up his stride a little and sidles up to me. His breath is just off the rhythm of my own, and I can feel the thump of his feet in the path. We go around a bend and lose sight of the others for a moment. He stays next to me, looking at me, the damp of his breath now and then grazing my arm. I pick up my stride, and for several steps, I pull ahead of him, but he gets up next to me again and stays with me, stride for stride. I'm running faster now than I want to, but I won't let him win. If there were no race, I'd run away from him, leave him standing in the trees. The path straightens out again, and it is like a nave, like a hallway, a series of long spindly arches reaching backward and backward. Dead trees and fallen branches. Black rot and white insects.

"Think you're going to win this race?" he says. His words puff out and sail off behind us. He has a sharp, slender nose that looks like you could cut paper with it. His face is red with the heat, and his hair is damp.

I say nothing.

"Don't think you will," he sneers, arms pumping, sweat on his lip. "Don't think you have any chance at all."

I close my eyes briefly, hoping that the rush of blood and the sound of my feet will bring music, will drown him out and carry him away.

"Just because you think you're some kind of goddamned animal," he says, spitting into the dirt, "doesn't mean you're going to win this race." His face is remarkable—pure hate. It makes no sense to me at all.

"Why don't you leave me alone?" I say.

"What's that supposed to do?" he says, focussing his voice so that the blond kid—even if he were nearer—can't possibly hear him. "Is that supposed to scare me? Is it? Well," he laughs, "that lipstick looks goddamned pretty on you. Goddamned pretty."

I say nothing, but something will happen.

"What are you going to do, wild man, bite me?" He tries to

laugh again, but it is swallowed by the air. "Even if I have to sacrifice this race, you won't win. I won't let you. Nobody wants you to."

I look at him. The veins in his neck are swollen with exertion. "Why bother?" I say, but talking pulls my head into the rush of everything, and I become aware of the sound of the woods, the rattling in the trees. I become aware of the blond boy behind us, keeping up steadily, doggedly.

"You think Coach Shaddock wants you to win? You think there's anybody at all who wants you to win?" Sweat gleams on his breastbone, beneath the straps of his jersey. His arms shine like plastic. He has perfect skin, so flawless it doesn't seem quite real.

I try to imagine Martin in the trees, somewhere invisible and painted, the forest so deep in his head and his arms and his chest —but there is nothing. Nothing but fine, black-boughed trees, rotting loam.

But then I see him, Martin, up the hill in the trees. My heart stops in my chest. The other boy doesn't see him. My sweat goes cold. I see the crossbow. I see him lift it. I see the shine of the razorhead bolts in the sunlight. And then the pale line the arrow makes in the air as it zips out toward us. I see the quick dark hole it makes in the boy's side, and the way he stumbles, regretting, near tears, trying to page back through the circumstances in his own mind and change things as they are. He falls, mouth open, and I can see Martin re-cocking the weapon. I look around, but the blond boy is nowhere in sight. And then I understand that the arrow was meant for me.

We bear to the right around a long curve. The blond boy, some twenty or thirty yards behind us but keeping a steady pace, disappears behind the swing of trees. The boy from my school drops behind me again and starts shadowing me. I slow a little, and he slows too. I speed up, he does the same. The leafy path swallows his noise. For a moment, he disappears completely. There's a rustling in the trees, and two squirrels shoot across the path. I look up, scan the trees, and suddenly my feet go out from under me like I've hit a trip wire. Adrenalin goes through me like a rocket. I reel forward, amazed, angry, and the path rises beneath me. I taste the leaves and dirt before I hit; the smell is already through my head.

His arms around my ankles, the boy goes collapsing onto my legs as we slide into the dirt. My knees skid and scrape. I roll onto my shoulder and kick out to break his grip. Rotting leaves are everywhere. "Son of a bitch," I say, and try to get up, but he pulls my leg down again and lunges forward, his mouth spraying, his eyes red and wild. He comes up quickly, and I swing out awkwardly, off balance, just to slow him down. I hit him in the middle of the face, catch my balance and hit him again. He grabs my shoulder and the bare skin is raw. His fingernails flash pink and then a bright pain shoots through the skin and he comes down, his weight pushing. The blond boy pads past us, his feet on the soft earth, his eyes invisible behind the glare of his glasses. His face is expressionless.

The boy swings and it catches me in the neck, and I stand up and back away, unable to breathe. I choke. My throat goes white, and I pull back, gasping. When he comes forward I hold my throat and kick out as hard as I can. My vision sparkles, my mouth turns to copper. He stops a moment, surprised, and sits frozen. I kick him again in the chest, and then, when I've got my breath again, I throw myself on him. I hold his head beneath me and pound it, my knuckles sliding over the round of his skull, on the slip and coarse of his hair. I feel him struggling but I hit him again, trying to make a smooth space of his nose and eyes. In my head I see vividly the look of his face that afternoon in the neighborhood when they got me, and I hit him because of the hatred that blooms and rushes in my chest. *Martin kicking the drunk.* I hit him again and again, because it's all right here, everything. I'd kill him, but the tall, lanky kid strides past us, and gives a funny, sickly laugh as he goes. And then I can hear voices around us in the trees, and the pound of feet. Suddenly the adrenalin is gone; my hands tremble and my chest feels weak. I get up and kick him. He cowers now, and he doesn't get up. I kick him again, this time in the leg to charley-horse his muscle, then I turn and start running again. My head feels full and swollen, and I've got a long way to go to catch up. I don't care any more. All I want to do now is run. I don't care.

I go slowly at first, trying to let the cool of the trees wash through me, trying to keep myself ahead of the others. I hear a flash of voices when the others pass the boy from my school, but I ignore it. I can see the lanky kid now in front of me, and I try to gauge the distance left in the woods. But my concentration is gone. The blond kid is out of sight, but there's still four miles down Division to the school.

I go up a hill and the earth of the path is black and damp and hard. In the center of the path is a rivulet eroded in past rains, and I straddle it, listening to my breath and my feet. And I'm alone again. If I closed my eyes and then opened them, it could be morning, and I could be at the Outskirts. If I turned off the path and went deep into the woods, I wouldn't have to come back. I could keep going toward the new forest. I could keep going until I got back to the mountains and found Martin and Carl. I can see it, can feel the way the weeds off the path would whip against my skin. But I don't. I don't know why I don't.

Martin, for days I sat in my room trying to understand what you meant by self-sufficiency. I wanted to know what it really meant, or if there was no meaning to the word. Every time you said it it seemed to mean something different, as though either it meant nothing or you were still trying to work out in your own mind what it really meant. I thought and thought, and the only answer I could come up with was that it didn't exist. Not really. I kept trying to think what it was like really to be alone, and I couldn't.

In and out, in and out of sunlight, the blackness of the boughs and the earth, the sweet pale green of the leaf ceiling.

Martin if we. . . .

My body begins to settle into a rhythm again, but this time I am tired, and everything is loose and foreign. It is like fever, the way the warmth moves along the shake of my bones.

When I come down the long hill, I start to pass the lanky kid. I can smell his sweat, the light brassiness of it. He has begun to lose most of his steam now, and the back of his jersey is dark with sweat, his breathing is open and burnt. I go past, and into a little clearing. The sunlight is hot and good. I want to turn around to see if the boy from my team is running again, but I do not. *Martin.* I try to remember what Kate said about Mahler's scheme of death and rebirth—about the earth, about the deaths of children, about God—and I wonder what kind of man he must have been. I can see the yellow and brown photograph of him Kate showed me in the library. He was sitting in a chair, reclining, not looking at the photographer but off into some abstract distance.

Then the woman's voice comes, singing through the trees, singing his face and hands, singing his head. I look around and the path is blank. Sweat comes into my eyes, and every bit of my vision blurs. I know where I am now, and I know where I have to go. Finally, as the music grows, running again becomes an end in itself. My body disappears, my mind disappears, and there is nothing left but the sunlight and the woman's voice modulating, rising. And soon the end of the path comes, and beyond it, the field below the picnic area. The sunlight is warm outside of the trees, and I see the blond kid across the grass, beyond the checkpoint, heading back toward Division. He's not as far ahead as I thought. Up above, at the pavillion, is the next checkpoint, and I head toward it, across the broad stretch of green grass, solid and perfect beneath the dome of blue sky.

I watch the road and the blond kid. I see his hair bouncing as he goes. I want to catch him, but it makes no difference if I do or not. It's enough just to run, just to be able to run.

When we come out of the park and head up the gravel end of the park road to the highway, the blond boy is about forty yards ahead of me. I haven't closed up the gap at all, but there is a long way to go. I'm beginning to enjoy myself.

When both of us have turned onto the highway, we run in a straight line, the blond kid and me. There is no one in sight behind us. I watch him closely, and count his steps. I'm just starting to get tired, and my breathing is getting raw. Because he's smaller than me, I start taking at least one stride for every stride he takes. I watch the flash of his legs. Study.

Along the flat highway there is no traffic. In the distance, somewhere between the boy and the blue huddle of low mountains is the high school and the stadium.

I wonder about my father, and I imagine him standing alone on the grass near the reviewing stand, nervous as a bat and smoking furiously. I want to be able to say something to him, but I don't know what it is. The music sketches in the air, the texture like the sky, like the slowly moving road.

I begin to gain on the blond kid. The nearer we get to the school, the closer I get. Forty yards, then twenty, then fifteen. He's pretty good—steady and dogged. But on a perfect day, I could outrun him forever. Soon I can see the pattern of tread on the bottom of his shoes. I can see the mesh of his shirt.

Half a mile away, I hear the dull sound of the crowd, then, closer, I see them gathered at the edges of the highway at the turn-off. You can tell when they see us, because they come close and line the pavement, shouting, trying to get a place to see. The color is brilliant in the sunlight. It undulates and shifts, like a breathing lung. I can see open mouths, and hear shouting. The blond boy is still ahead of me—five, maybe ten yards. I see the strain in the pink-white flesh of his legs, I see the strain in his arms as he pulls at the air. I stay with him, matching every stride. I move up, and I know he hears me now, hears my breath, the pound of my shoes. We get closer and closer, and I know what's going on in his mind. I can see it as clearly as I see my own thoughts.

I can make out distinct, singular faces in the crowd now, and they seem different to me from what they were when we started. The music goes, and my legs are sore and tired, yet they do not exist. I try to look away from the crowd, concentrate on the boy, the pavement. I've never kept up this kind of speed this long before, and I can feel the crashing of my heart, can feel the pull of the veins of gravity at my shoulders. The sweat goes cold on my face in the breeze.

Kids run out to the edges of the crowd when we approach, some of them calling my name, some of them calling the other boy's. I don't know any of them. When we start to get into the crowd, my breath is raw and desperate. I look for my father, but he is not here. He's probably down at the reviewing stand.

I look for Emily or Kate, but I don't see any faces I recognize. The sound around us is shrill and constant. I'm only a yard away from the boy now, close enough to reach out and touch him, and I see the taut muscles of his face, the way his jaw is set, the way the heat reddens his cheeks. I'm right next to him now and I kick the air, pulling, pulling, and in the far side of the crowd, near the turn-off, is Martin.

His curly hair bobs above the heads that surround him, and even though he's fifty yards away and in the midst of the crowd, I see that it's him, standing there in a blue nylon windbreaker.

I drop a little bit, but then hurry again. I'm even with the kid. When I look back through the crowd again, I can't find Martin. I look to where he was, but he's gone. The crowd closes up like a whirlpool as we go around the turn and into the last several hundred yards of the race.

I see Emily and she waves and jumps up and down, then coughs. Seeing her picks me up, and suddenly I'm moving past the blond kid, shoulder beyond his shoulder, touching, forcing. I know my father is on the edge of the crowd, smoking, waiting, and I push it.

And then, as we get down to within sight of the reviewing stand, Martin is there again. The crowd screams and I go faster, nothing at all real in the world but my legs and the pavement and the thought of my father, gentle and human and smoky and waiting for me, as if at the edge of something, and so I push it, I force it. The road trembles and my arms begin to ache and Martin watches and I'm not on the ground anymore, I'm in the air, floating through the ocean of voices, two yards, five yards, then ten then a million miles away from anyone who could touch me. And when the finish line comes into sight the boys from my own team bunch up in a clot of red and shout and jump as if I'm their friend and there's Shaddock, amazed and confounded, jumping and shouting too, rubbing his balding head and I close my eyes and open them and my father is there at the side of the road. His face is red and he yells and punches the air when he sees me. I feel my heart in my chest, the wind pulling at my shoulders, and there is Martin by the reviewing stand on the slight grassy knoll behind. He's naked but for shorts and his body is dark and streaked with clay and dirt and the crowd opens up around him, between him and me, like a sea parting, and what goes through me is a bolt of anger and hatred, and love and recrimination. What goes through me is that it's finally over, this mad spring, and I'm free of it. I am my breath, I am my legs, I am the past the future the end of everything.